DISCARDED

Something True

A TRUE LOVE NOVEL
BY KIERAN SCOTT

SIMON & SCHUSTER BFYR

NEW YORK LONDON TORONTO SYDNEY NEW DELHI

The Library of Congress has cataloged the paperback edition as follows:
Scott, Kieran, 1974–
Something True / Kieran Scott. — First paperback edition.
pages cm. — (A true love novel ; [3])
Summary: Eros, the Goddess of Love, in her guise as True, a modern-day New Jersey high
school student, tries to match a third couple, the last one required for her to be reunited
with her own true love, Orion, and return to Olympus.
ISBN 978-1-4424-7724-7 (hardcover) — ISBN 978-1-4424-7723-0 (pbk.) —
ISBN 978-1-4424-7725-4 (eBook)
1. Eros (Greek deity)—Juvenile fiction.
[1. Eros (Greek deity)—Fiction. 2. Goddesses, Greek—Fiction.
3. Mythology, Greek—Fiction. 4. Dating (Social customs)—Fiction.
5. Love—Fiction. 6. High schools—Fiction. 7. Schools—Fiction.] I. Title.
PZ7.S42643Som 2015
[Fic]—dc23
2014012392

For my newest true loves, Brady and Will

ACKNOWLEDGMENTS

Special thanks go out to all the people who have believed in this series since the beginning, including Zareen Jaffery, Sarah Burnes, Justin Chanda, Julia Maguire, Logan Garrison, and Madison Randall. Thanks also to Valerie Shea, for her attention to detail, and to Chloë Foglia and Bobby Haiqalsyah, for the beautiful, eye-catching covers. Big ups to Sooji Kim, Veda Kumarjiguda, Siena Koncsol, Paul Crichton, and Anna Worrall, for helping me get people psyched about the trilogy.

To my incredible support team and self-appointed publicists, Jen Calonita, Elizabeth Eulberg, and Jennifer E. Smith, my undying gratitude. I'd also like to thank all the bloggers and fans who were part of the True Love Matchmakers Club. You really got the word out about the first book, and I couldn't be more grateful. Thanks also to some super-supportive authors who've helped out on Twitter, Instagram, Tumblr, and at various events, including Katie Sise, Stephanie Kate Strohm, Lauren Morrill, E. Lockhart, and Melissa Walker.

To the Woodside Kindergarten moms who've attended the parties and events and helped me get the word out, thank you! I'm touched and humbled by your support. And to awesome Indy owners Tom Downs (Shaw's Book Shop, Westwood, New Jersey) and Kenny Sarfin (Books & Greetings, Northvale, New Jersey), thanks for your undying support. To all the incredible bookstore owners and librarians who've shown their love for these books, I couldn't be more grateful. I hope to one day visit all your stores and libraries to thank you in person! Of course huge thanks to Laura Leonard and the Hillsdale Library for everything you've done and continue to do.

As always, thank you to my mom, who is with me every moment of every day.

Finally, thank you to my biggest fans, my family and friends, especially Erin, Sona, Wendy, Shira, Sharren, Kristy, Courtney, Jessica, Rachel, Maura, Meredith, Ian, Mom and Dad V., and the Viola Boys—Matt, Brady, and Will. I could never write a word if it wasn't for the joy you guys bring to my daily life, so thank you!

PROLOGUE

"I demand to see the queen! I demand it!"

I screeched until my voice nearly shattered, but the faces of the guards outside Queen Hera's chambers remained unaltered. They were ever fixed in indifference, as if the sight of a powerful goddess raging before them was an everyday occurrence. But then, they worked for the queen, so this was probably the case. My twin brother, Apollo, meanwhile, lounged in the corner, picking his teeth with his fingernails, no help to me.

I grabbed the nearest guard by his sinewy throat. In my free hand, a fireball rivaling the temperature of the sun sprang to life.

"Let me in or I will burn you, hair by tiny little hair," I said through my teeth.

The doors behind the terrified guard whipped open and there Hera stood, framed by the pointed archway. Her white gown ruffled in the breeze, and her dark hair flowed freely behind her.

"Oh, come inside already, Artemis. I tire of your constant cater-wauling. You, too, Apollo," she added, her gaze flicking past me.

With that, she turned on her heel and reclaimed her throne. Her dozen ladies-in-waiting immediately descended upon her, offering fruit and wine, combing her long tresses, laying out flowers and new gowns and ropes and ropes of jewels for her approval. Apollo followed me inside, and the guards closed the doors behind us.

"How did you manage to whirl inside the castle walls in the first place?" Hera asked, reaching for a grape. "Lesser gods and goddesses should not have such power."

"Ah, but my powers have grown these last two millennia," I said, striding toward her, barely refraining from kicking one cream-skinned lady aside. "Or have you not noticed, my queen?"

She arched an eyebrow at me but betrayed no surprise. "What do you want of me? I'm rather busy, as you can see."

"I want you to send me to Earth, as I have asked of you these last fourteen days."

"And I have said no for fourteen days," she replied coolly. "The king has sent Eros on a mission to reignite her passion for creating lasting love on Earth. He has promised your Orion to her as her prize once she succeeds. I dare not foil his plans without good reason, and until now you've not given me a good reason. What makes you think I'll change my mind today?"

"Because I have new information," I told her, placing my sandal on the step just below her throne and leaning in. "It was not Ares nor Aphrodite who tore my Orion from the stars for Eros to toy with, but Eros herself."

It took what was left of my meager self-control to keep from exploding into furious flames as I conveyed this news, humiliating as it was to my own ego. I had tried for centuries to bring Orion back to me—tried everything from dark magic to pacts with Hades to offering human sacrifices to the stars—but nothing had worked. Meanwhile, if the rumors around the Mount were true, Eros had managed what I had not with a mere snap of her fingers. If I ever found her—

when I found her—I was going to wring her scrawny neck.

Hera paused with her hand in a bowl full of strawberries. Her dark eyes flashed with anger.

"Eros did this herself?" she asked, withdrawing her hand and sucking on each finger in turn. "My, my. All you little goddesses are displaying new powers, aren't you?"

"But it is Eros who uses hers to mock another goddess. To mock me," I said, the sour need for vengeance burning inside my gut. "Orion is mine. He was the day he died and he remains so today. Let me take him back. Let me exact my vengeance on Eros."

The queen sat forward, seemingly interested for the first time. "And how, pray tell, would you exact this vengeance?"

"We'll kill her," Apollo said bluntly, shrugging. "What else?"

Hera's lips twitched ever so slightly. She and Eros's mother, Aphrodite, had long been fierce rivals. I knew that the idea of taking Aphrodite's most precious daughter from her would intrigue my queen.

"But you would never win," Hera said without blinking. "You saw the earthquake she caused. The girl has regained some of her powers."

Yes. There was that. Once banished to Earth, a lower god or goddess's powers are always stripped. Normally only upper gods are allowed to wield their powers on Earth.

"About that, Your Majesty," I said slowly, carefully. "You don't think it's possible that Eros is somehow becoming . . ."

Apollo glared, telling me to tread lightly. But what other way was there to say it?

"An upper goddess?" I finished.

"Of course not," the queen snapped, sitting up straight. "How dare you even imagine such a thing?"

But there was fear behind her eyes. It was as plain as the nose on her face. Hera did not want to believe that Eros's powers had grown to the point that she might ascend to a new level, but she had no other explanation.

"Well then. Why not send us to Earth with our powers?" I suggested. "I will dispatch that weakling with one hand tethered behind me."

"No." The queen shook her head. "This I cannot do. You three would cause far too much destruction, and over what? The love of one mortal soul? Did we not learn our lesson from Helen of Troy?"

"Then bind her powers and send us without," Apollo said, grabbing a grape from one of the ladies and tossing it into his mouth. "Even the playing field. You should be able to do that as long as she's not expecting it."

"Of course I can bind her powers!" the queen roared. Her bellow shook the stone floor beneath our feet. A silver pedestal vase crashed to the floor, spraying roses and water everywhere. "Have you forgotten who I am?"

The guards froze in place. I shot Apollo a warning look, and after the briefest hesitation he bowed his apology to the queen. But it was clear she was uncertain. She didn't know how much power Eros wielded now, any more than we did. All the more incentive for her to allow us to kill the backstabber. Besides, Apollo was right. As long as Eros wasn't forewarned and didn't have a chance to deflect the binding, it should be easy for the queen.

"You would do this?" Hera asked me. "You would consent to be earthbound without your powers?"

I bit back a denial. I couldn't imagine being without my powers for even a minute. But the queen was considering it, so I held my tongue. Anything to get me to Earth, to get Orion back, to teach that bitch of a goddess a lesson. Anything.

"I agree to these terms," the queen said.

"You do?" I breathed. After a fortnight of begging, I barely dared believe her. "But what about the king?"

"I will handle the king," Hera replied, adjusting her robes on her throne. "He's not the only one around here who gets to have a little fun. Besides, Eros's job on Earth has been far too easy. It would be nice to throw an obstacle in her way in the form of you two." She ate another strawberry and leaned back, assessing me with a long, pointed glance. "She plucked him from the stars herself, did she? She has that amount of power?"

My lips pursed. "Yes, Your Majesty."

"Then go. The both of you," she said lifting a hand. "Do what you will with Eros. Once you have this Orion in your clutches, I will bring you home again."

"We have your word on that?" Apollo, ever the suspicious soul, asked.

The queen looked toward the tall windows that lined her chambers, and the clear blue sky beyond. I could feel her ladies-in-waiting holding their breath. "You have my word."

My chest expanded as I rose to my feet, weightless triumph filling my lungs. With the queen on my side, there was no way I could lose. Before long, I would be with Orion again, and we would live out his days in a state of amorous bliss. Eros would know real pain. She would know loss. She would bow at my feet and beg for her life. It was only a matter of time.

"We're done here," the queen said.

And then, with a flick of her fingers, we were gone.

CHAPTER ONE

True

I woke up when my face hit the hardwood floor next to my bed and was still processing the shattering of my cheekbone when I jumped up, grabbed my bow and arrow, and whipped around, ready to let fly. My breath heaved. My heart pounded within my throat. My face throbbed. But there was no one there.

On my bedside table, my cell phone vibrated so hard it shimmied toward the edge. That must have been the culprit. Not Artemis and Apollo bursting into my room, wielding hunting knives and whips and machetes. I saw my friend Wallace Bracken's face smiling out at me from the screen, shoved the bow under my arm, and grabbed the phone.

"Hello?"

"Hey, True," he said. "I just wanted to tell you that me and Mia? We're not gonna work out."

I dropped the bow and slumped back down on the bed. A dart of white-hot pain shot from the crest of my cheekbone through my eye. I touched it gingerly.

"Ow."

"Huh?" Wallace asked.

"Nothing," I said. "What happened with Mia? I thought you guys were having fun yesterday."

"We were, but it turns out she's a PC girl," Wallace said. "And I cannot go out with a PC girl."

"Wait, what? You mean she's politically correct?"

Wallace laughed heartily. "No, no, no. She has a frickin' Dell computer. And a Windows 8 phone. I'm an Apple guy. The two don't mesh."

I sighed. "Wallace. You can't be serious."

"Trust me."

He was. Dead serious. The boy lived for his tech. And besides, he couldn't have liked her much in the first place, if he was willing to let her go over something so trite.

"Okay, fine," I said. "Well, you tried."

"Yeah, I guess. Thanks for your help. Maybe I'll stop by Goddess later and drown my sorrows in a peanut butter cupcake."

"It's on me," I told him.

We hung up the phone, and my shoulders curled inward. Late last night, when I hadn't been able to sleep, I had started to foster the tiny hope that Wallace and Mia might be my third couple. They'd looked so happy yesterday at the football game. Maybe they'd find true love, finally fulfilling my bargain with Zeus, and send me and Orion home to Mount Olympus to live happily ever after. But of course, it couldn't be that easy. Nothing was ever that easy.

I got up and winced again as my cheekbone throbbed anew. It wasn't fun, being the hunted. It wasn't restful, either. Nor did it make one pretty, if the glimpse of my reflection in the nearest looking glass was any indication. I leaned toward the pedestal mirror on my desk, right next to the hulking sand timer, which was already mercilessly running, marking the time I had left to make my next—and final—love match. Among the details that greeted me were dark circles under my eyes, sallow skin, ratty hair, a sleep crease as deep as the Grand Canyon from my ear to my chin, and a small red bruise forming on my cheek.

Lovely.

But still, I'd made it through the night. Which meant that Artemis and Apollo, my two greatest nemeses who had shown up on Earth the previous evening with the purpose of stalking me like prey, had at least not been sent here with their godly powers. If they had, they certainly would have found me and annihilated me by now. That was something. And after my minor shopping spree at Murdoch's Outdoors last night, I was now armed with a workable bow and several arrows. When they did find me, I'd be ready.

Suddenly the door to my bedroom flew open. I whirled around with an arrow set in the shelf, string drawn. My mother stood in the doorway, hand on her chest, her short blond hair grazing her perfect chin. Her blue eyes went from bright with concern to soft with relief, and her whole body relaxed. Apparently the fact that there was a deadly weapon trained on her heart didn't register.

"Oh, good. You're alive," she said, dropping her hand. "Between you and your father, you're going to give me a coronary."

"My father?" I lowered the bow.

She sighed the particularly weary and yet indulgent sigh that she always reserved for Ares, the God of War, who also happened to be my dear old dad. "He's downstairs. The brute whirled in five minutes ago with no warning, of course." She angled herself toward the hallway, holding the door for me. "Come. He wishes to speak with you. And make haste. Hephaestus is sitting with him."

I dropped my bow and arrow on the bed and pushed my long, tangled hair behind my ears as I slipped by her. My best friend

Hephaestus, formerly the God of Fire and Smiths, was not a big fan of my father's, nor my father of his. They had both been in love with my mother at one time, which normally wouldn't be a big deal, because pretty much everyone has been in love with Aphrodite. But this was different. A couple of millennia ago, my mother and Hephaestus had been married, and she'd cheated on him with Ares.

So, no—the two of them alone together was not ideal.

When we walked into the kitchen at the back of the house, Hephaestus sat in his wheelchair at the small wooden table, drumming his fingers on its surface. My father stood with his feet planted in front of the sink, his massive arms crossed over his chest, eyeing Hephaestus beadily. Every muscle of his body was clenched, as if he was prepared to pounce at the slightest provocation. His dark hair stood on end, and tiny beads of sweat dotted his upper lip. He wore gray-and-black camouflage pants and a tight black T-shirt with a silver cuff on each wrist, the right one dented and deeply scratched. The other was spattered with dried blood.

"Father," I said, by way of greeting.

"Eros," he replied, relaxing only slightly.

I crossed to Hephaestus and sat in a chair next to him. His dark skin shone from his morning workout, and the white T-shirt he wore was soaked through with sweat. He still sported his weight-lifting gloves, which were grayed and torn from use, and his light eyes brightened considerably now that he had more company.

"Good morning," I said to him.

"If you say so," he replied, shooting a look past me at Ares.

My mother went right for the coffee, poured herself a cup, and then added some caramel-colored alcohol to it. My nose wrinkled, but I couldn't exactly blame her.

"What news do you bring from the Mount, Father?" I asked,

trying to appear casual and unaffected as I leaned back in my chair.

"You are aware that Artemis and Apollo are here," he said gruffly. "You are aware they're out for blood."

I exchanged a glance with Hephaestus. "My sister Harmonia told us as much. She said Hera sent them here to retrieve Orion, and that the queen knows of our relationship."

"Does the queen not comprehend that Artemis will kill Eros for this infraction?" Aphrodite asked. "She must realize that Artemis believes Orion to be her own property—that Eros has stolen him from her."

"I believe the queen wants to see a fight and wouldn't mind very much if one or the both of you wound up dead," my father said darkly.

He may as well have grabbed a knife from the butcher's block and gutted me with it. "What? What quarrel does the queen have with me?"

"She knows your powers have grown. Artemis's as well. She sees the both of you as a threat to her throne, to her ultimate power," my father explained. "What better way to deal with it than to let the two of you deal with each other?"

"And if the girls do that, she won't have to answer to Zeus for the crime," my mother said slowly. "They will have done the idiot deed themselves. It's brilliant, really."

"Thank you, Mother," I said acerbically.

Aphrodite rolled her eyes to the heavens. "I didn't say I approve!"

"You have to avoid them," Hephaestus said. "Make your next match as quickly as possible. Then Zeus will bring you and Orion home, and this will all be over. Once you're back on the Mount, you'll have your entire family on your side. They'd be imbeciles to attack you living under Aphrodite's roof, with the two of you and Harmonia at your full power."

"No, no, no. You have to take the fight to them," Ares said vehemently. "Go on the offensive. Surprise them. Hunt them down and take them out."

"What a shock. The God of War wants to start a war," Hephaestus chided, causing my father's lips to curl.

"How dare you condescend to me?" my father spat. "I could smite you where you sit."

"Boys, if you'd like to engage in a pissing match, I'd rather you do it outside," my mother said wearily, rubbing her forehead with one hand. "You've already given me a headache with your mere presence."

Hephaestus's nostrils flared, but he kept his calm. Barely, if the fingernail marks on his armrests were any indication. "Is Zeus still willing to stick to the bargain he made with Eros?"

My father spoke through his teeth. "Yes. He fully intends to restore Orion's memory and return you both to Mount Olympus if and when you are successful," he said, bracing one hand against the side of the refrigerator. "If anything, Hera sending Artemis and Apollo after you has only heightened his resolve. There's nothing those two like better than a battle of wills. She may wish to distract you and see you engaged in battle, but he wants you to succeed, and he'll do everything in his power to make sure that you do. Then he gets to gloat."

"The king does love to gloat," my mother said under her breath before taking another swig. "Congratulations, my daughter, you've just won the role of pawn."

"Well, it's a relief, at least, to know the king is on my side," I said, absently pushing at the puffy spots under my eyes. "But still. Maybe Ares is right. Maybe I should fight the twins and get it over with. If I can best them, then perhaps I can sleep again."

"What?" Hephaestus said. "True, you know how psychotic the twins can be. And there are two of them and one of you. I will fight the best I can, but without my powers or the use of my legs—"

"But I have my powers and they don't," I replied, glancing at my father for confirmation. I was still unsure of why my powers were returning to me, but I was glad they were.

"We don't know that for sure," he admitted. "Just because they haven't found you doesn't mean they don't have their strength, their telekinesis."

"Plus, as your mother mentioned, they must be righteously pissed off," Hephaestus reminded me. "It's bad enough she knows you rescued him when she couldn't for all those years, but if she has any clue that the two of you are in love . . ."

"*Were* in love. He doesn't currently have any clue who I am, remember?" I said bitterly.

"Is that really what you want to focus on right now?" Ares demanded.

"Of course she does! Orion is the love of her existence!" my mother said. "Or have you forgotten what love means to those of us who can actually feel it?"

"Don't get on me about that right now, woman! I'm just—"

"Enough!"

I stood up, knocking my chair back against the wall. My chest heaved as I fought for breath. I was already so tense I could scarcely see straight. I didn't need to listen to their bickering on top of everything else. My mother and father stared at me, surprised. It wasn't often I stood up to them on their own, let alone both of them at once. My fists clenched at my sides as I fought to control my emotions and thoughts. I had to focus.

"Hephaestus is right. If I can make one more love match, this will be over. As far as I'm concerned, I still have a mission to complete."

I strode past them, out the kitchen door and toward the stairs.

"Where are you going?" my mother asked.

"To work," I told her. "I'm supposed to be there in half an hour."

Her jaw dropped, and she set her coffee mug aside. "How can you even consider going out there with the twins on the loose? Powers or no powers, Artemis can still set a trap. She can still stage a sneak attack."

"She's right, you know," my father said from the kitchen. "You must be prepared for anything."

"What would you have me do?" I asked, throwing up my hands. "Hide here for the foreseeable future? Wait to see what happens if the sand timer runs out and I've yet to complete my mission?" My mother and I stared into each other's eyes, both wishing the other had the answers. "Don't you want to go home?" I asked quietly, appealing to her most precious desire. My mother hated it here. She had resented me every moment since our arrival for being the one who got us banished to Earth.

"Of course I do. But not at the expense of your life," she said, reaching out to tuck my hair behind my ear.

I smiled, tears shimmering in my eyes. It was rare that Aphrodite had a maternal moment, and I relished it. Hephaestus wheeled up behind her.

"I'll go with her," he offered. "Keep an eye on things."

"Thank you," I said, then lifted my chin as I gazed as confidently as possible at my mother. "If we want to go home, I have to complete my mission. One more couple. How hard could it be?"

I jogged up the steps with her on my heels and went to my room. My father decided to follow as well. I could hear his heavy footsteps straining the ancient stairs. I pretended neither of them were there and went to my closet. When I whipped open the door, it gave off a soothing sort of breeze. My eye went directly to a red cotton dress, and I yanked it off the hanger, grabbing a black-leather laser-cut belt that was carved to look like a string of flowers. Couldn't hurt to dress the part.

"And what will you do if Artemis and Apollo storm your little cupcake bakery?" my mother asked, coming up behind me.

The thought sent a chill right through me. If there was one thing I knew about Artemis and Apollo, it was that they gave little value to human life when it stood in the way of something they wanted. I reached back into the closet and tugged a black duffel bag off the bottom shelf.

"This should do," I said, unzipping it.

I tossed the dress and belt onto the bed, lifted up my bow and a few arrows, and stuffed them inside. I'd simply have to tell my boss that it was full of workout gear for after my shift. The very thought of having a bow and arrows nearby considerably lightened my mood. There wasn't much in the heavens or on Earth that could best me when I was armed with my most trusted weapon. I glanced over my shoulder at Aphrodite and my father behind her, giving them a wry smirk.

"Better safe than sorry."

My father grinned from ear to ear. "That's my girl."

CHAPTER TWO

Orion

I hate waking up and not knowing where the hell I am. Not that it happens to me often. Actually, no. That's a lie. It does happen to me a lot. Sometimes even when I'm in my own room. I wake up and everything feels wrong, like I don't belong there. Which is weird, because it's my room. Then a second later it passes and everything is fine.

But this morning I wasn't in my room. And what was really disturbing was, I was staring at a pair of feet. Guys' feet, with a big toe half sticking out of a hole in a ratty white sock.

"Greg! Gregory Howell, did you pass out playing video games again?"

I sat up straight. A door creaked open and then footsteps pounded down the stairs. My buddy Greg groaned and scratched his armpit. We had both sacked out on top of wool sleeping bags in his basement and yes, in fact, the Call of Duty home screen was up on his TV.

"I knew it."

Greg's father, a youngish dad with shaggy black hair and a serious jones for plaid flannel, stood with one foot on the floor and one on the third stair. The man was tall, like six foot four, but was still an inch shorter than Greg. He ran Howell's Farm, the huge stretch of land that Greg lived on, and took it beyond seriously. Right then he had a stern look on his face.

"Morning, Orion," he said to me.

"Hey, Mr. Howell." I got up, found my kicks, and shoved my feet into them.

"Dad?" Greg was still coming to. One eye was squinted as the other one looked around, confused.

"Greg, I need you to wake up and get your butt over to Goddess Cupcakes," his dad said. "They have the guest booth at the market today, and their van broke down. I need you to help them load up the truck and bring back whoever's gonna be working the stand. Got it?"

While Greg's dad was giving this speech, Greg had already gotten up, pulled a sweatshirt on over his wrinkled T-shirt, and started lacing up his work boots. Meanwhile, I felt weirdly alert. Goddess Cupcakes. That was where True Olympia worked.

"Got it," Greg said.

When the door slammed, I sat down next to Greg on the old, itchy couch where we'd spent three hours playing video games last night.

"Dude, I'm so coming with you." I reached for my varsity football jacket. It was still pretty new, since I'd just moved to Lake Carmody a couple of weeks ago, and the sleeves squeaked when I put it on. I couldn't wait until it was broken in, soft and stained. Then I'd really feel like part of the team.

"What're you so excited about?" Greg asked, grabbing a hat and pulling it low over his dark hair.

"Cupcakes for breakfast?" I semi-lied. "Are you kidding?"

We stepped over empty bags of chips and soda cans on our way toward the stairs, Greg shaking his head.

"I think you're the first person I've ever met who eats more than I do," he said.

I raised my palms. "Football players need carbs."

Greg laughed and I couldn't stop smiling, but not because of my joke. I was just psyched, hoping True might be there. I mean, I had a girlfriend. An awesome girlfriend. But True was fun to flirt with. There was something about her that just intrigued me.

Maybe it was the fact that the first time I'd ever laid eyes on her, she'd already laid her lips on me. It was a case of mistaken identity in the end, but a kiss from her wasn't the worst way to start my first day at my new school.

Greg grabbed a set of keys off the hook near the door. His mom was in the kitchen, with a huge breakfast of pancakes, sausage, eggs, and hash browns laid out. Greg's little brother, Billy, and a couple of the guys who worked the farm were sitting there, chowing down. My stomach grumbled.

"You kids want anything before you go?" Greg's mom asked with a smile. She was always smiling. Which was one of the reasons I liked hanging out at Greg's. Most of my friends were on the football team, and they lived in these big houses closer to town with parents who were either never around—like mine—or always seemed stressed out. I'd met Greg when I joined yearbook as a writer, and we'd gotten to talking and sort of hit it off. I liked that his family was old-school and his house was like something out of a black-and-white movie. There was something about it that was comforting and familiar. Which made no sense, since my house was totally modern.

"Maybe a couple for the road," Greg said, kissing his mother's cheek.

He snagged some pancakes and tossed me one, then took a few sausages as well.

"Heathen," his mom joked. "At least take some napkins."

"Thanks, Mrs. H!" I said, reaching over Billy's back for the napkin holder.

"See you later, Orion! Tell your mother I said hi!"

I gave her a wave and we headed outside. After I shoved the whole pancake in my mouth, I checked my phone. There were ten new texts from Darla Shayne, my girlfriend, starting late last night. I must not have heard the alerts, because we'd jacked up the volume on the game. We'd won our football game yesterday afternoon, and afterward I'd asked her to homecoming. (She said yes.) Then last night she'd wanted me to come over and hang out, but I'd already told Greg I'd hang with him. Darla had been really disappointed, so I already felt guilty for ditching her, and now I felt even guiltier for ignoring her.

CAN'T WAIT FOR HOMECOMING!
DID YOU GET A TUX YET?
WHERE ARE YOU? CALLING UR HOUSE.
UR MOM SAYS YOU'RE STILL AT GREG'S. CALLING UR CELL.

Yep, sure enough, there was a missed call.

GOING TO BED. WHERE R U??? CALL ME IN THE AM.

Apparently, being an attentive boyfriend was not one of my special talents. I hit the call-back button as Greg led me over to a big blue pickup and got in. I put the phone against my shoulder and reached for the handle on the other door. It squealed like a pig when I opened it.

"Guess I should oil that one," Greg said with a laugh.

"Orion!" Darla answered the phone as I slid onto the old vinyl bench seat of the truck. "I thought you were dead."

I laughed. Darla was dramatic like that. It was one of the things I liked about her. Everything was a huge deal with her. It made life exciting.

"Sorry. I didn't hear my phone," I told her. "What are you doing today?"

"Working! I have a shift at ten."

She sounded excited about it. Which she probably was. She loved helping people pick out clothes at the shop where she worked downtown. She also loved to get out of her house. She lived alone with her mom, this high-powered motivational speaker who was always traveling to give speeches to companies. Most people would love having that big house to themselves, with a housekeeper the only adult around, but Darla hated being alone.

"We're headed into town to go to Goddess. Do you want to meet me and grab coffee or something?"

I slammed the door, and the engine rumbled to life.

"Sure!" she said. "I'll be there in twenty minutes."

"Cool."

I ended the call and sat back for the seriously bouncy ride in Greg's dad's truck, taking a bite of my sausage link. The sun was shining, the breeze was blowing, the leaves were turning all kinds of awesome colors, and I was on my way to maybe see True and then meet my gorgeous girl and have cupcakes for breakfast.

Sometimes it was almost unreal how good it was to be me.

CHAPTER THREE

Darla

"I'm so excited. You must be *so* excited!"

I held my phone to my ear as I maneuvered my white BMW convertible into a space near the center of town. I know, totally illegal, but sometimes you can't just hang up the phone, and this was one of those times. We were talking about homecoming court. I mean, come on.

"I know. I can't wait. Do you really think I have a chance?"

Mariah Gatewood's sharp intake of breath on the other end of the line almost startled me into rear-ending the car in front of mine. I hit the brakes, closed my eyes, and silently counted to ten.

"Of course you have a chance!" Mariah gushed. "Who else could it be?"

I put the car in park. "Well, we know Veronica's gonna get it."

"Of course."

"Of course."

Veronica Vine was my best friend and the most popular girl in the junior class, if not in the whole school. She had been on homecoming court every year, and this was not the year there would be some random snafu that would leave her out. She and Josh

Moskowitz were practically married, which did nothing but sky-rocket her stock, and she'd gone up an entire cup size but down an entire dress size over the summer. Any boy with a pulse would vote for her.

I got out of the car, making sure to plant my stiletto boots firmly before standing, because I'd already splatted on my face in these shoes once, and I was pretty sure I'd die of embarrassment if it happened again.

"But there's only one other spot for a junior, and there are tons of girls who could get it," I told Mariah. "You could get it!"

"Um, please. No," Mariah said. "But you're Veronica's BFF. And now that you've got Orion you're, like, a lock."

Okay. That stung. Because clearly she thought that without Orion I wouldn't have a chance. Which was true, but she didn't have to say it.

Still, I took a deep breath and let it go. My mother always said it was better to let the little things go, and she made a seriously awesome living giving inspirational speeches from coast to coast, so this was a mantra I tried to live by. I mean, I knew Mariah was right, so why bother snapping at her about it? There were certain things a person needed to do to be considered popular. I knew this better than anyone. And ever since the first time Trevor McKay had called me Darbot the Geek back in seventh grade when I still had my back brace and retainer and glasses, I had been working my butt off to get where I was.

It was the reason I had learned to put in contacts, even though the very idea of touching my eye skeeved me out. It was the reason I had spent my entire eighth-grade year solidifying myself as Veronica's publicly declared BFF and not just the girl who sometimes helped her out with her homework. It was the reason I had walked around my house for hours in these stupid heels until I could actually do it without looking like a deranged T. rex with a drug problem. And it was the reason I had locked down Orion on his first day at school before he could even look at anyone else. For years I'd been watching the popular kids, taking note of what it took to be noticed, to not be invisible. And now I wasn't invisible anymore. And if I could make it onto homecoming court, then everyone would know who I was. I'd be important. Finally, important.

"Thanks, Mariah."

I walked around the back of my car, and my heel got caught in the seam between the brick lining of the sidewalk and the actual sidewalk. I steadied myself on the parking meter and looked around, but luckily, there weren't that many people out. It was still kind of early for a Sunday.

"No problem. You're so lucky he moved here."

I swallowed back a bitter taste in my mouth just as my phone beeped. Call waiting. I looked at the screen.

"It's Veronica," I told her.

"Tell her I said hey!"

No arguments. That was how it was. When Veronica called, you took the call. It was just accepted fact. I clicked over.

"Hey, V!" I said, my fingers going to the diamond D pendant around my neck, a gift from Veronica for my sixteenth birthday. It was exactly like her V, but slightly smaller. She hadn't given one to Mariah or our fourth, Kenna Roy, so it meant a lot to me.

"Hey, D! Listen, I wanted to tell you that I bought a new dress for homecoming, and it's blue."

I stopped halfway across the sidewalk. "What? But mine's blue."

"I'm sending you a pic right now."

My phone beeped with a text. I opened the photo and just about died. The dress was not only the exact same shade of blue as mine, but it was almost the exact same cut. Except this one had more of a plunging neckline. With her hair curled into perfect tendrils and her lips shellacked in deep red, Veronica looked like she was walking the red carpet at the VMAs. I would kill to look that good, just once.

"I don't get it," I said into the phone, ducking into the shade under the pink-and-brown-striped awning of Goddess Cupcakes. "We shopped together. I thought you liked the red dress you bought."

"Um, hello? When are you going to tell me how much you *love* the new one?" Veronica asked.

A harried-looking mom with a double stroller walked by me, and one of her mop-haired kids dropped his striped sock on the ground. I bent to retrieve it and jogged as best I could to catch up with her.

"Miss? Your son dropped this," I called.

She stopped and looked at me with tired eyes. "Thank you!" she gushed. "He would've screamed the whole way home."

I smiled at her and waved at the little guys as they took off again. One of them waved back. Too cute for words.

"Darla? Are you there?"

I flinched. I'd almost forgotten I was on the phone.

"No! I mean, yes. Sorry. The dress is awesome," I said. "But aren't you worried that we're going to look . . . I don't know . . . like matching bridesmaids or something?"

"Of course not. Because after school tomorrow we're going shopping for *your* new dress."

Suddenly I felt very, very hot. I turned around and pressed my forehead into the cool glass window of Goddess, my fingers gripping my phone so tightly they hurt. I loved my dress. Veronica knew I loved my dress. It made my waist look tiny and my legs look longer and the cap sleeves totally hid the fact that one of my shoulders was slightly higher than the other—something my back brace didn't entirely fix.

I took a breath, choosing my words very carefully. "That's really nice of you to offer, V," I said. "But I like my dress. And it was on sale, so you know I can't return it."

"So you'll wear it to prom," Veronica said, like the conversation was over. "Or give it to your mom or something. It probably wouldn't make *her* hips look huge."

"It makes my hips look huge?" I asked, lifting my head.

"Well, when your waist is cinched that small, your hips naturally stand out by comparison." Veronica was getting impatient. "Why are we still talking about this? Tomorrow we'll go shopping and find you something even better, I promise. I gotta go. Mom's trying to force-feed me an omelet, so I *must* go get her head examined."

"Okay. Bye."

Veronica was already gone. I gazed down at the picture of her again, feeling suddenly exhausted. She, of course, looked perfectly proportioned in her dress. I flicked through my photos to the one we'd taken of me in the dressing room when I'd decided on mine.

Oh my God. My hips *were* huge! How had I not noticed that before? I blanked the screen and shoved my phone back in my purse. There. Gone. I could obsess about that later. Right now I was late to meet my boyfriend.

Shaking my hair back from my face, I reached for the door handle, but froze. There, not five feet away inside the shop, was Orion, and he was talking to . . . no, *flirting with* True Olympia.

They were totally oblivious to me standing there. True laughed, tipping her head back to expose that long, swanlike neck, and Orion watched appreciatively, giving her a ravenous look that should have been reserved for me.

Everything inside me clenched. He was my boyfriend. Mine. I'd worked hard for this moment, for this relationship, the guy who finally proved to the world that I was the girl I'd always wanted to be. There was no way I was going to let that weirdo sweep in and ruin it for me.

Deep breath, Darla. Let it go. Deep breath. Let it go.

No. Not this time.

Homecoming court was going to be announced tomorrow. If Orion and I were nominated, there would be posters to make and campaigns to wage and speeches to write. I couldn't have my boyfriend flirting with other girls. It would make me seem weak. Pathetic. Unworthy.

Then I remembered my second mantra—the one that my mother had nothing to do with. This one I'd come up with myself to get through moments just like these:

What would Veronica do?

I yanked open the door and strode across the tile floor toward Orion. True took one look at me and her face fell.

Don't trip, I thought. *Don't trip, don't trip.*

"Hey, baby!" I trilled, throwing my arms around Orion's neck. I did sort of trip at the last second, but it just made it look like I was really enthusiastic about the hug.

"Hey!" he replied.

I kissed him right on the lips, leaving no room for misinterpretation as I moved my hips against his and pressed my chest into his rough wool jacket.

"Miss me?" I asked.

"You know I did," he replied, smoothing my hair behind my ear in that way that sent a shiver down my neck.

"Hi, True," I said blithely, smiling at her expressionless face. "Can I get a coffee? Skim milk, two sweeteners?"

"Sure," she said.

Then I turned and dragged Orion to the corner booth, where I sat half on his lap with my legs crooked over his. He couldn't take his eyes or his hands off me. It was like there was no one else in the room.

"You ready to be my homecoming king?" I asked, cuddling against him.

Not that I ever thought I could win. A senior almost always won, and if it wasn't a senior, it would be Veronica. But I could pretend. I spent half my life pretending.

Orion smiled sexily. "You're gonna be the most beautiful queen ever."

I smiled back. This was much better.

CHAPTER FOUR

True

I couldn't stand behind the counter for one more minute. I was in such close proximity to Orion and Darla's smacking lips that I could actually hear the slurping, see the saliva when it caught the sunlight just so. If I didn't move soon, the resulting meltdown would probably involve someone getting an entire vat of decaf dumped over her head. Which, while momentarily satisfying, would be bad for everyone in the long run.

"Tasha?" I turned to my coworker, who was pouring out coffee for a middle-aged dad with a six-year-old who'd just picked up his birthday cupcakes. "I'm taking my ten."

"Oooookay."

She had a dubious look on her pretty face. Probably because we'd only been working an hour. But when a girl needed a break, a girl needed a break. I lifted the pink Formica counter open at its hinge and walked over to the table on the far side of the room near the front window, where Hephaestus had settled in for his stakeout. He gave me a wry look as I sat down across from him, my back to the happy couple.

"You okay?" he asked.

I wanted to put my head in my hands, but I refused to slump.

Not in front of her. I had recognized the look she'd given me when she'd thrown her arms dramatically around Orion's neck. Triumph. Plain and simple.

"He was flirting with me, wasn't he? Before she got here," I whispered hoarsely. "I'm not making that part up."

"You're not making that part up, no." Hephaestus slowly folded the newspaper he was perusing and laid it aside. With the red-and-blue-striped scarf hanging around the neck of his open leather jacket, the steaming coffee, the newsprint, he looked like a young, hot college professor. "But does it really matter? As soon as you make your next love match, the two of you will be reunited and you'll be out of here, anyway. What happens today is irrelevant. Soon all of this will be vapor, like a waking nightmare."

I looked down at my hands, the fingertips raw from practicing with my bow for hours last night after so many days without touching a string.

"It doesn't feel irrelevant." Darla giggled loudly. "Though nightmare is about right."

Someone rapped loudly on the window and Hephaestus and I both jumped, but it wasn't Artemis or Apollo. It was Wallace. He waved, then made a move for the entrance. At the same moment, Darla extricated herself from Orion's arms and started across the café toward the bathroom. Wallace opened the door, still looking in my direction, and slammed right into Darla's side. What can I say? I was powerless to stop it.

Well, actually, I could have stopped it with my powers, but I didn't. My bad. There are worse things than hoping to see your rival fall on her butt.

"Oh God! I'm so sorry!" Wallace said, grasping her arm to steady her.

"It's okay. I'm fine," Darla said, flustered.

Then they looked at each other. His eyes widened. She blushed. For the first time I think they were really seeing who they'd each just bumped into, and it definitely had an effect on the both of them.

"Oh, um . . . hey . . . Darla." Wallace shoved his hands into the pockets of his heather-gray wool jacket.

"Hey, it's . . . Wallace. I mean, hi."

"I didn't see you," Wallace said. "I mean, I did see *someone*, but it was too late to stop, so I tried to zig and then you—"

"Zagged," Darla said.

They smiled. Together. Like mirror images. Like they were both thinking the same thing. It lasted half a second, before Darla shyly averted her eyes to look at the floor, but I saw it. Something flipped inside my chest, and my pulse began to race. There was way more going on here than the average person could see.

They liked each other. More than liked. I could feel it in my bones.

But Wallace Bracken, the proud tech geek with a 4.0 in awkward behavior, and Darla Shayne, the boy-crazy, clothing-obsessed, popular chick with the vapid friends? How was that even possible? Until now I'd never seen the two of them speak to each other.

"Yeah," Wallace said. "Anyway, I guess I should go—"

He pointed at me and Hephaestus.

"Me too."

She lifted her hand in a sort of wave, then click-clacked toward the bathroom without looking back. Wallace turned slowly and joined us. His dark hair fell over his warm brown eyes, and he checked his iPhone quickly before shoving it back into the deep pocket of his black cargo pants.

"Hey, True . . . Heath." Wallace made a big show of looking over the newspaper. "What's happening in the world? Anything good?"

Hephaestus smirked. "Is there ever?"

Wallace laughed a fake laugh and glanced in the direction of the bathroom alcove.

"Um . . . what was that?" I asked.

He lifted his shoulders, Mr. Casual. "What was what?"

"That." I lifted a thumb toward the ladies' room door. "You and Darla. It seemed . . . awkward."

"Oh. That." He sat heavily in the chair next to mine. "We used to be friends. A long time ago. No big."

He was avoiding my eyes. Wallace never lied, but he also never avoided my eyes. Which meant he was lying now. For the first time since I'd known him. Or at least not telling the whole truth.

"So," he said, leaning forward and finally looking at me. "Where's my cupcake?"

Way to change the subject. There was something going on here. What if Darla and Wallace were a love match? What if they were meant to be? On the outside, they were complete opposites and totally wrong for each other. But maybe he could ground her a little with his penchant for straight talk and total disregard for social acceptance. And maybe she could help him live a little—introduce him to new people, stray his attention from his iPad every now and then with a party or something.

And if they could find true love, then she would break up with Orion, and Orion would be . . . free.

"Coming right up," I said with a smile, rising from my seat.

I walked back to the counter, feeling much lighter than I had when I'd left it, and shot Orion a big, bright smile—which he returned in spades now that his girlfriend wasn't around. This could be it. This could really be it. My third pairing. Match this couple and Orion would be mine, one way or another. Mine, all mine.

CHAPTER FIVE

Darla

"Claudia! Peter! Wait up!"

I jogged as best I could in my Jimmy Choo boots to catch up with Claudia Catalfo and Peter Marrott in front of the school on Monday morning. It wasn't easy, considering the pencil skirt I was wearing and the fact that the point on the bottom of the heels was about one millimeter square. When Claudia turned around, her eyes widened. I hoped because I looked so hot and not because I looked like I was about to deck.

"Hey, Darla," Peter said, his brown hair flopping over his forehead adorably, like always. He looked me up and down. "Wow. You look—"

I paused in front of them, half panting. He didn't finish his sentence. Just kind of winced. Claudia had a grip on his hand like she was afraid I might tear him away or something.

"I know," I said, tossing my hair over my shoulder. "Well, homecoming court is being announced today, so I thought I'd dress up."

Not just me, of course. Veronica and I had spent an hour on our phones last night, texting selfies back and forth until we found the perfect outfit. She was wearing a red cardigan and white tank top with a dark-gray miniskirt, and I was wearing a pink cardigan with a gray tank top and a black miniskirt. I had chosen the boots myself.

Claudia's green eyes flicked to my cleavage and her nose wrinkled. A blush crossed my face, but whatever. The girl never wore makeup and dressed like a grandmother half the time in these turtlenecks and leggings, her hair always in a bun. I wished she would come into My Favorite Things, the boutique where I worked. When you're that tiny, it's practically a sin to wear baggy clothes. Plus, if she would give me five minutes, I could totally show her how to accentuate her cheekbones and make her eyes look five times bigger. But then, she'd landed Peter Marrott with her current look, so she must have been doing something right.

"Okay," Claudia said, glancing at her watch. "So . . . did you need something?"

"Oh, right. I want to join Boosters," I said as a school bus roared by us, leaving behind a huge cloud of acrid exhaust. "Orion Floros and I are going out, and I think I should take over as his . . . booster person."

"But he already has a booster," Claudia said.

I rolled my eyes. "I know, but True Olympia? Come on. He doesn't even like her."

Lie. He did like her. Possibly, he was even attracted to her. But it was one tiny white lie for the sake of the greater good. I hadn't asked Orion yet, but I was sure that if I did, he would say that he would totally want me, his girlfriend, to be his booster instead of some random person who wasn't even part of our crowd. It just made sense. Plus, I loved the idea of doing the things for him that a booster was supposed to do, like baking brownies and decorating his locker and leaving little gifts at his house. Projects were totally my thing.

Also, I didn't like the way it felt, seeing them together yesterday. I didn't want to be jealous, but I was. Orion was my ticket to homecoming court. He was the last piece of my popularity puzzle. He wasn't supposed to be looking at other girls like he wanted them. What would people think?

"Well, there she is now," Claudia said, gesturing toward the parking lot. "If she doesn't mind stepping down, then it's fine." She waved to True, who was walking toward the front door of the school with Heath at her side. The girl said something to Heath and came over to us alone. She was wearing a long, colorful, flowing skirt and a form-fitting white top. Very pretty. She'd definitely turned her whole look around since she'd first moved here. I had to admire that, at least.

"Hey, guys. What's up?" she said, greeting the most popular guy in school and his girlfriend as if they were old friends. Color me confused.

"Darla wants to take over as Orion's booster," Claudia said, hugging a book to her chest. "Would you mind giving him up?"

I narrowed my eyes at True, trying for my best *don't mess with me* look, which I'd learned by watching Veronica.

True laughed. "Um, yeah, I would."

My jaw dropped, and an indignant sort of bleat came out. "Seriously?"

"Seriously," True replied.

I was so stunned I felt myself start to shrink. As hard as I tried, confrontation had never been my thing. When someone stood up to me, I became that girl again—the loser wallflower that no one listened to or cared about. The one who would sooner die than speak up for herself. My throat closed over, and I started to sweat. So, very, gross.

Get a grip, D. What would Veronica do?

I took a deep breath, lifted my chin, and looked down my nose at True.

"Excuse me, but he's *my* boyfriend."

Peter hid a laugh, badly, behind a cough. True sucked in her cheeks as if she'd just tasted a sour apple. "I'm aware. But if you wanted to be his booster, you should have signed up the day he made the team, like I did."

"Okay, ladies," Claudia said. "Let's not make this a thing."

True and I stared each other down. There was no way I was going to blink first. But then, out of nowhere, her expression changed. She lit up like she'd just been spritzed with cooling cucumber spray.

"I have an idea," she said. "Why don't you join Boosters anyway? You can help Wallace plan the pancake breakfast this weekend!"

Claudia smiled. "Yes! That's a great idea."

"Wait, Wallace Bracken?" I asked, even though there was only one Wallace in the entire school.

Claudia, Peter, and True started walking again, and I fell into wobbly step with them.

"Yep. He's sort of our manager," Claudia said. "And he's great with the organizing and everything, but not so much with the creativity and motivating. I bet you'd be incredible at that."

My spirits perked up at the compliment, but only slightly. Wallace Bracken was my next-door neighbor. When we were kids, we used to play Harry Potter in our backyards together, making up elaborate stories and going out on dangerous adventures to slay Lord Voldemort. In middle school we were in all the same classes and we used to study at his house, eating the crazy cake combinations his mother was always trying out on us. Sometimes I'd even have dinner there while my mom was off establishing her career.

But then, Darbot had happened. And I'd decided that I was going to make myself Veronica's best friend so that people would stop seeing me that way. But if you were Veronica Vine's best friend, you couldn't hang out with people like Wallace Bracken. She'd made that perfectly clear to the world in some pretty awful ways.

So I'd stopped being his best friend. We were still in almost all the same classes and he still lived next door, but we hadn't so much as said hi to each other in, like, four years. Until yesterday, when he'd slammed into me at Goddess. But I don't think that counts as much of a conversation.

"Wallace could handle the assignments and the budget, and maybe Darla could take care of decorations and getting everyone psyched to do their part," True suggested oh-so-helpfully.

"Perfect," Claudia said at the door to the school. "I'll let Wallace know you're coming to the meeting tomorrow afternoon, okay?"

"Um, sure," I said. "Sounds good."

"This is gonna be so great!" True exclaimed. Then she rushed to catch up with Heath on his way up the ramp.

I bit my tongue as I watched her go. If I had to deal with Wallace, then I had to deal with Wallace. At least if I was on the Boosters I could keep an eye on True and Orion at the events the team and the club had together. I could keep them from flirting, keep people from seeing them act couple-y when they weren't.

Claudia and Peter turned as one to go inside.

"And hey! Good luck today!" I called after them.

"With what?" he asked.

"You know. Homecoming court? It's being announced in homeroom?" I said.

They looked at each other sort of blankly. "Right. Thanks. You too," Claudia said.

Like it didn't matter to her one bit. I supposed when you were a total lock like they were, you had the luxury of pretending it was no big deal.

"Hey, D!"

"Hey, V!" I called out, pivoting on my heel.

The smile froze on my face when I saw Veronica striding toward me. She wore skintight jeans and an off-the-shoulder royal-blue sweater the exact shade of the Lake Carmody High blue. Her blond hair was as glossy and bouncy and perfect as ever, hanging straight down her back, and her diamond studs sparkled in her ears. But it was her boots that were the jaw-dropper. Calf-high, slouchy, creamy suede Michael Kors limited edition. They were thousand-dollar boots. I knew because I'd torn them out of *InStyle* last month and tacked them to my style board above my bed—the board full of the things I daydreamed I'd one day have.

"Where did you get those boots?" I blurted.

She lifted a shoulder and checked her phone, shooting off a quick text. "They were on my bed when I got home from spin last night. Daddy got them in L.A."

What that really meant was that she'd asked her father's assistant, Penelope, to get them for her, and Penelope had pulled a few strings, as always. Veronica's dad might be a high-powered entertainment lawyer constantly jetting back and forth between New York and L.A., but his idea of high fashion was polka-dot suspenders and an only slightly stained tie.

"I thought we were dressing up," I said, looking down at my outfit. Standing next to her, I was seriously overdressed.

Three tiny lines appeared in Veronica's perfect brow. "You didn't get my text?"

I whipped out my phone. There was a text from Veronica sent fifteen minutes ago.

CHANGED MY MIND. GOING CAZ.

To which I had texted back on my way to school:

WHAT DOES CAZ MEAN?

"I got it. I just didn't understand what it meant," I said.

"Caz. You know, casual?" she said, striding past me.

"Oh. Okay." I wished she'd texted me a little earlier so I'd had a chance to change. And also used words in the English language.

"So, isn't this exciting?" I asked as I held open the door.

Veronica checked her phone again and sent another text. "What?"

"You know."

Suddenly her face lit up, and she shoved the phone into her leather messenger bag. "Right! Homecoming announcements! Do you think you'll get it?"

She breezed past me into the school, total confidence. She knew she was in. I followed her into the main hall, the buzz of conversation around me humming in my veins. It felt like the revving of the engines before a big race.

"I hope so," I said. "What do you think?"

We paused in the center of the hallway. Her locker was on one side of the school and mine was on the other.

"I think that whatever happens, we're going to have a kickass time at homecoming," she said.

I felt like I'd been slapped, and my face fell. "So . . . you don't think I'm going to get it."

"No! Of course I do! I voted for you!" Veronica said. "I'm just saying, it's not the biggest deal. I mean, if you don't get it. That's all. Don't be disappointed. It's not like it's *so* much fun to ride around the football field in a convertible, freezing your ass off in your tiny dress."

Maybe not if you've already done it twice. I swallowed hard, trying not to let her get to me. She was just preparing me for the worst. That's what friends are for.

"And speaking of dresses, don't forget! Shopping this afternoon!" She grinned excitedly, as if she didn't go shopping every afternoon of her life.

"Right. My new dress."

Last night I'd spent way too much time staring at myself in the mirror wearing my blue dress, and honestly? I still loved it, even if my hips did stand out a tad. I didn't want a new dress. I didn't need a new dress. But now was not the time to debate it. We had to get to homeroom.

"Well, good luck, V," I said. Not that she needed it.

"Good luck, D!" she replied.

We hugged, the bell rang, and it was time to face the announcements.

Fifteen minutes later I sat in homeroom, experiencing what it must feel like to have a heart attack. Or a stroke. Or both at the same time. My heart was fluttering and making me hiccup. I could feel the blood running through the veins and arteries in my wrists. I kept having hot flashes, followed by extreme cold blasts that made me shiver. Under my desk, my knees were pressed together, my hands clasped palm to sweaty-ass palm.

"The chess club recorded its first victory of the season last night, beating Jamestown High eight to one," the vice principal announced over the loudspeaker. "Their next match will be held at Oak Ridge High this Thursday, so come on out and support the team!"

My teeth clenched. Who cared about the damn chess club? Get to the homecoming announcement already! Homecoming!

"Hey, Darla! Did you finish the calc homework?"

I glanced over my shoulder. Rusty Shipman was leaning forward in his desk, his ever-present spray of acne shining particularly red this morning. I wished someone would get the kid some Proactiv for Christmas. He was actually pretty handsome, but the zits were so distracting.

"Yeah, why?" I asked.

"I can't get number ten. Can I see your notes?"

"Yeah. No problem." I fished through my bag for my homework and handed it to him. From across the room I saw Kenna eyeing us curiously as she toyed with one of her short black braids, and faced forward again. She wouldn't tell Veronica I was whispering with Rusty in homeroom, would she?

"And now, for the moment you've all been waiting for, the announcement of this year's homecoming court as voted on by you, the students of Lake Carmody High."

I just about fainted and glanced at Kenna again. Her glossy smile was excited and encouraging. I felt so weak I could barely bring up a smile back.

"If your name is on this list, please come to room 128 immediately after school today for an informational meeting about campaign rules and regulations."

Yeah, yeah, yeah. Get on with it!

"First, the freshman representatives. The freshman princes will be Nico DeLeo and Scott Rasmussen. The freshman princesses will be Zadie Carlson and Vanessa Vine."

Kenna and I locked eyes. So Veronica's little sister had made it in her first year. Shocker.

"For the sophomore class, the princes will be Liam McKinley and Shane Westwood. The princesses will be Christa Jennings and Tara Schwartz."

I couldn't breathe. Oh God. I couldn't breathe. I sat back in my chair to keep myself from putting my head on the desk.

"And for the junior class . . ."

I swear every person in the room turned to look at me. Was that a good sign, or a bad sign? The juniors voted only for the junior representatives during nominations. Did this mean that a lot of them had voted for me? Or did they just know that I was nervous and they wanted to see me have a major breakdown when I didn't get it?

I would not break down. No. I would not break down. If I didn't get it, I would not break down.

Oh God, please let me get it.

"The junior princes will be Orion Floros and Josh Moskowitz."

My heart leaped. If Orion got it, then I had such a better chance at—

"And the junior princesses will be Darla Shayne and Veronica Vine."

I squealed so loud everyone laughed, and then they applauded. For me. Kenna jumped up and ran over to me, enveloping me in an awkward standing-to-sitting hug. My whole body flushed with relief, then ecstasy.

I was on homecoming court. I was on homecoming court. Darbot the Geek had made homecoming court!

"Back to your seat, please, Ms. Roy," our homeroom teacher grumbled.

Kenna air-kissed me, then went back to her chair by the window. It was so loud now I barely heard the seniors get announced, but Peter and Claudia's names were, obviously, mentioned. Then my phone buzzed and I grabbed for it, my hands shaking. It was a text from Orion.

CONGRATS! I KNEW YOU'D GET IT, MY PRINCESS!

I laughed, so overcome I almost cried, then texted back.

YOU TOO, MY PRINCE!!! XOXO

I sent the text, then texted Veronica.

CONGRATS, V! THREE YEARS IN A ROW! YOU ROCK!

I watched the phone as the VP finished his announcements, my smile so wide it was starting to hurt my face.

"I knew you'd get it," Jenica Stalb said, leaning across the aisle. "I totally voted for you."

"Me too," Rusty said, passing my homework back to me. "And thanks."

"Thank *you!*" I replied, my heart full.

The bell rang, and everyone began to gather their stuff. I got up and glanced at my phone. No reply from Veronica. A few more people congratulated me as we shuffled up the aisles toward the front of the room, and I waited for Kenna to join me before heading for the door. She wrapped her arm around mine and held me tight.

"So? How does it feel to be a princess?"

"Pretty damn good," I replied, glancing at my phone again.

My heart sank just a touch.

"What's wrong?" Kenna asked.

"Nothing. Just . . . I texted Veronica congratulations and she hasn't texted back."

"Oh." Kenna's face went serious for a second, so I knew I wasn't overreacting. "Well, she's probably just busy with people congratulating her. I'm sure she'll get to it."

"You're right. I'm sure that's it."

I didn't want to make a big deal out of it, but I still held on to my phone the whole way to first period, and she never texted me back. Not one word. Was she mad at me for something? Had I done something wrong? I thought it would be so cool, doing the homecoming thing together for once. Didn't she want me there?

By the time I sat down in honors chem, my smile was considerably less bright.

"Hey. Congratulations."

I looked up to find Wallace Bracken hovering next to my lab table on the way to his.

"Oh, um, thanks," I said.

I felt touched that he'd bothered, considering.

As he moved back to his own table, my cell phone vibrated in my hand. I was so startled I almost dropped it. It was from Veronica. Finally!

CONGRATS

My heart sank. That was it. No smiley face. No exclamation points. But at least it was something. I wasn't going to let a lack of punctuation get me down. I was nominated for homecoming queen. We were going to meet after school. Just us. Just the elite of the school. Veronica, Orion, Josh, and I were going to have the best time.

I took out a notebook and started to sketch out ideas for posters. No time like the present. It felt like the first day of a brand-new life.

CHAPTER SIX

True

Ninth period, Monday. We'd gotten through an entire day of school and no sign of Artemis and Apollo. Please, Gods, let this Wallace and Darla thing work. Let me be right about them. I just wanted to hold Orion in my arms again. I just wanted to hear him say he loved me. Please, please, please.

As I cleaned up my paints at the end of class, carefully twisting the crusted, corroded caps onto the tiny tubs of color, I kept an eye on Orion two easels over. He was wearing a black sweater that made him appear sophisticated beyond his years, and his dark, wavy hair had grown out a bit since he'd arrived on Earth, giving him a casual, sexy look. He shoved something into his backpack, zipped it up, and glanced my way.

"Hey," he said with a smile. "How was the rest of your day yesterday?"

I dropped the paint tubs onto the counter and grabbed my stuff, my heart pitter-pattering as I approached him. "Uneventful."

Thank the Gods.

"Congratulations on the whole homecoming court thing," I said drily. "I guess that makes you a pretty big deal around here."

He puffed up his chest. "Yeah. Don't get bigger than me." Then he laughed. "Whatever, it's just kind of cool to be nominated when I'm so new here, you know? Darla's all over me to come over tonight and make posters and stuff, but it seems kinda pointless. At my old school, the seniors always won."

Whatever he said next was completely lost on my ears, because I'd just caught sight of his painting, and the entire world around it had faded to a muted gray. He had painted the arrow again—our arrow—the one that hung from the pendant I'd once given him, but that now lay flat against my own chest. I could tell because the fletching was uneven, with nine striations in the feather on one side and eight on the other, which would, of course, make a real arrow imbalanced. In fact, he'd joked when I'd given it to him that I was trying to throw off his shot so I could beat him at target practice.

But this painting was different from the last. This time Orion had painted the arrow flying through the sky over a near-perfect rendering of the cabin we'd lived in together for the last six months in Maine. The six months before we were caught, that is.

Orion was not supposed to remember that cabin. He wasn't supposed to remember the arrow. Was he actually starting to recall our time together? Was he starting to realize who he really was? Maybe I'd been right from the beginning. Maybe our love was so strong it could survive even a brainwashing by Zeus himself.

"What?" Orion asked, shifting his feet self-consciously as I gaped at his painting. "Is it that bad?"

When he turned briefly to the side, I saw the tiny white scar near his temple, the spot where Artemis had struck him with an arrow those many millennia ago. I felt a surge of something huge and unstoppable inside me, and I knew what I had to do.

"No. I just . . ." I looked into his eyes—the eyes I knew so well I could have painted my very own copy of them down to the last tiny gold fleck. Holding my breath, I reached up and tugged his arrow pendant out from beneath the collar of my T-shirt.

Orion did a double take. The smile fell from his face. He looked at his painting, then back at the arrow. Then, so slowly it felt as if it took an eternity, his eyes met mine. At the easels around us, students gathered their things, dropped brushes into cans, chatted about their days, shuffled toward the door, but the two of us simply stood there, locked together inside our own little world.

"Orion," I said.

He opened his mouth to speak, and someone in the hallway screamed.

"Get out of the way, cretin!"

There was an awful slam, as if a body had been shoved against a locker door, and a few people shouted.

Orion grabbed my wrist. We stared at the open classroom door. Our teacher, Mrs. Fabrizi, had left for the bathroom or the teacher's lounge or had gone out to the parking lot for a smoke. We were entirely alone.

"Have you seen this girl? Do you know her?"

The skin on my back began to crawl. That was Apollo's voice. They had found me.

A door banged shut, and someone cried out in pain. I had to protect Orion. A quick glance around the classroom gave us few options. We were on the second floor, so going out the window would be dangerous, and the entire space was open, with nothing but flimsy easels to hide behind. I saw the handle on the supply closet in the corner and made a snap decision.

"I'm really sorry about this," I told Orion. Then I opened the door, flung him inside, and started across the room.

"Hey! What're you doing?!"

The closet's handle started to turn. There was a lock on it, of course, but I was halfway across the room. Clenching my jaw, I lifted my palm toward the handle and willed it to lock.

Nothing happened.

I tried again. The door began to open. My brain went weightless. My powers. What had happened to my powers?

Using my entire body, I slammed the door closed as hard as I could and turned the key, which Mrs. Fabrizi had carelessly left in the lock.

"True? What the hell? This isn't funny!"

Ignoring him, I pocketed the key, darted to the classroom door, and peeked ever so carefully into the crowded, end-of-the-day hallway. My heart stopped beating. Artemis and Apollo were dressed in their battle gear. He in short pants, laced boots, and a gold breastplate, she in a short skirt, long sleeves, and a leather vest, and they also looked pissed, which was never a good thing. At least the kids in the hallway were smart enough to be cowering near the walls, staying out of their way. They were showing around a picture of me, which they'd gotten from Zeus knew where, and shoving aside anyone who refused to help them.

Every fiber of my being told me to bolt, but Orion was just twenty feet away, rattling the door and getting louder by the minute. How the hell was I supposed to protect the both of us?

"True." Hephaestus's voice rose up behind me. "You're going to want to run."

He sat in his wheelchair near my side, his fists clenched atop his knees, the tendons in his neck protruding. At that moment, Artemis turned, and her dark eyes zeroed in on me. We held each other's gaze for a fury-filled moment as all movement around me seemed to slow. My mortal enemy. She who would as soon rip out my throat as take a breath. The goddess who coveted my love.

"True," Hephaestus said through his teeth. "Run!"

I whirled around, adrenaline, anger, and liquid terror coursing through my veins. I had to protect Orion. I had to stay alive long enough to restore his memory and regain our love. They were, at that moment, the only objectives that mattered.

I raced back into the art room, closed the door, and shoved a heavy but low supply cabinet up against it as best I could. Orion had grown frantic in my absence. If—no, when—Artemis and Apollo got through the outer door, they would surely hear him and discover him, their prize, sitting like a caged animal.

I pressed my face against the closet door.

"Orion, listen to me," I said desperately.

"True, what the—"

"Listen! Please!" I screeched. "There are some very dangerous people in the hallway and they're looking for me, but they won't hesitate to hurt you if they find you."

"What?!?! What the hell are you talking about?"

"Please!" I cried. "Please just stay quiet until they're gone. Please, Orion."

"True, I don't understand. Why are they after you?"

"Just trust me. Stay here and I'll explain everything to you later. Okay?"

Not that I had any idea how I would do that, but I had to say something. There was a pause. "Will you be all right?"

A tear rolled down my cheek at his concern. "I'll be fine."

"Hephaestus?" Apollo's voice shouted. "What in the name of Hades are you doing here?"

They were right outside the door. It was time for me to go. And the only way out was through the window. I ran to the pane farthest from the door, cranked it open, and kicked out the screen.

The door opened and slammed into the metal cabinet with an earsplitting clang. I whipped around and saw Artemis's livid face pressed into the small opening.

"You're dead!" she shrieked.

I hardly needed more motivation than that. I hooked one leg out the window, then the other, sitting on my butt on the sill. The ground looked so very far away. I had never been afraid of heights before becoming human, but now I realized with every fiber of my being how much it would hurt if my mortal body fell that distance. Artemis slammed against the door again, and then the cabinet went over, shattering glass bottles from the shelves across the linoleum floor. There was no more time to contemplate. I turned around and slid down, hanging by my fingertips out the window, the cold steel rim along the sill cutting into my fingers. There was nothing left to do but drop.

Someone nearby screamed as my body plummeted heavily to the ground. I landed on my feet, but the pain that bolted up my legs sent me immediately sprawling onto my side. I scrambled to my knees, doing a mental check for breaks, and realized with a sigh of relief that my bones were intact. I bounced up to my feet, and ran, flying by a few curious and disturbed bystanders in the courtyard.

"Are you okay?" one pudgy girl with braces asked.

I didn't answer. I just kept running. Only when I was about to turn the corner at the end of the building did I look back, and I saw both Artemis and Apollo leaning out the window, cursing after me. I gave them a triumphant smile and sprinted into the trees alongside the school. As I leaped over fallen branches and sloshed through muddy, leaf-filled puddles, my breathing grew ragged and I imagined Orion standing terrified inside the closet, trying not to move.

My heart suddenly seized up and I stopped running, bracing my hands over my knees. Was he okay? Had they found him?

Through the trees up ahead I could see the backs of a few massive houses, the backyards and patios dotted with lawn furniture and play sets. There was no one outside, and I leaned against a towering maple tree and pulled my phone from my pocket.

It was finally becoming clear to me how these things could come in handy. I hit Hephaestus's photo, and the phone began to ring.

"True? Thank the Gods," he whispered harshly. There was no noise behind his voice, as if he'd slipped into a vacuum. "Are you all right?"

"For now," I said. "Are you?"

"I managed to give Apollo a bloody lip before he got away from me," he said giddily. "Now I'm in the back of one of the janitor's closets. I'm gonna stay here until the coast is clear."

"Good." I dug my nails into the rough, wet bark of the nearest tree. "Hephaestus, I have a problem."

"Another one?" he joked.

"My powers. They didn't work," I told him.

"What? Why?"

"I don't know. Someone must have bound them. Zeus . . . Hera . . ."

"Hera," he said, then sighed. "It makes perfect sense. If your father is right and she wants to see you and Artemis do battle, she couldn't let one of you have an unfair advantage. She might not have been able to do it if you were back home, or if you'd known it was coming, but—"

"She caught me with my guard down." I swallowed hard. "So we're to fight as mere mortals, then?"

"Looks that way."

But there were two of them and one of me. Hardly a fair contest. We were silent for a moment. I didn't want to fight Artemis and Apollo. I didn't want to fight anyone. All I wanted was to be with my love again, to be at peace. If only my father had never found us. If only Zeus and Hera had stayed out of it. But of course they couldn't. They were upper gods. They had to control everything.

But they couldn't control me. I wouldn't let them.

"I have one more favor to ask of you," I said.

"What's that?"

"Before you head home, could you go back into the art room and get Orion out of the supply closet?" I asked. "He's locked inside. You might need a crowbar."

"What?" Hephaestus blurted. "How'd you manage that?"

"I have my ways," I murmured regretfully.

"Okay," he said, his voice turning serious. "I'll take care of it."

I felt sad, suddenly, thinking of Orion. I'd missed my opportunity to spill everything, and now that I had some distance from it, I knew it would have been a mistake. I could never tell him the truth about who he was, about who we were. There was no way he'd ever understand. I was just going to have to be patient and do my job. Plus keep the both of us alive long enough for me to succeed.

I saw a flash of something from the corner of my eye and my heart hit my throat, but it was just a robin, taking flight into the trees. Even so, it was a reminder that any false security I'd felt before today had been obliterated.

"I'd better get going," I said, gazing back in the direction of the school. "And Hephaestus?"

"Yeah?"

"When you do leave for home, make sure you're not followed. They know where we are now," I told him. "It's a whole new world."

I clicked off and darted out of the trees, putting as many mansions and play yards as I could between myself and my enemies.

CHAPTER SEVEN

Orion

WORKING ON POSTERS. R U COMING?

I stopped outside Goddess and stared at my phone. It was almost crazy how psyched Darla was about homecoming. I just didn't get it. What was the big deal if you got to wear a plastic crown? I knew it meant you were mega popular or whatever if you won the vote, but we both knew it was a long shot. And besides, the dance was almost two weeks away. We had plenty of time.

But I still felt the tiniest bit guilty when I texted back. Not for saying no as much as for saying no and being where I was.

CAN'T TONIGHT. SRY. CALL U LATER.

I shut off my ringer and pocketed my phone. Through the windows I saw True behind the counter, handing change over to a little girl. Even though Heath had told me that she was okay, I still let out a breath. Her hair was pulled back in a low ponytail, and she wore a pink T-shirt under her brown Goddess Cupcakes apron. The silver chain hung around her neck, but I couldn't tell whether that arrow—the one that looked exactly like the one I kept painting—still hung from it. The end was tucked under her collar.

Every time I thought about her showing me that necklace that afternoon, I got this weird tingling sensation at the back of my skull. The first time I'd painted the arrow, the assignment was to pick a symbol—any symbol—and an arrow was the first thing that had popped into my mind. I didn't know why but I thought hey, arrows are cool, and I went with it. But why did my arrow look exactly like True's arrow?

I must have noticed it on her at some point. I must have seen it that day she kissed me or when we had talked about Boosters. It made perfect sense.

But that didn't explain why I'd felt so . . . excited when she'd shown it to me that afternoon. I'd felt as if something was about to happen, but I had no idea what.

I shoved my hands through my hair and opened the door. True was handing two red velvet cupcakes to a couple I vaguely recognized from school. Heath sat at a corner table, reading a paperback novel. Dude sure hung around this place a lot. True's face lit up when she saw me.

"Orion! Hey!"

"Hi." I leaned into the counter, as close to her as I could get. My heart was pounding. "Are you okay?"

"Yeah. I'm fine. I'm so sorry about locking you in that closet," she replied. "It was the only thing I could think to do."

"It's fine. I mean . . . it sounded like those people were out for blood, so . . . thanks. I guess." I glanced up and down the counter. There was no one nearby, other than one of True's coworkers, who was sitting at a small table, tapping on a laptop with the end of her braid in her mouth. Monday nights weren't the most happening nights at Goddess. "What the hell happened? Who were those guys?"

True cleared her throat and looked down at her hands. Her fingernails were gnawed away, and there was a tiny cut on the back of one knuckle. She brushed a few crumbs off the pink countertop.

"They went to my old school, and we kind of had a . . . falling-out," she said, biting her bottom lip. "I didn't really hang out with the greatest people . . . before."

"So . . . what? You were in a gang or something?" I asked with an inadvertent laugh.

"A gang? Yes!" she exclaimed, weirdly excited to share this information. "That's perfect!"

"What?" I said, confused.

She shook her head and smiled. "No, I mean, that's exactly right. I was in a gang." Her expression shifted to a serious frown in a snap. "And I didn't want to be in the gang anymore . . . but they didn't want me to leave so . . . anyway, we moved away, but clearly . . . they found me."

"But why?" I asked, standing up straight. "Why come after you? Did you do something to them?"

True scratched her forehead and turned away. Crap. I was prying or something. But what did she expect? It wasn't every day a girl you liked—I mean, liked as a friend—told you she was on the run from some street gang.

"I . . . um . . ." She picked up the glass coffeepot and poured some into a cup, then chugged it down. Her slim hand was shaking. "I kind of told the police that they were . . . selling drugs. You know, at school." She turned her profile to me. "I was their star witness."

"Wow. So I guess they got off," I said, gripping the edge of the counter.

Her brow knit as she turned around again. "Got off what?"

I laughed. "Well, they're not in jail, so . . ."

"Oh, right! Yes. Of course." She laughed. "So that's why they hate me. Because I . . . turned on them."

I stared at her. Didn't she realize how serious this was? If drug dealers had busted up a school looking for her, then she was in major danger.

"What?" she asked, fiddling with her ponytail.

Or maybe I was wrong. She was clearly nervous. Maybe she did get it. And I didn't want to say anything to make her feel worse.

"You just . . . you don't really seem like the gangbanger type."

Which was true. She was way too beautiful. Too elegant. Too graceful and kind and intelligent to get sucked in by people like that.

True arched one eyebrow. "I'm tougher than I look."

I smirked. "That I can believe."

I stared into her eyes. There was something about them. Something familiar. An image hovered just at the edge of my mind—her eyes with strands of her hair tossed across them, a smile on her face—but then it faded, and the harder I tried to call it back, the murkier it got. It must have been a dream or something. Whatever it was, it was gone.

"Okay, I really don't want to talk about this anymore," True said. "Can I get you anything?"

"Sure," I said. "I'll have a french toast cupcake and coffee."

"Black," we both said at the same time.

I tilted my head. "How did you know?"

True smiled. "Just a hunch."

She poured the coffee and placed the mug on the counter, then opened the display case, smiling up at me through the glass. There

was that tingling warmth again. Like I was on the verge of something, but I didn't know what. When she turned to get a plate, I
ran my hand over the back of my neck. Was it possible to betray my
girlfriend just by smiling at another girl? Because that was what it
felt like I was doing.

"Speaking of breakfast food, we should talk about the pancake
breakfast," True said, sliding the plate toward me.

A customer came up behind me, but then the back door to the
kitchen opened and a tall guy in a black T-shirt with an eyebrow
piercing walked out. He gave True a nod and went to hang by the
register.

"I can help you over here!" he called, rescuing True from having
to work.

"What about the pancake breakfast?" I took a sip of my coffee
and reached for the cupcake.

"It's something the boosters and football team do together, and
tomorrow I'm gonna have to volunteer us for a job." True tugged a
folded piece of paper out of the back pocket of her jeans. "I happen
to be friends with the guy who's organizing everything, so I have
the list."

She flattened the paper on the counter, and we both leaned over
it. Our shoulders brushed, and my skin basically exploded. I shifted
position to try to separate from her, but somehow ended up getting
closer.

"Balloons, streamers, signage, cups and plates . . ." I read down
the list, trying to pretend like that's what I was thinking about.
What I was really thinking about was the lock of True's hair that
was brushing the back of my hand. But then I heard a laugh across
the café, a laugh that sounded a little like Darla's. I had to get a grip.
I stood up straight again and took a huge bite of cupcake.

"Design the place mats?" I asked, my mouth full of frosting.

There. Me being gross should break the mood.

"Oh yeah, apparently that's a big thing," True said. "Every year there's a different school-spirit-themed design."

"That sounds cool." I shoved the second half of the cupcake into my mouth. "I'm in."

"Yeah?" She fiddled with the paper. "Because it's going to take some work. We might have to get together a couple of times to figure it out."

My face was weirdly hot. I chewed. And chewed. And chewed some more. Then I swallowed and chugged some coffee, scalding my throat.

"Get together a couple of times?" I repeated. "Like, alone together?"

She lifted one shoulder, a little twist of a smile on her face. "Maybe."

Damn, she was pretty. And I was not going to feel guilty for thinking it. I could have a girlfriend and be attracted to other girls. It happened all the time. The key was not doing anything about it. That was the key.

"I think I can handle that," I said. "Place mats it is."

"Shake on it?"

True thrust her hand across the counter. I stared at her fingers. It was a weird thing to shake on, but what the hell? I grasped her hand and tried to breathe, telling myself that I was just imagining how perfect her fingers felt inside mine.

CHAPTER EIGHT

True

"I still don't like this," Hephaestus said as we headed for the front door of Lake Carmody High on Tuesday morning. "They know we're here. They're going to come back."

Overhead, storm clouds gathered, turning the world a murky gray. A sudden wind kicked up and someone screeched, sending my heart into overdrive. But it was just a girl chasing her lost book report up the pathway from the bus drop-off point. I lifted my hand hopefully and tried to use my powers to stop it for her, but nothing happened. My powers were still bound.

"Nothing?" Hephaestus asked.

I shook my head. "I kept trying all night. They're just gone."

"My mom didn't even want me to come to school today," a girl said to her friend as they hurried by.

"Did you hear about Mason Lange? He has a concussion!"

"What?"

"Yeah. That's what you get for asking what the hell some stranger is doing in your school wearing a costume."

"Omigod . . ."

Everyone was buzzing about Artemis and Apollo's attack

yesterday. The tension was almost as thick as the humidity.

"That's the girl," a redhead with thick glasses said, eyeing me suspiciously. "The one they were showing a picture of."

Her boyfriend shot me a scathing look, put his arm around her protectively, and squired her away.

"Great. So glad that's gotten around," I said under my breath.

"It's so chivalrous how he's protecting her from the danger that is you, though," Hephaestus joked. "You should at least appreciate that."

"Fair enough." I paused and took a deep breath. "Look, I know Artemis and Apollo are not just going to give up," I told him, glancing furtively over my shoulder as my hair whipped in front of my face. "But I can't just leave Orion here alone like a sitting duck. I have to be here to protect him. You'd do the same for Harmonia."

Hephaestus's eyes shadowed. "That I would."

"Have you heard from her lately?" I asked.

"Not since she warned us of Artemis and Apollo's arrival," Hephaestus said under his breath. "But it's not unusual for her to go silent for a few days. We try not to use the mirror too much to avoid detection by the upper gods." His right wheel got stuck in a divot and I waited while he shoved it free, which he did, gritting his teeth. "At least Orion came up with a cover story for you. Now if he sees them lurking, he'll think he knows why."

I shook my head and smiled. "I still can't believe it. A gang. Why didn't I think of that?"

We paused as we came around the corner. There was a huge crowd in front of the two double doors to the school. The people in the back were on their toes trying to see, and almost everyone was texting like mad. I noticed more people pointing at me and staring and tried to ignore it, but I'll admit it stung. I was just getting used to *not* being a pariah around here. One more reason to hate Artemis and Apollo.

A broad-chested white-haired man in a dark uniform walked up from behind us and strode to the melee, pushing through the throng like a butter knife through cream cheese. There was a shout, and suddenly the group fell silent.

"What's this about?" Hephaestus asked.

"New security measures."

Orion's voice, as always, warmed me from the inside out, melting away my tension. He stepped up next to me, surveying the crowd with appreciative eyes, as if they were his loyal subjects. He was wearing a red-and-blue-striped turtleneck sweater over jeans and looked so gorgeous I didn't understand why the girls at this school didn't mob him like he was a boy band member every time he stepped foot on the grounds. My mouth actually watered at the sight of him.

"Security measures?" I asked, trying to recover my senses.

He nodded. "After I saw you at Goddess yesterday, I told my mom about this whole gang-members-out-for-revenge thing, and she called the school board. They decided to hire a private security company to make sure those two kids don't get on school grounds again."

"You're kidding," I said.

"Nope. They got a bunch of pictures from people who got them on their phones yesterday, so they know who to look for."

Hephaestus and I exchanged a look—a very happy look—and together the three of us joined the crowd, which the man in charge was now organizing into four neat lines. I saw one of the security guards hold up a tablet with a semi-blurry picture of Apollo's face on it.

"Orion, this is genius," I said. "Thank you."

"Don't thank me. Thank my mom. If there's a school safety issue, that woman is on it like leather on a football."

Unbelievable. First Orion had unwittingly supplied the perfect explanation for Artemis and Apollo, and now he'd saved the day without realizing it. He'd saved himself, really. Artemis and Apollo might have easily made it past the usual lame guards who policed the school, but an entire trained security detail? Not a chance.

He was so my hero. He just didn't know it.

"So . . . do you want to meet up at lunch and talk about our pancake breakfast project?" I ventured, hugging a couple of books against my chest.

I saw Hephaestus eyeing me in an amused sort of way as we inched forward in the line, but I chose to ignore it. I must have looked so human to him in that moment. I *felt* human—vulnerable.

Orion scratched the back of his neck, his telltale gesture of uncertainty. The sight of it caught my heart, as any sign of his former self seemed to do. It reminded me that he was still in there somewhere—my Orion—and that sooner or later he'd come back to me.

Sooner. Sooner. Sooner. Please let it be sooner.

"Um, I usually have lunch with Darla. . . ."

"Oh." I looked away. "Right. I just thought we were going to . . . you know . . . make a plan."

"We are. No. You're right. If we're gonna do this, we should do it. We only have a couple of days," Orion said. "Lunch is cool. I'll make it happen."

"Cool," I replied, grinning.

"Cool," he said again.

"So very, very cool," Hephaestus joked.

I whacked the back of his head just as we reached the front of the line. The security guard, a man with a wide neck and almost no hair whose name was Eugene, according to the gold tag on his pocket, held up a picture of Artemis next to my face. I glanced at Orion to see if he registered any sort of recognition at the sight of his former love.

"Wow," he said. "This must've been some hot gang you were a part of."

I rolled my eyes.

"You can go through," Eugene said.

"Thank you."

I walked into the lobby and stopped in my tracks. Tacked to the wall directly across from the door was a huge black-and-white picture of Orion and Darla, holding hands and laughing. It was at the center of a blue poster with silver lettering that read FLOROS & SHAYNE: PERFECT TOGETHER. HOMECOMING KING & QUEEN. Darla was busy putting up another one over the window in the cafeteria door. She hopped down and helped the sophomore girl next to her reposition her own poster so that it hung straight.

Which was nice. I'd give it to her. But most of the other posters were just of one person. I saw a pretty picture of Zadie sitting alone in a park, and another of Gavin Dunnellon in his football jersey. Why did Darla have to post a picture of herself hanging on Orion? She couldn't pose for a photo alone?

Hephaestus wheeled up beside me. "You okay?"

"I think I just died a little bit inside."

He reached out and squeezed my hand. "Hey. You scored lunch."

I gave him a grateful smile. "I did, didn't I?"

Suddenly Darla spotted Orion and ran to him, throwing herself into his arms like he was a soldier just returned from the Battle of the frickin' Bulge.

"When did you do all this?" he asked her.

"I was up half the night and got here at the crack this morning," she said. "Do you like it?"

"You're kind of amazing, you know that?"

My heart felt like it had turned to ash. He leaned in for a kiss and I turned away, headed for my locker, Hephaestus trailing along at my side. Orion and Darla were the perfect high school couple. He clearly cared about her. And I was clearly nothing but a peripheral distraction. If I was going to get Darla and Wallace together, I had to do it fast, before these two got any closer.

"It's gonna be okay, True. One more couple and you get him back."

Hephaestus was right, of course. And there was plenty to feel positive about. The school was safe from Artemis and Apollo, I had a lunch date with Orion, and today Darla would be attending her first Boosters meeting as Wallace's assistant.

But still, I couldn't help wishing that Orion's love for me was big enough to overcome anything, including a brainwashing by the mighty Zeus. I couldn't help wishing that Orion—*this* Orion— would choose me.

CHAPTER NINE

Orion

"I don't understand why you have to sit with her," Darla said, crossing her arms over her chest in this pouty, sexy way. She pushed out her bottom lip as she glared across the courtyard. "I mean, look at her. What a total freak."

True was alone at a picnic table, laid out on the bench with her eyes closed. Her long hair spilled to the ground, where it had caught a couple dozen fallen leaves. The sky was covered in gray clouds, but two tiny shafts of sunlight had broken through and were trained right on her face. Usually she was with Charlie and Katrina or Wallace and/or Heath, which would have made the convincing so much easier. But for some reason, today it was just her.

"Don't you care what people think?" Darla asked.

I blinked. "Um, no. Not really."

"Excuse me, you two." The white-haired guy in charge of security came up behind us and cleared his throat. "Would you mind moving this a bit farther inside? We want to keep all entries and exits clear."

Darla and I moved closer to the wall, away from the door to the lobby. The guy continued into the cafeteria, his head swiveling left and right methodically. He looked like a robot.

"It's so weird, having them here," Darla said, rubbing her arms like she'd gotten a chill. "I feel like I'm living in a TV movie."

"I know, but if it keeps everyone safe . . ." I looked over at True again.

I hadn't told anyone what I knew about those people being after True and why, or that I was there for the big attack. I just didn't feel like talking about it 24-7, which was what would happen if I spilled. But the gangsters, or whatever they were called, had shown True's picture to enough people yesterday that everyone knew she was somehow involved.

Darla followed my gaze, then gave me an irritated look. "What's Veronica gonna say if you go out there?"

I sighed. This was pretty much the only thing I didn't like about Darla. Veronica's opinion meant everything to her. I'd watched her wait to order food until Veronica ordered hers, then copy Veronica's order. I'd seen them wear almost the same outfit to school half a dozen times. If Veronica hated a movie, Darla hated that movie. If Veronica liked a song, Darla liked the same song. It was borderline scary.

"I don't care about Veronica," I told her, rubbing the sides of her arms. "I care about you."

"Well, *I* think you should sit with me." She shook her chestnut-brown hair behind her shoulders and lifted her chin. "Homecoming is in less than two weeks. Perception matters. You can't be hanging out with some gangbanger."

"She's not a gangbanger." I laughed. I couldn't help it. "It's one lunch!" I wrapped my arms around Darla's waist and pulled her to me, so close that she had to put her hands on my shoulders.

"Besides, don't the seniors usually win these things?"

"You'd think so, but there was this one year that a junior won. Her name was Ruma Sen. But she was Miss Teen New Jersey *and* she was going out with the senior captain of the basketball team, so . . ." Darla shook her head, like she was clearing away an unpleasant smell. "Anyway, that's not the point. The point is you're *my* boyfriend. A fact *she* seems to keep forgetting."

I chuckled. "True and I are just friends."

"Please. That girl has 'I want to be Orion's girlfriend' stamped on her forehead," Darla said.

I glanced at True. Really? Did she actually *like me* like me?

"Orion?"

Right. So not what I was supposed to be thinking about.

"That would be one big forehead," I joked, and Darla laughed. "Look, it's one lunch," I said again. "And I promise that tonight I will come over with Chinese food and watch as many episodes of *Say Yes to the Dress* as you want."

"Really?"

"I'll even pretend I understand the difference between princess and . . . what's the other one that you like?"

"A-line."

"Right. A-line."

Darla leaned in and pressed her lips to mine. My heart did the crazy swelling thing it did every time we kissed, like it practically couldn't take it. She tasted like cherries and sugar, and her body was soft and hard at the same time. I would never understand how this girl was single when I moved here. Did the guys in Lake Carmody not have eyes?

"You have a deal, Mr. Floros," she said, looking at me through her thick lashes.

"Can't wait," I replied truthfully.

Darla turned and sauntered off slowly, knowing exactly how awesome her ass looked in her jeans, and tossed me a smile over one shoulder. As I walked away, one of the youngish security dudes who was stationed near the door shot me this look like *Nice*.

I grinned back. *I know, right?*

I grabbed some cafeteria grub from the food line and headed outside for True's table.

"Comfortable?" I asked.

She opened one eye, then sat up, her hair bringing the leaves with her. "I was, yes, thanks for asking." She reached for my tray and snagged a couple of fries, shoving them into her mouth.

"Sure. You can have some. Feel free," I joked.

True rolled her eyes. "What is it with people and food? This place has tons of it on offer. It's not like we're in the middle of the Greco-Persian Wars or something. Back then you'd trade your mother for a crust of bread, but now—"

I sat down across from her. "The Greco-Persian Wars?"

True blushed and plucked a leaf from her hair, tossing it up into the breeze. "I'm kind of a history buff."

"Right." I shoved my straw into my soda and smiled at her as I took a sip. True stole another few fries. This was a person who didn't give a crap what people thought of her.

"That's an interesting lunch," she said, eyeing my tray. "Are you going into hibernation soon?"

I looked down at my plate, which was piled high with two burgers, an extra-large order of fries, a helping of macaroni and cheese, and a chocolate chip cookie. She had a muffin, a yogurt, and a banana on her side.

"You're the one who keeps bogarting my fries," I joked. "And I bet I finish this before you get through that yogurt, and when I do, I'm taking your muffin."

"My muffin is your muffin," she said, which, for some reason, made me blush. Then she reached into her backpack and pulled out a bunch of laminated paper. "Now let's talk place mats. These are the ones from the last five years."

"They save the place mats?" I asked, shoving a forkful of macaroni into my mouth as I looked them over. The worst was a totally amateur drawing of a football with a hand-lettered school logo. The best was a wide-angle picture of the whole football team in uniforms, cheering, with football helmets shoved in the air.

"I like that one," I said.

"You would." True laughed.

I arched my eyebrows. "What?"

"Anything to get your face out there," she teased me.

I blinked. Was I that bad?

True tapped her chin with her index finger. "I like the idea of a photograph instead of a painting or a drawing, though."

"Okay. But if not the football team, then what?" I asked, lifting my chin at Josh and Veronica as they walked by on their way to our usual table. Josh nodded back, but Veronica gave me this look like I was a pile of puke. Like I gave a crap. I didn't like the way she treated Darla, and I couldn't care less what she thought of me. "The cheerleaders?" I suggested, grinning.

True took a spoonful of yogurt. "A sexy place mat?"

"Who said anything about sexy?" I asked, raising my palms. "You just assumed, which is very sexist of you, by the way."

"Uh-huh."

From the corner of my eye, I saw Darla stride by us, pointedly looking away. I wished she didn't feel hurt by the fact that

I was having lunch with someone else. I wished things were less complex for her. But I'd make it up to her later with two hours of mind-numbingly shallow TV. Who else offered to sit through *Say Yes to the Dress?* I was the best boyfriend ever.

"Okay, we could take a picture of the front of the school," I said, narrowing my eyes. "Or of the logo on the basketball court . . ."

"The football field!" True exclaimed, dripping some yogurt onto her chin. "It's really pretty out there in the afternoons when the sun starts to go down. I bet that would look amazing."

"Sounds good to me," I said, handing her a napkin. "Maybe I could get my friend Greg to take the picture. He's one of the year-book photographers."

"That would be perfect." She quickly and unself-consciously wiped her face and fingers, then crossed her arms on the table. "So, can I ask you something?"

"Shoot," I said.

"Why football?"

"What do you mean?" I asked.

Her shoulders rose. "Why play football? What made you pick that?"

I took another bite of mac and cheese. "I dunno. I've been play-ing since I was six years old. It's just something I've always done."

True looked at me strangely, like I'd said something she didn't understand. Then she shook her head and sighed. "Okay, but why do you still play it now? What do you like about it?"

"Um . . . I don't know. I like the team vibe thing," I said. "The competition . . . I think it's cool, like, lining up right across from these guys. You get to look 'em in the eye and sort of try to psych them out. And then, once the ball is snapped, it's about survival. Who's stronger, who's faster, who's smarter. It's very . . . primal, I guess."

True laughed, and the sound sent a warm flood over my stomach. "What?" I asked, blushing.

"Nothing. Nothing. It's nice." True looked down at her food. She shoved her spoon into her yogurt and swirled it, like a tornado. "I mean it's good. It's good to have something in your life you really . . ."

I swallowed, waiting for her to finish her sentence. True looked up at me, those clear blue eyes full of pain. And not just regular pain, but a lot of it. A lifetime of it, if I had to guess. I tried to look away, knowing Darla was probably watching us, knowing that staring into another girl's eyes was in no way gonna fly. But I couldn't. I literally could not look away.

"Something you really what?" I said.

"Something you love," True said quietly.

My heart banged against my rib cage. True picked up the plate with the muffin on it and passed it to me. "Here," she said, her eyes never leaving mine. "I'm not going to eat it anyway."

"Um . . . okay."

I glanced down, and all of a sudden I was somewhere else. The plate was a different plate—ceramic with blue flowers—and the table under it was made of raw wood, not plastic. I saw True's hand as she passed it to me, but it wasn't her hand as it was now. It was softer, paler, whiter. And her nails were perfectly shaped and pink. But it was her hand. I knew it somehow. Then she looked up at me and smiled. Her hair was loose over her shoulders, and behind her, a fire crackled inside a stone fireplace.

"What? What's wrong?"

Suddenly I slammed back into the now. It was like being sucked down a long straw and splatting up against a glass window at the end of it. At least, it was what I imagined that might feel like. My whole face radiated with pain, and my skin felt tight over every inch of my body.

"Orion? Hey! Are you okay?" True snapped her fingers in front of my face. She'd already put the plate back down. The pain moved from my cheekbones into my skull and took root at the back of my brain, pulsating angrily.

"Yeah. Yes. I'm fine." Both my hands gripped the edge of the table, but I didn't remember putting them there.

"Good." She looked concerned. "I thought I lost you for a second there."

"No. I'm okay." My fingers shook as I released my hold. "I think I just had déjà vu or something." I cleared my throat and reached for my soda. After a few quick gulps, the pain subsided. Not totally, but enough that I could focus. "That ever happen to you?"

The look she gave me was both understanding and confused—somehow sad and somehow hopeful. She released a sigh and smiled.

"It happens all the time."

CHAPTER TEN

Darla

I didn't even look at True Olympia as I strode into the auxiliary gym for the Boosters meeting on Tuesday after school. The room stank of stale sweat and dusty, forgotten equipment, but since it had been pouring buckets outside since sixth period, they couldn't meet outside. Everyone was sitting in groups on the floor, making signs for the game that coming weekend. From the corner of my eye, I saw True glance at me, but I ignored her. She was not worthy of my notice. At least, that was the image I was trying to project to the world.

I walked past a couple of girls who were whispering about "the attack" on Monday, which was what everyone was now calling it, and casting suspicious glances at True. I wondered if it was possible, what people were saying—that True was somehow involved. Not that I would be surprised to find one more layer of weirdness about her. When I saw Wallace sitting on the bottom bleacher, I hesitated. I actually felt nervous, not that I would admit that to anyone, ever. But what if he hated me?

Then Wallace looked up from his iPod and smiled. Which, okay, was a good sign, but . . . what was wrong with him? You didn't smile at the person who completely ditched you as a best friend four years ago. You just didn't.

"What's up, Ding Dong?" he asked in full voice, clearing off the area next to him. "I heard you were joining our ranks, but I didn't dare believe it until right now."

A few girls nearby snickered.

"Don't call me that, *Wall-E*." I sat down in a huff.

"Someone's in a mood," he said, shaking his dark hair off his brows. He had these very dark-brown eyes that were soft like a puppy's. Why he hid them with his hair I had no idea. "Shouldn't you be psyched?" he asked. "Your beautiful face is plastered on every wall of the school."

I blushed slightly and flicked a speck off my sweater. "Whatever. No one's going to vote for me if people think my boyfriend would rather hang out with True Olympia," I said, shooting her a dirty look. Ugh. So much for ignoring her. I turned toward Wallace, putting my shoulder between me and True. "Did you *see* them at lunch today? Why does he want to slum it with the losers?"

Wallace blinked. "Isn't that kind of what you're doing right now?"

I froze. Awkward! "You are not a loser," I said, with as much certainty as I could force into my voice.

Wallace laughed and tapped at his iPad. "Yeah, right. That's why you haven't talked to me since seventh grade. Because I'm the coolest of the cool."

"Come on. Don't say that," I muttered.

"Say what?" He lifted his shoulders. "The truth?"

"Whatever." I really didn't want to talk about this. Not here. Not now. Okay, if we're being honest? Not ever.

"Yeah, whatever. And by the way, True's not a loser. She's a friend," Wallace said, sliding his iPad aside on the next bleacher up. "So I'd appreciate it if you didn't trash her in front of me."

Yeah. This was going well. "Well, I'm here. So what are we working on?"

"We have the pancake breakfast this weekend," Wallace said, handing me a list. "At the end of the meeting today, we'll ask people to sign up to take care of each of these things with their football player. Why don't you look it over and see if you can think of anything I missed?"

I glanced down the page. Only one item had already been claimed. Next to "Place mats" he'd typed in "True & Orion." Just seeing their names together like that made me taste bile.

"Why does she get first pick?" I asked.

"Apparently, that was the job your boyfriend wanted," Wallace said, looking down at his iPad. "Don't you want him to be happy?"

What I wanted was for a huge lightning bolt to pierce the gym roof and fry True Olympia where she sat. Was that really too much to ask? Mercifully, my phone beeped. I dug it out of my bag and was relieved to see a text from Veronica. Someone from my normal life! At least, I was psyched until I read it.

AT THE MALL! WHAT ABOUT THIS DRESS 4U?

I had avoided dress shopping yesterday afternoon by claiming I had a Skype call scheduled with my mom, and I'd kind of hoped that Veronica would just forget about it and move on to something else. Apparently, I was not that lucky. The picture popped up, and I almost gagged. A headless mannequin was sporting a pink dress that looked like something out of a nightmare movie from the eighties. I typed back,

YOU'RE KIDDING, RIGHT?

But I hesitated before sending it. Because what if she wasn't kidding? Then I'd be insulting her taste. I sighed and my posture slumped. What was the right thing to text back? How to be diplomatic about this and not set her off? Sometimes text etiquette could be very complex. Especially when it came to Veronica.

"What's wrong?" Wallace asked.

"Nothing."

He angled for a look at my phone and snorted. "Halloween costume?"

"Apparently, it's the dress Veronica wants me to wear to homecoming," I said.

"What dress do *you* want to wear to homecoming?" he asked.

I scrolled to the pic of me in the blue dress and held it up so he could see.

"You look awesome in that," he said boldly. "What's wrong with it?"

"Nothing. I mean . . . you don't think it makes my hips look fat?" I asked, tilting my head.

Wallace snorted. "Did Veronica tell you that?"

"No. Well, yes," I admitted, my shoulders slumping. "But she was right."

Another text from Veronica popped up.

HELLO???

I shoved the phone deep inside my bag. I was just going to pretend I didn't get her text yet. How was that for diplomacy?

Wallace let out this snarky laugh and shook his head. "The girl's good."

"What do you mean?" I asked, leaning my elbow on the upper bleacher and my cheek in my hand. I was mildly distracted by a group of freshman girls who were kneeling around a half-done banner, trying to figure out how to best outline the letters with gold glitter.

"She's trying to sabotage you," he said.

My jaw dropped. "You're crazy."

"Do I look crazy?" he asked.

I let my eyes travel slowly over his outfit. Black Vans sneakers, brown-and-black-plaid cargo pants, a black T-shirt with R2-D2 on it, and a leather bracelet wrapped five times around his wrist. Plus, there was black ink pretty much covering his left arm. An equation of some kind, it looked like. Of course, aside from the arm ink, the look worked for him, but he'd given me such an opening.

"Do you really want me to answer that question?" I joked.

Wallace turned sideways on the bench, pulling one knee up under his chin so he could better face me. "Let me ask you this. How did she react when she found out you were nominated? Did she squeal and scream and shower you with air kisses?"

"Um . . . not exactly," I said cagily.

"Right! Because she was hoping someone else would be nominated. Someone who wasn't a threat. Someone totally beatable. You've got Veronica Vine spooked, Ding Dong," he said, lowering his voice so the snickering girls wouldn't hear, at least. "And now she wants you to look like a pink cotton candy disaster to kill your chances."

He couldn't be right, could he? I mean, Veronica Vine could never feel threatened by Darbot the Geek.

"You're not Darbot the Geek anymore," Wallace said, like he was reading my mind. Which kind of got under my skin. We weren't friends anymore. He had no right to think he knew what I was thinking. Even if he did.

"Okay, first of all, Veronica is my best friend, and while she may be a tad self-centered, she would never sabotage me."

Wallace laughed and started to interrupt, but I lifted a hand to stop him. On the floor, one of the freshmen was about to dump a whole canister of glitter on a skinny, uneven line of glue.

"I'm sorry, can we pause this conversation?" I said.

Without waiting for an answer, I got up and crouched next to the girls and their sign.

"No, no, no, ladies. First, you should use a paintbrush to even out the glue and make a thicker line," I said, grabbing a clean, flat brush to demonstrate. "Then you carefully scatter the glitter."

I demonstrated, shaking the glitter out like it was salt, then blew away the excess. Voilà! A perfect outline. "See?"

"Wow. Thanks," one of the girls said, looking at me as if in awe.

"Just let me know if you need any more help. I'll be right over there," I said, pointing at Wallace. I got up and perched myself next to him again. He smirked at me.

"What?" I snapped.

"Nothing. Unpause," he replied.

I sighed. "Okay, secondly, I have *zero* chance of winning. The only junior ever to win homecoming queen at Lake Carmody High was Ruma Sen, and she was like a goddess among girls. And even if a junior *could* win, it would definitely be Veronica, not me." I paused and toyed with the zipper on my messenger bag. "It's an honor just to be nominated."

"Can I talk now?" Wallace asked.

"Sure," I replied tartly. "Knock yourself out."

"Okay, first of all, everyone hates Veronica Vine."

I pressed my lips together. If anyone in the world had a total right to hate Veronica, it was Wallace. I averted my eyes, trying to figure out what to say.

The girls on the floor continued their glitter line and high-fived, which made me smile. See? I was totally good at projects. I should have joined Boosters ages ago. If only Orion could see me now, he'd totally ask for me to take over and boot True to the curb.

Just thinking her name made me look at her, and she quickly looked away. Why was she staring at me? Freak.

I took a deep breath. "Okay, I get it. But 'everyone'? Really?"

"Look, people *pretend* to love Veronica because they think they have to," Wallace said with that *I know everything* look on his face that annoyed me even back when we were friends. "She's mean, Darla. She's mean to everyone. Even her boyfriend. Even you."

"She's not mean. Not . . . not anymore, anyway. She's just opinionated. Men are intimidated by women who know what they want, so they label them as bossy or mean or bitchy, but she's not. She's confident."

"No, no. She's bitchy." Wallace reached for his iPad and brought some kind of list up on the screen. "Have you ever asked yourself why Ruma Sen won homecoming queen as a junior?"

"She was a super-popular gorgeous beauty queen with a hot boyfriend," I replied, flicking my hair over my shoulder, glad to be off the touchy subject of Veronica. "Duh."

"Wrong again," Wallace sang, which made me want to slap him. "It's all about the numbers, Ding Dong."

"Don't call me that," I said again, but this time through my teeth.

"Here's how it works," he said, tapping his iPad screen.

Nice. Just ignore me. Why was I ever friends with this person?

"Each class generally votes for the kids nominated from their own class, except for a handful of the freshmen and sophomores who vote for juniors and seniors because they think they should," he explained, the rectangular glow of the screen lighting up his face.

"And you know this how?" I asked, studying my nails as if I was *so* uninterested. Although my interest was officially piqued.

"I'm on the homecoming committee. I helped count the votes the last two years."

"*You're* on homecoming?" I didn't mean to sound snotty, but I did.

"Gotta round out my college apps somehow," he said. "And you know how I love to crunch the numbers. Anyway, back when Ruma Sen was a junior at Lake Carmody, the junior class was bigger than any other class at the school. Thus, she won most of the vote. I went into the records and double-checked."

"So?" I said.

Wallace turned his iPad screen toward me, holding it straight up against his thigh. His case was covered in planets and comets and shooting stars.

"So, right now the junior class is bigger than the senior class by seventy-two kids, and bigger than the sophomores by sixty-three," he told me, pointing to the official school census. "That means a junior could win this thing. *You* could win this thing."

I pulled the iPad closer to me, making sure that what I was seeing was correct. Wallace was right. The junior class was huge compared to the others. And if those were the people who nominated me, then maybe they would also vote for me. And if they did . . .

My mouth went dry. I imagined myself standing in the center of the tricked-out gymnasium, a sparkly crystal crown atop my head. Suddenly I could practically feel the hard plastic band against my skull.

But then my phone beeped again and the sensation died.

"You mean Veronica could win this thing," I said, pushing the iPad back toward him.

Wallace rolled his eyes and slapped the cover closed over the screen. "Okay. You just keep telling yourself that."

I smiled slightly. His mom used to say that to us when we were feeling down on ourselves about a project gone wrong. He must have picked it up from her. Suddenly it felt as if no time had passed. As if nothing had changed.

"You really think I could win?" I asked, glancing over at the freshmen as they held up their completed and totally perfect sign, then brought it over to the corner to dry.

Wallace followed my eyes and smiled. "Yeah. I really think you could."

CHAPTER ELEVEN

True

"So, you don't think those guys are going to come after you again, right?" Claudia asked me after Boosters that afternoon. We stood in the front hallway under one of the big banners advertising the pancake breakfast this weekend, which we'd secured with about four rolls of tape.

Apparently word really had gotten around that Artemis and Apollo had been showing people a picture of me yesterday after school. And also that I'd thrown myself out a window to avoid them. So far no one seemed to know about Orion's involvement in the whole thing, though, which was good. I didn't want him to have to try to explain that I'd locked him in a closet. It wouldn't do much for his reputation as a male, or mine as a non-weird person, which I was still trying to cultivate.

"They get distracted easily," I lied. "Anyway, I'm sure the school is safe, at least, with all the added security. And my mom and I have an alarm system at home." Another lie. But maybe we should get one.

"Okay then. Well, be safe."

Claudia surprised me by reaching in for a hug. I hugged her

back and smiled. Physical contact was so rare around here, it was nice to share actual affection.

"See you tomorrow?" she said when we parted.

"Yep." I couldn't stop smiling as she strode back toward the gym to meet Peter. "And tell Peter I said hi."

"I will."

Peter and Claudia. A happy, beautiful couple, reunited because of me. It hadn't been easy, but I'd figured it out, and look at them now. They not only seemed closer than ever, but were practically a lock for this homecoming king and queen insanity. And Charlie Cox and Katrina Ramos, my first couple, were going strong. Whenever I saw them together, they were holding hands or whispering in each other's ears or sneaking kisses. Totally in love.

I could do this. I could match another couple. I just had to stay positive. I took out my phone and texted Wallace.

HOW WAS IT W/DARLA 2DAY?

He texted back immediately.

FINE. WHY?

YOU GUYS LOOKED LIKE YOU WERE HITTING IT OFF.

His reply said merely:

????

Ugh. Maybe it was time to stop being coy about this and tell him my suspicions. If he did like her, it would make it much easier to match the two of them with him on my side.

"Hey, True!"

I looked up to find Charlie and his friend Brian walking past, soaking wet from cross-country practice in the rain. Charlie's usually floppy blond hair was slicked back from his face, and Brian's dark skin shone under the fluorescent lights.

"Hey, guys!" I said with a smile, flipping my hair over my shoulder.

"Are you gonna be at Goddess later?" Charlie asked, walking backward as he passed me, his sneakers making awful, wet squeaking noises with each step.

"Not tonight. Tomorrow."

"Ugh! I was so looking forward to some free cupcakes," he said with a wink.

I laughed as I rounded the corner into the main hall, and I realized that my heart felt light and giddy. It wasn't so bad, being a normal, human teenager. Once you had friends, once you had a purpose, once you developed a sense of style. In fact, I was starting to get comfortable in my own skin. Earth wasn't the hell it was cracked up to be. I hooked a left and headed for the door all smiles, and then my foot was nearly crushed by a wheelchair wheel.

"Hephaestus! Are you *trying* to maim me?"

"No, actually, I'm saving your ass," Hephaestus said, turning me away from the front of the school. There were still two security guards posted at the doors, but they were chatting about some football game and not paying much attention to the scant number of students coming from after-school activities.

"Why? What's wrong?" I asked.

"The twins are out there," Hephaestus said under his breath. "Apparently they've figured out they can't get on school grounds, so they're lurking at the deli across the street. You have to go out the back way." He glanced down the hall at the sound of male laughter, and we both saw Orion headed toward us along with Josh Moskowitz, Trevor McKay, and Gavin Dunnellon—a wall of wet hair and varsity jackets. "And you have to get Orion to go with you."

So much for my normal human moment. I had to protect my amnesia-ridden boyfriend from the fallen deities looking to kidnap him and kill me. Awesome.

"How?" I asked.

"I don't know, but just do it. I'll get the van and meet you in the back parking lot."

He gave my wrist a quick squeeze before wheeling toward the exit. My skin felt hot and prickly as adrenaline began to course through my veins. I had no idea what the twins might do with Orion if they got their hands on him, but I wasn't willing to find out. The guys were fast approaching. I grasped at the only thing I had going for me, and turned to face them with a smile.

"Hey, guys!" I said brightly.

"Hey, True," Orion said as the others added their greetings. "What's up?"

I grabbed Orion's arm and turned him around, steering him through the crowd of his friends back toward the gym. "*I* am taking *you* out to dinner."

"You are?" he asked, one hand clutching his football duffel, the other his backpack strap on his shoulder. "Why?"

I hurried him away from his friends, out of their earshot. Luckily, none of them seemed to care in the slightest that I was dragging him away. They simply went on their merry way toward the front door. Boys. Honestly, it seemed as if nothing ever fazed them.

"It's a booster thing," I told him as we passed by Lester Chen's locker with its big, glittering #85 on the door. "It's . . . take your player to dinner night!"

"Really? But none of the other guys—"

"Are you really gonna turn down a free pizza?" I interjected. "You can even get extra peppers if you want, as disgusting as it is."

Orion stopped walking. "How did you know I like extra peppers?"

Oh, Hades. Just when I was so close to home free. I ran my hand over the back of my neck as my brain scrambled frantically for a response. But I'd never had pizza with Orion in this version of our life. I'd never even been in a pizza shop while he was eating when I could have overheard his order.

"Darla!" I blurted suddenly. "Darla told me. She joined the Boosters, and so I asked her what you'd want to eat and she said pizza with extra peppers."

Orion looked so stunned I thought he might fall over. "Darla helped you?"

"I know," I said. "I was as surprised as you are."

"But I'm supposed to go to her house tonight. For Chinese. We had a plan." He looked almost forlorn, which broke my heart. The thought of Darla potentially ditching him made him that sad.

"Like you can't have pizza now and then Chinese in a few hours. Are you not a teenage American male?" I ventured.

Orion smiled. "Excellent point."

In the lobby, a door slammed. I glanced nervously over my shoulder. "So can we go?"

"Sure," he said finally, shrugging. "I could eat."

I breathed a sigh of relief and shoved open the back door next to the gym. The rain had slowed to a light drizzle, and the cool autumn air felt like nirvana against my hot skin. I just hoped he didn't say anything to Darla later about my lie. But there was nothing I could do about that now. The most important thing was that I was saving him from Artemis and Apollo. For now, anyway.

Tomorrow was an entirely different nightmare for an entirely different time.

CHAPTER TWELVE

Darla

"Thanks for picking me up," I told Veronica as I slipped into the passenger seat of her black Mercedes. My hair was misted with rain, and I was shivering under my lightweight trench. "I'll have my car back tomorrow."

Once every three months my mother's mechanic showed up like clockwork to take my car into the shop for a bunch of routine maintenance. Today was that day, so our housekeeper Lisa had dropped me off this morning, but she was too busy with errands to pick me up. Orion was supposed to get a ride home with Josh, so I'd tried to find them after Boosters, but no luck. Thank God Veronica had been done with the mall.

"No problem. It was on my way."

Veronica tossed her hair over her shoulder, and I noticed the many shopping bags neatly lined up on the small backseat of her car.

"Get anything good?" I asked as I plugged in my seat belt.

"Eh. Slow day."

I almost laughed. Her slow day was another girl's shopping spree. She hit the gas without checking a single mirror, and the car lurched away from the curb.

"Did you get my text?" she asked.

Snagged. I'd been hoping she'd be too busy cataloging her many purchases to remember the homecoming dress thing.

"Oh yeah," I said. "I just checked my phone before I called you for the ride."

"What did you think?"

We came to a stop at the edge of the parking lot, the windshield wipers gliding lazily back and forth over the wide windshield. Across the street, half a dozen cars idled at a red light, so Veronica had to wait to make the left. She instantly began to drum on the steering wheel. Veronica hated to wait almost as much as I hated to eat alone.

I couldn't wait to get home, crawl into some comfy yoga pants, and order up a Chinese food feast for me and Orion. Lunch had been a skimpy salad, as always, and my stomach had growled all the way through eighth and ninth periods. Wallace had given me half a Snickers at Boosters, but I still felt semi-faint.

"Darla? My lips *are* moving, right?"

"Yeah, um . . ." What was I supposed to say about that awful dress? Was Wallace right? Was my best friend really trying to sabotage me? "It was—"

"Omigod!"

Suddenly Veronica's hand reached out and grabbed mine. The light had turned green and cars had started to slowly move forward. Inching up right in front of us was a big black van, and sitting perfectly framed by the back window was Orion. But that wasn't what had caused the *Omigod*. It was the fact that True was leaning back from the front passenger seat to talk to him, and her buddy Heath was driving.

"What is he doing with them?" Veronica demanded as Heath gunned the engine and they drove off.

I felt sick to my stomach. Orion had met up with True after Boosters? Why hadn't he met up with me? "I don't know."

"You don't know?" Veronica demanded as she turned out into traffic, her jaw dropping in shock or disgust or both. "How do you not know? I know where Josh is every minute of every hour of every day."

"I know, but—"

"It's the only way you're going to keep him in line, Darla. The only way," Veronica warned me as we zoomed through the now yellow light. "With a guy that hot, you have to keep him on a short leash."

"I can't tell him what to do," I said, toying with the zipper on my bag as I thought about our conversation at lunch. He said he cared what I thought, but he made it pretty clear he was going to do what he wanted anyway.

"Yes, you can! You have to!" Veronica took a blind turn way too fast and slammed on her brakes at another red light. "Look, D. Hot boys don't transfer to LCH that often. You were lucky he showed up after the whole Charlie debacle. Orion Floros has put you on the map. Unless you want this whole homecoming thing to become one huge joke, you cannot let that girl snake him."

My teeth clenched. The whole Charlie debacle? Like it was somehow my fault that he'd turned on me? She was the one who'd hinted—not so subtly—that he needed a makeover. She was the one who'd practically forbidden me from going out with a band geek. And why did she make it seem like no guy was ever going to date me unless he was a transfer? I knew it had taken the guys in my grade a couple of years to forget about the Darbot the Geek I'd been before, but I'd had boyfriends in high school. Not as many as she had, but still.

"She's not going to snake him," I said as calmly as possible.

"She better not, because you know how it's gonna feel if you're sitting in some car during the homecoming parade with the guy who just dumped you for the freaky klepto chick with the violent streak? Not good."

My insides felt twisted and lumpy. If Veronica really was trying to sabotage my chances at homecoming, and she thought that Orion was the only reason I made homecoming court in the first place, then wouldn't she want me to screw things up with him? Wouldn't him defecting to the land of the weird with True be the greatest thing ever?

"Can I ask you something?" I blurted.

"What?" she asked, hitting the gas the second the light turned green.

"Do you think I have any shot at winning homecoming queen?"

Veronica's laughter filled the car. It filled the town. It filled the entire universe. She laughed so hard I thought she might actually drive us off the road. My face burned, and tears welled up in my eyes. When we came to the stoplight across the street from Moe's Diner, she finally caught her breath and glanced at me.

"Omigod, you're serious."

I didn't trust myself to speak without my voice cracking. Instead I weakly lifted a shoulder.

"Darla, no junior has won homecoming queen since Ruma Sen," she said in this totally condescending voice. "And I'm sorry, but you're . . ."

"No Ruma Sen," I finished for her.

She widened her eyes like, *obviously*. Suddenly I found myself staring at the car door handle. I saw myself opening it and jumping out of the car. Imagined what it would feel like to slam the door on her and just walk away. She was my best friend, and I'd felt like nothing but crap since my butt hit the heated leather seat of her car.

"Neither of us are," she added in a kinder voice.

Okay. Well, at least she saw us as equals. Or at least equally not in Ruma Sen's category. I felt myself start to uncoil.

"Are you hungry?" Veronica asked. "Wanna hit Moe's?"

My favorite diner was right there, bursting with the after-extracurricular crowd. "But you hate Moe's."

Veronica had once said that you could gain a hundred pounds just by inhaling Moe's grease-filled air.

She lifted her shoulders. "I'll get a smoothie."

I sighed reluctantly. I knew that if we went in, we'd probably bump into Mariah and Kenna and some of the guys, and at the moment I didn't have the energy to be social. But then, Orion wasn't coming over anytime soon, and being seen was important. Especially right now.

Not that I had any chance at homecoming queen, but I wanted to at least get a few votes.

"Okay. Sure," I said, just as the light turned green.

Veronica hit the gas and turned into the crowded parking lot, cutting off an oncoming car so closely I saw my life flash before my eyes. Which wasn't pretty. It was mostly me as Darbot the Geek. Me as a loser. Orion flirting with True, having lunch with True, laughing with True.

"What should I do?" I heard myself say meekly.

"About what?" Veronica pulled into a space and killed the engine.

"Orion." I looked at Veronica and, instead of imagining what she might do, decided to ask her point-blank. "What would you do?"

"Call him," she said firmly. "Call him and tell him you know who he's with. Remind him whose boyfriend he is. Put the boy in his place. Don't be a doormat, Darla. You're better than that."

I whipped out my phone and hit Orion's speed-dial.

"Just be cool," Veronica whispered.

Whatever that meant.

"Hey, babe!" Orion answered.

Veronica got out of the car, so I did the same, blinking against the rain. "Hey! Having fun with True?"

"Yeah, I am, actually. Thanks for—"

"Well, that's great," I said, surprised. I'd expected him to be shocked that I knew. Or at least hem and haw. "But you're still coming over later, right? To visit your girlfriend. Who would be me, by the way."

He hesitated, and I glanced uncertainly at Veronica as we headed for the front of Moe's. Had I gone too far? She gave me an encouraging nod. No. I hadn't.

"Yeah, of course. I'll be there around seven thirty. Is that cool?"

Cool. Be cool.

"Yep. That's perfect. I'll have our SYTTD marathon all cued up," I told him.

"Great. I'll see you then," he said.

"Oh, and Orion? I think you should bring the food. And get me an extra spring roll, okay?"

I hung up the phone and yanked open the door for Veronica.

"That was perfect," she said.

"Thank you."

I grinned, feeling so much better. Sometimes I had no clue where I'd be without Veronica Vine.

CHAPTER THIRTEEN

True

"Wallace? We need to talk."

I dropped my tray and sat down across from Wallace at the lunch table he'd chosen in the corner of the cafeteria, since it was, once again, storming out. I was starting to think Hera was responsible for this weather. What better way to squash burgeoning love than to douse it with a few straight days of torrential downpour and gray skies?

"That's ominous," Wallace said, looking up from his iPad and popping a pretzel into his mouth. He was wearing a white T-shirt under his gray vest, and somehow the combination made his brown eyes seem deeper. Drawn up his left arm was a series of intricately detailed spaceships.

"It doesn't have to be, as long as you answer my next question honestly."

I took a no-nonsense posture, back straight, arms folded on the table. Eye contact, crucial.

"Shoot," he said, leaning back in his chair.

"Do you like Darla Shayne?" I asked him. "*Like her* like her, I mean."

Wallace froze. I think he stopped breathing. Somewhere in the cafeteria something crashed, and dozens of people laughed. Wallace didn't flinch.

"Wallace?"

"Okay, yes." He suddenly collapsed forward, his forehead hitting his iPad. "How did you know?" he asked the table.

My heart skipped around like a gymnast twirling a long, trailing ribbon. "I have a sixth sense about these things," I told him. "The good news is, I can help you get her. Just like I helped you get Mia." For all the good that did him.

I reached for my apple juice, popped it open, and took a few long gulps. My pulse was pitter-pattering in my veins. This was it. This was so it. I was going to match my third couple, free up Orion in the process, and return to Mount Olympus the victor. Maybe I could even get out of here without ever having to face Artemis and her obnoxious brother.

Wallace sat up straight. "That is never going to happen."

"Why not?" I asked. "You're a nice guy, she's a nice girl. . . ."

Okay, I hiccuped a bit when I said she was "nice." But she wasn't horrible. She *had* once tried to help me when that awful Veronica person was posting horrible pictures of me online with embarrassing captions. She had her positive qualities. And clearly Wallace saw something in her. If a guy of his quality could love her, then she must be a good person.

"Like that's all that matters," Wallace said, slapping the cover over his iPad. "First of all, she has a boyfriend."

"Yes, but—"

"And also, she's popular." Wallace lowered his voice as a pair of cheerleaders passed close by our table. "And she wants to stay that way, believe me."

"So? Who's to say she can't go out with you and stay popular?" I capped my juice again and took a bite of my bagel.

Wallace barked a laugh. "Honestly, sometimes it's like you come from another planet."

My face flushed, and when I swallowed the bagel, it felt like a knife going down my throat.

"Also, there's history. History you don't just get over," Wallace muttered, pressing his hands into his jeans.

History, huh? Gods, how I wished for my powers. If I had them, I could simply call up this so-called history. Find out exactly what had happened between them and know, in an instant, how to fix it. But I couldn't do that, and I didn't have the time required to conduct a therapy session right now. I had been on this planet for over four weeks, and my sand timer was getting perilously close to the midway mark. Plus, Artemis and Apollo were out there somewhere, just waiting to spill my blood and kidnap my love. This had to happen, and it had to happen now.

What I had to focus on here was the fact that Wallace liked her. And Darla clearly had some sort of feelings for him. It was the blush that had told me. The blush she'd gotten when she'd seen him at Goddess on Sunday. It wasn't just any old blush. It was the blush of love.

"Wallace, trust me. I can make this happen," I said confidently. "You guys looked pretty cozy at Boosters yesterday. What were you talking about?"

"Homecoming. I think she can win. She doesn't," he said flatly. "It's pretty clearly important to her," he added, glancing past me at a huge poster Darla had hung in the cafeteria—her and Orion laughing over Zeus knew what.

Wallace fiddled with a string hanging off the corner of his iPad case. The tingling beginnings of an idea danced inside my mind.

"So show her she can win," I said slowly.

"What?" Wallace asked.

"Do your thing with the numbers," I said, twiddling my fingers at his iPad. "Create an app for that or whatever. You're good at that stuff."

"I guess I could take a poll or something," Wallace mused, narrowing his eyes.

"Yes! Perfect! Take a poll and show her where she stands," I suggested. "You could even . . . I don't know . . . offer to be her campaign manager or something."

"Then she'd have to be seen with me." Wallace snorted a laugh. "She would never—"

"Okay, okay. Baby steps," I said. "But you can do it, right? Come up with a projected vote or whatever?"

"Well, yeah. Of course. I just need a good sampling of voters," he told me.

"So do it!" I told him. "Show her you care about her. That you want her to succeed. Use your powers for good!"

"Okay. I think I will."

Outside, thunder rumbled, but Wallace was already tapping notes into his iPad. I watched his fingers fly over the screen, feeling a giddy glow deep inside. This was going to work. I was going to secure love for one of my best friends, set Orion free from his relationship, and complete my mission.

It was a win-win-win. And the game was officially on.

CHAPTER FOURTEEN

Darla

My pinky toes were killing me. I should have known when I bought these stupid wedges that I'd never make it through a whole day of school in them, but they made me six inches taller, so I'd pretended it wasn't an issue. But as I hobbled to my locker after the final bell, I was sure I could hear the poor little digits audibly screaming.

It was my father's fault. I hadn't seen the man in five years but was totally jinxed with his short-person DNA. It was so unfair. The guy who was going to completely bail on you shouldn't also get to saddle you with their unsavory genetic material.

Why couldn't I have been tall and willowy like my mom? But then, she wasn't winning the Greatest Parent Award either. She'd totally blown me off for room service last night after Orion had gone home, claiming jet lag. About the only pep talk I'd gotten from her was "Sleep well!"

But that was her life. It was rough traveling back and forth across the country and giving speeches all day long. Sometimes she didn't have the energy for a long Skype call. I just had to get used to it. I *was* used to it.

I came around the corner and saw Liza Verdanos, the other

senior girl nominated for homecoming queen besides Claudia, holding court in her cheerleading uniform, standing in front of a huge poster of herself, also in her cheerleading uniform. She was handing out little LCH megaphones, which, by the way, was totally against the rules. And also unfair.

What would Veronica do? I asked myself.

Gritting my teeth, I strode over to her, holding back a wince with every step.

"Hey, Liza," I said, giving my hair an expert toss. "I thought handing out campaign swag was against homecoming policy. You should be careful. You could get disqualified."

The smile on my lips was completely false. Which was fine, because the smile Liza shot back at me could have cut ice.

"They're not campaign gifts. They're for the game this weekend. The cheerleading squad paid for them, not me."

"Wow. That's a great line. Did you practice it in front of the mirror while you were doing your herkies or whatever?"

I didn't wait for a response, but I did see her glower at me as I turned away. I think the pain in my feet was making me extra sour.

"Darla! Hey, Darla!"

I paused. The whisper was coming from somewhere nearby. I turned in a slow circle until I saw Wallace sticking his head out of the computer lab, waving me over. I glanced around to make sure no one was looking, then slipped inside.

"What are you doing?" I asked.

"I figured you wouldn't want to, you know, talk to the likes of me in public, so here we are."

The computer lab. I hadn't been inside its walls since freshman year, when we were all forced to take a semester of programming.

It smelled exactly as I remembered it, like manufactured dry heat, warm rubber, and mint gum. Two guys worked at a computer in the corner near the shaded windows, and Mr. Ryan, the computer science teacher, sat at his desk playing Dots on his phone.

Mr. Ryan was actually pretty cute for a teacher. If he'd get some sun and maybe trim his beard, he could probably get a date and find himself a life out there.

"Why are we here, exactly?" I asked, crossing my arms over my stomach.

Wallace sat down in the nearest chair and pulled out his iPad. "I polled some people during lunch and worked up a spreadsheet." His eyes flicked over my legs to my shoes. My ankles were quivering. "Wanna sit?"

Thank God. "Sure."

I sat down next to him, and my toes started to throb intensely. Still, it was better than the biting pain when I was standing. My phone vibrated with a text from Orion.

@ UR LOCKER WHERE R U?

I hesitated for a split second, not wanting him to know I was hanging in the computer lab, but then changed my mind. If I was supposed to be keeping tabs on him, might as well invite him to join us. I typed back:

COMPUTER LAB. COME BY. ☺

"Check it out." Wallace turned the iPad toward me. "With my current model, I have Liza Verdanos in the lead, with you trailing behind her by only three points. Claudia's a close third, and Veronica comes in fourth. If you can scour yourself up a few more votes, you could win this thing."

I looked into Wallace's eyes in disbelief, then snatched the iPad from him. He'd shaded my vote tally in purple, my favorite color, and he was telling the truth. It was almost the same length as Liza's vote tally and longer than Claudia's. Veronica's was centimeters behind.

Could this really be true? Were more people willing to vote for me than they were for Veronica? She would die if she knew this.

"You made this up," I said, tilting the screen toward him.

"What? No. I'm insulted you think I would fudge any numbers, ever." He sat back, indignant, his legs splayed wide in his dark-blue jeans. There was more doodling on his arm today, a line of Star Wars ships. Plus, he'd drawn a whole mess of elaborate curlicues around them.

"When did you have time to do this?" I asked.

"I polled people between classes and at lunch, then made up the formula to predict the rest of the student vote during calc," he said, hooking one arm over the back of the chair. "I'm so far ahead Mr. Berkowitz doesn't mind if I work on apps and stuff during class."

That I could believe. Mr. Berkowitz had practically worshipped the ground Wallace walked on ever since Wallace had won the state math award as a freshman. There was a rumor that they'd driven into the city for Comic-Con together last year, but I chose not to believe it. Because weird.

"Anyway, you should really start campaigning," Wallace said, closing a notebook and shoving it into his backpack. "You and Orion together are like a dream team. He's got the new-guy mystique, you've got the popular crowd *and* the smart kids. It's perfect."

This was insane. Like, truly insane. I thought back to Veronica's hyena fit in the car yesterday and felt something break open inside me. To her, the very thought of me winning homecoming queen was hilarious, but little did she know, I had a shot. A real and honest shot.

I could beat Veronica Vine.

"Can I ask you something?" I asked.

"You just did." Wallace smirked. He looked cute when he smirked. It was too bad more girls weren't into the sci-fi skater genius type.

"Why do you care? About me winning homecoming?"

Wallace slowly zipped his bag closed, as if he was carefully considering his answer. "I just really can't stand Veronica Vine. Like, at all."

Right. Of course. It was about beating her, not seeing me win. Which made sense, after everything she'd done back in middle school to make his life a living hell. When I'd started hanging out with Veronica, she'd basically staged a war against Wallace. She used to complain loudly about his BO, which he totally didn't have. She started a rumor that he'd built a robot for himself—which he had—but she'd said he'd done it because he didn't have any real friends—which was not true. She told everyone she'd seen him pick his nose and eat it after lunch, like it was dessert. Totally gross and totally false.

I don't know if it was because she wanted me to stop talking to him so that she wouldn't be associated with him in any way, or because she really didn't like him, or because she was somehow threatened by him, but it had worked. The more unsavory she made him, the clearer it was that I had to stop hanging out with him if I wanted to stop being Darbot the Geek. So we had stopped hanging out. And the rest was history. Until now.

I tried to swallow this awful, sour lump that had settled in my throat. Usually I tried not to think about that stuff Veronica had done—the stuff I hadn't stopped her from doing—but whenever I did, I felt like this.

"Wallace, I'm really . . . I'm sorry," I said. "About everything. You know. Seventh grade."

He stared me right in the eye. I couldn't make myself stare back.

"Yeah, that sucked," he said.

I looked down at my angry toes. "Do you hate me for it? Do you think you could ever, like, forgive me?"

"Sure. Of course," he said lightly. "I did that already. A long time ago."

"Yeah?" I asked.

He shrugged. "You didn't want to be picked on anymore. I get it. People do what they've gotta do."

He was right. I had done what I had to do. Exactly right and I knew it. So why did I feel so squirmy?

"Anyway, I think it'd be cool if you won," he said, changing the subject. "If a junior won. Very antiestablishment."

I still couldn't believe that the junior with the chance to win was actually me. If I won, Veronica would be crushed. Suddenly I felt hot with fear. I couldn't imagine how she'd react if they called my name at the homecoming dance. She would probably have the meltdown to end all meltdowns. She might never talk to me again.

But also, it would be kind of cool.

The door to the lab opened, and Orion walked in. I felt relief at the sight of him, like a cool breeze. He shot Wallace a curious look as he joined us.

"Hey, sweetness." He leaned down and planted a kiss on my lips. "What's up?"

"Do you know Wallace?" I asked.

The two of them exchanged a guarded kind of look. "Yeah. True's friend," Orion said, rounding his shoulders. "How's it going?"

God! Could I not live through five minutes without that girl's name coming up?

"Good. You?" Wallace tilted his head.

"Good."

They were having some kind of standoff, which I just did *not* get. But I knew I didn't like it.

"Ooookay, well, Wallace is a total genius with numbers," I said. And yes, I was sort of sucking up to try to make up for the awkward. "And he ran this formula that says the two of us could totally win homecoming."

"No way," Orion said, his eyebrows rising. "Lemme see."

Wallace showed him the iPad, first the graph for the girls, then one for the guys.

"Right now you and Josh are splitting the junior vote down the middle. If you can find a way to edge him out, you could definitely win," Wallace explained, standing and lifting his backpack onto his shoulder.

"Wow," Orion said, a spark of interest in his eyes.

"So *now* will you help me campaign?" I asked, grasping the sleeve of his varsity jacket with both hands. "If you start to take this seriously, we could make history."

"Make history, huh?" He looked at me and smiled. "All right. If it means that much to you, maybe we should get on this thing."

"You think?" I got up, ignoring the stabbing pain in my feet. I was too giddy, suddenly, to care. Orion was showing an interest in homecoming. A real interest. "Does that mean you'll help me make more posters?"

"Totally," Orion said, handing Wallace back his iPad. "Tonight? My place?"

I took a step closer to him. "I'm in."

Orion pressed his lips to mine, and I wrapped my arms around his neck. This was more like it. This was what a couple nominated for homecoming should be doing. Making plans. Smooching in public. Well, inside the cave of the computer lab, but still. There were people here. They could tell other people what a perfect couple we were.

"So, um, I guess I'm gonna go then," Wallace said.

Orion broke off the kiss. "Thanks for the info, man."

"Yeah, Wallace." I leaned my head on Orion's shoulder, trying as best I could to convey my gratitude with my eyes. As much as I was thinking about the homecoming study, I was thinking about the other stuff too. "Thank you."

"You're welcome." Wallace looked me right in the eye and smiled. "For you? Anytime."

CHAPTER FIFTEEN

True

"How'd it go?" I asked, the second Wallace walked over the threshold at Goddess on Wednesday night. The place was packed with kids from a handful of local schools, and he glanced around before answering.

"You know the battle at the end of the second *Star Trek*?" he asked. "The new ones, I mean."

My coworker Torin looked up from the box of cupcakes he was filling. "Dude. That was brutal."

"Yeah. About like that," Wallace said.

My heart sank as I handed change to the girl I was helping. She shot Wallace a sympathetic look as he slumped against the counter in front of me.

"It can't have been that bad," I said, biting my lip.

"She likes Orion. It's blatant to the world," he said with a groan.

"Maybe she does like him, but that doesn't mean they're meant to be," I replied. Okay, maybe snapped.

Wallace lifted his head. "So what do we do?"

I smiled. At least he wasn't ready to give up.

"Tell me a little about this history you were talking about

before," I said, tilting my head toward the end of the counter, away from the hustle and bustle. Cassie, one of the few employees over the age of twenty, cleared tables nearby. Other than her, the only people close enough to overhear us were two scrawny guys sitting together, each listening to their own music on their earbuds. "The other day you said you used to be friends. What did you guys used to do together?"

Wallace sighed and drew doodles on the countertop with his fingertip. "I don't know. We were just kids. I tutored her in math, she schooled me in science. We used to swim in my pool and play adventure games."

My forehead crinkled. "Like what?"

"Harry Potter and Hermione, Spiderman and Mary Jane, saving the world. That kind of thing."

I laughed. Loudly. "Sorry. I just can't imagine Darla doing any of that."

"Yeah, well." Wallace gave me a mournful look. "It was a long time ago."

I nodded, setting aside my mirth. "Okay, that Darla is still in there somewhere. Deep, deep inside. I'm sure you can find some common ground. Spend more time with her. Figure out what you guys have in common in the here and now."

"Well, we do have Boosters again tomorrow. And afterward we have to do some shopping for the pancake breakfast on Saturday," Wallace said.

"Good! There you go!"

Wallace's phone beeped. He checked the screen. "I should go. My mom's expecting me to come home with pizza. I'll see you later, True."

"Okay. And don't worry! It's all going to work out!"

As Wallace shoved open the door, I heard an angry shout. I

glanced over, and the blood rushed from my face. Artemis and Apollo stood right outside the shop, not twenty yards away. They were dressed in modern clothing now, head-to-toe black with a definite vinyl-and-leather vibe. Artemis's brown curls were pulled back from her face in a bun, and Apollo's hair hung in scraggly black locks over his ears. He was glaring at Wallace, who had raised his hands in an apologetic *don't shoot me* kind of way. The twins let him move on, then turned. I hit the floor so fast I smacked my kneecap on the tile and my leg exploded in pain.

"True? What the—"

"Shhh!" I scrambled toward the back of the shop, squeezing past Torin's legs and pushing open the door with the top of my head. Inside, I jumped to my feet, ignoring the fact that my knee felt shattered, and raced for the break room, where I yanked my duffel bag off the bottom shelf of the storage area and opened the zipper with shaking hands. Bow and arrows in hand, I backed up against the wall, held my breath, and listened.

Nothing. No yelling, no crashing, no explosions. Maybe they hadn't seen me. Maybe I was still safe.

"True?" Torin called out.

Crap. I quickly shoved the bow and arrow back into the bag and kicked the whole thing under the storage shelf. Torin's curious face appeared in the small round window of the break room door. He spotted me, then slowly pushed it open.

"Are you okay?" he asked.

He was wearing a black T-shirt with the Superman *S* emblazoned across the front. If only such a hero actually existed. I wouldn't mind having him on my side right now.

"Yeah, sorry," I said, swiping my hands on the back of my jeans. "I just saw some people I'm trying to avoid."

"Ah." His face flooded with understanding. "Been there. Stalker exes. Not good."

I laughed and sat down shakily on the old couch near the back of the room.

"Hang out here until I lock up," Torin said.

"Thanks."

He left, letting the door swing closed behind him, and I leaned back into the cushions. My hands were trembling, and my heart felt like it was trying to wrecking-ball its way out of my chest.

The twins were clearly closing in. I wasn't sure how much longer this avoidance plan of mine was going to work.

CHAPTER SIXTEEN

Orion

"I still can't believe we could actually win this thing," Darla babbled, leaning over my shoulder as I scrolled through pictures of us on my computer. "I mean, can you believe it? Darla Shayne, homecoming queen."

I could believe it. Mostly because she'd said it so many times by now it had been hammered into my brain. I would have paid good money to talk about anything else, but we were here to make homecoming posters, so there wasn't much opportunity to change the subject. Instead I kept staring at the screen as photo after photo of me and Darla flashed by.

It was insane, how many pictures she had when we'd only known each other for two weeks. Pics from the diner, from football games, in the cafeteria, in the hall, at some park I didn't even remember going to. I swear her and her friends were like amateur photojournalists.

"I like that one," she said, just as I flipped past it.

I went back and smiled. She was sitting on my lap, laughing, with my arms around her waist. She looked really happy. It wasn't posed. It was real.

"Me too. Should I send it?"

"Go for it."

She kissed my cheek. "Just . . . don't tell Veronica, okay?"

I swiveled in my chair. "Tell her what?"

Darla pressed the pen she was holding between her two palms. "What Wallace said. That we could really win. If she finds out, she'll freak."

"She's your best friend. She should be happy for you."

Like that was even possible. But maybe if I said it she'd see how one-sided her relationship with her best friend was. She dropped back to the floor, where a new poster was laid out, and began carefully outlining her name.

"Please." Darla rolled her eyes. "If she thought I could potentially be more popular than her, she'd be furious. She'd probably stop talking to me. No one's more popular than Veronica Vine."

More logic I did not understand. I mean, I got that Veronica Vine was a bitch and people were scared of her, but technically, that wasn't popularity. It was dictatorship. I didn't want to argue with her about it, though. Darla had a sensitive spot when it came to Veronica.

With a sigh, I dropped the image into the email we were sending to her mother's assistant, who could apparently rush print anything in any size. Darla laid out on her stomach, crossing her legs at the ankles behind her. Her hair trailed down onto her poster and her lips screwed up in concentration. From that angle, I could see almost all the way down her shirt.

God, she really was hot. And she was in my room. Lying down. And the door was closed. What were we doing talking about Veronica Vine?

"You're cute when you're busy," I told her, tilting off the chair to lie down next to her.

"I'm always cute," she joked back.

"Can't argue with that." I moved her hair off her shoulder, then leaned in to kiss her neck. Darla stopped coloring or glittering or whatever she was doing and turned to look at me. My lips met hers and I moved in closer, wrapping one arm around her back. She turned onto her side and pressed herself into me, deepening the kiss. I ran my hand down her side until my fingers rested on her hip, then moved them back over her totally perfect butt.

"Orion, your sister's right next door," she whispered. It was a protest, but her heart wasn't in it. Her hips moved closer to mine even as she said it.

"So? She never comes in here," I said, pulling her into me.

Darla dropped her marker and ran her hand up my side too. She clenched me to her and my hand traveled under her sweater, my fingers sliding over the warm skin of her flat stomach.

Then my phone rang.

"Dammit," I said under my breath.

"Just leave it," she said, kissing my cheek.

I pulled myself away with some serious effort. "I would, but I have to talk to Greg about the place mats. That's probably him."

I grabbed my phone off the desk, hot all over, and blew out a calming breath. Then I saw the name on the front of my phone, and it wasn't Greg. It was True. My lungs clenched around my heart.

"I'll be right back."

She shrugged and went back to her work. Meanwhile, my brain was vibrating inside my skull, danger warnings flashing everywhere. I slunk out into the hallway and closed the door quietly behind me.

"Hello?" I said into the phone.

"Orion? Hi, it's True."

"Yeah, hey." I locked my arm around my stomach and grabbed my shirt at the side. My skin pulsated.

"Why are you whispering?" she asked.

"Am I?" I turned away from my room and walked toward the bathroom at the end of the hall. "Sorry." I slipped inside and half closed the door. "Is that better?"

"Yeah. That's better," she replied.

I shoved the small window open and breathed in the gush of cool air, then looked into my own eyes in the mirror. I looked like a guy who was totally scared. Why? I could talk to whoever I wanted on the phone, and Darla knew that True and I were friends.

"How are you?" True asked. "I didn't see you much today."

"Were you looking for me?" I teased.

Damn. Stop flirting, you idiot.

"Maybe," she said, playing along. "But I guess you're pretty busy being Mr. Popular Homecoming Guy."

I turned my back on my reflection. "I'll never be too busy to talk to you."

What? What the hell? I had to get control of myself. My girlfriend was two doors away.

True, meanwhile, sighed. She sounded content. Like I was saying exactly what she wanted to hear. The thought made my throat close over. I liked it. I liked that she felt that way.

Ugh. It was like there was something fundamentally wrong with me.

"So what's up?" I said finally, trying to steer the conversation in the right direction.

"Oh, right. Did you have a chance to talk to Greg about taking a photo for us?" True said.

"No. Not yet."

"Orion?"

It was Darla, calling me down the hall.

"One second!" I called back.

"Where'd you go?" she asked.

"Who's that?" True asked.

I could hear Darla approaching on the hardwood floor. Her foot hit that one board in the center that always creaked. She was less than three steps away. My hand went slick. For a split second I considered telling True it was my mom, but then the door pushed open and there Darla stood in her bare feet and skinny jeans looking vulnerable, and I knew I couldn't do it. I shouldn't do it. Maybe she was a tad obsessed with homecoming, but she was still my girlfriend. She was still the person I had asked to go to this stupid dance with me. The least I could do was not lie right in front of her to spare someone else's feelings.

"It's Darla," I said. "We're making posters for homecoming."

There was a long pause on the other end of the line. Then, "Oh."

"I should probably go," I told her.

"Right. Okay. But you'll talk to Greg tomorrow?" True asked, her voice tight.

"Yes. I'm on it. See you then."

I hit the end button and shoved the phone deep into my back pocket.

"Who was that?" Darla asked in a tentative voice that made me want to punch myself.

"It was Greg," I replied instantly. Apparently I *would* lie to save *her* feelings. "Like I said."

"You have to hide in the bathroom to talk to Greg?" she asked.

"The connection was bad." I slid by her into the hall, feeling gross over how easy the story was flowing from my lips. "I kept moving until I could hear him."

"Oh."

Her "oh" sounded almost exactly like True's. This wasn't right, the lying. I didn't like the way it sat inside my stomach, like a big, fat, festering blob. I wasn't this guy. I didn't play. I didn't cheat. It just wasn't me. But I really liked Darla, and I really liked True.

Sooner or later, something was going to have to give.

CHAPTER SEVENTEEN

Orion

I was kind of glad to have a yearbook meeting at lunch on Thursday. Usually it sucked because, obviously, lunch is the best period of the day, but this way I had an excuse to avoid Darla and True being in the same room together. On top of which, the endless homecoming talk was getting old. I mean, I wanted to win—actually, I wanted Darla to win, because it was really important to her—but I didn't think it was *that* big of a deal, and it was getting harder and harder not to blurt it out. Like the next time I heard Veronica Vine say, "If it's humid that day and my hair frizzes, I'll die," I might just up and say, "You know there are kids in the world, right now, who are *actually dying*."

Which would probably not be good for my social life. Or Darla's.

Greg and I sat at the end of one of the U-shaped tables while our adviser, Mrs. Mattia, blabbed on about mixing it up in the layouts—going for the unexpected. Greg was scrolling through pictures on his camera, while I tapped my pencil against the edge of the table until Dani Trainor, the editor in chief, brought her hand down on top of the eraser. She had a star tattoo on the back of her thumb, which had to have caused some serious pain to have inked, and wore so much eyeliner it was as if her eyeballs were staring out at you from the bottom of some huge sinkhole. Not the kind of girl you wanted to mess with. I dropped the pencil, and she watched it roll noisily across the table with narrowed eyes until it finally hit Greg's arm. When Mrs. Mattia was done, Greg rolled the pencil back.

"I got an idea, why don't we do a layout that's all words and no pictures?" he suggested under his breath. "That would really be mixing it up."

"I think the girls of the school would revolt," I joked back. "The first thing they do is flip through it for pictures of them and their friends, right?"

"That is *so* sexist," Dani said, shoving her chair back. She stormed across the room, dropping her huge yearbook binder on the front table with a *thwap* and staring me down the whole way. I really hoped she didn't know how to make a voodoo doll, because if she did, I was screwed.

Greg laughed and got up to walk to one of the computers near the wall. "You wanna work on the Boosters layout?" he asked. "I got a few good shots at the game last weekend."

"Sure."

I turned my chair around to sit next to him as he plugged in a USB. The ancient screen went blue and then actually groaned as it tried to load the pictures.

"We could be here a while," Greg lamented. He reached into his bag and pulled out an apple, then tossed one to me.

"Thanks." I crunched into it, and the juice ran down my chin. "So listen, you wouldn't happen to have any good pictures of the football field, would you?"

"Probably, why?" Greg asked.

"Me and True are in charge of the place mats for the pancake breakfast on Saturday," I explained. "We thought it would be cool to use an image of the field. Problem is, we need it today so we can get it to the printer tomorrow."

"Shouldn't be a problem. If I don't have one you like, I can take a few after school," he said, lifting his chin toward the computer. "We'll look through my files once this dinosaur finally warms up."

At that moment, the first picture blinked onto the screen. It was a close-up of True, wearing a blue-and-white Boosters T-shirt, shouting in the stands. The second I saw her, I had a sudden flash. True was in this huge, rolling field under a clear blue sky, bending to pick wildflowers. Her long hair trailed over her shoulders and tickled the tips of the pink and yellow petals. She was wearing some kind of long white dress, and the strap slipped off her shoulder, but she didn't seem to notice. She was totally unself-conscious and confident. She looked back at me and laughed, her eyelids falling heavy as she watched me approach.

I wanted her. I wanted her more than I ever knew I could want anything.

". . . I mean the pictures are really awesome."

I blinked, Greg's face and the computer screen coming slowly into focus. Part of me was still stuck back in that field, and I felt as if I could reach out and touch True—as if I *needed* to. Every inch of me longed for every inch of her. The back of my skull radiated pain into my eyes, down my tongue, and to the very tips of my ears.

"Dude. Are you okay?" Greg asked me, his brow wrinkling.

"Sorry," I said to Greg. "What?"

"You look like you're gonna throw up or something." He pushed his chair back, away from me, a few inches. "You need a garbage can?"

Suddenly the rest of the room snapped into harsh relief. The colors, the laughter, the scents of dry paper, bad pizza, and spilled soda. I still held the apple in my right hand, and the juice leaked over my palm. My stomach turned. Maybe I was going to be sick. I put my head between my knees and breathed. The image of True was fading, but the way I felt was not. I had this awful, physical urge to see her. Worse. To hold her. To kiss her. To . . . do other things with her.

It was like she'd cast some kind of spell on me.

I shook my head and laughed. Voodoo? Spells? Maybe all those TV shows my sister was obsessed with were starting to seep into my subconscious.

I pushed True out of my mind and thought of Darla. Her eyes, her hands, her lips, her body. Darla. Yes. Darla.

I lifted my head and took a breath. "I'm okay."

Greg looked me over and seemed to believe me. He edged his chair back toward the computer.

"Got a caption for this one?" he asked.

I shook my head, staring past his shoulder. Honestly, I was afraid to look at the screen again. "Go to the next one."

The next picture was of Claudia, Wallace, and Claudia's friend Lauren. I took another breath. The pain in my head was easing.

"Anyway, your posters are great," Greg said, reaching for the mouse. "You guys have my vote."

"Posters?" I said.

"Yeah. For homecoming." Greg's light eyes were disturbed under his black hair. He must have said something while I was off in that field with True. Something I hadn't heard. "You and Darla? King and queen? I'm gonna vote for you."

"Oh, right," I said, nodding. "Thanks."

After this I'd have to track down Darla and tell her we'd scored another vote. Darla. Sweet, cherry-flavored Darla. She was my girlfriend. She was the one I wanted.

"So do you want to find some pictures for True?" Greg asked.

"What?" I blurted. "I wasn't thinking about True."

"Dude, seriously? Maybe you should go to the nurse and lie down."

I blew out a sigh and reached into my bag for a bottle of water. "Let's just look at some pictures of the field. I'll be fine."

I just had to convince my frantic pulse and jackrabbity heart that it was true.

CHAPTER EIGHTEEN

Darla

I walked past the football field after school that afternoon, my eyes on my beautiful boyfriend, who stood near the bleachers in his practice uniform, deep in conversation with his coach. It was a warm autumn day. The leaves were falling. I had worn sensible but stylish flats, so my feet weren't killing me, and I'd just gotten back an A on my chem lab. Best of all? Like, ten different people had told me today they were going to vote for me for homecoming queen. Ten!

Everything was right in the world.

"Read over this list and tell me if it's right."

Wallace shoved his iPad in front of me just when I was about to wave to Orion. We were supposed to check in at Boosters and make sure everyone was ready for the pancake breakfast on Saturday, then head out and do the last-minute shopping for decorations.

"You're the champion list maker of all time," I told him, pushing the iPad away. "I'm sure it's fine. And I called the florist. The centerpieces I ordered will be delivered in the morning, and she's giving us a twenty percent discount since it's for the team."

"Sweet." Wallace grinned. "I called ahead to the party place, and they're going to have the balloons all bundled and ready."

"Nice." I paused as he clicked something off on the screen. "We make a good team after all."

"We do, don't we?" he replied, tilting his head. "Don't look now, but your Romeo approacheth."

Orion jogged over to us with this massive smile on, like he'd just won a Golden Globe or something. He leaned in to kiss me, so hard I had to bend back at the waist.

"Wow. What was that for?" I asked.

"Coach just told me we're going to run the wildcat tomorrow night, and he wants me to QB it," Orion said.

I literally had no idea what that meant.

"Wow, man. That's awesome," Wallace said, and sounded sincere.

"Yeah," I agreed. "Totally awesome."

He looked so happy. Like, purely happy. I tugged my phone out of the side pocket of my bag, and trained the lens on Orion.

"What're you doing?" he asked.

"Taking your picture. You look so cute right now I can't help it."

Orion clucked his tongue but smiled. As I clicked the picture, True walked by with Claudia, wearing a pretty red dress that made her already long legs look way longer. Orion watched her go by. He even turned his head and sort of craned his neck so he could keep watching her go by. Wallace shot me a look. The humiliation hit me like a sledgehammer.

"Um, hello?" I snapped at Orion.

Orion's face turned purple. Snagged.

"What the hell?" I demanded. "Why are you staring at her?"

"I'm not. I mean, I wasn't," he said.

"Oh, please. Wallace? Was he staring at True or not?" I demanded.

Wallace raised his hands and took a step back. "I'm neutral. I'm Switzerland."

I groaned. "So . . . what? Do you like her? Are you, like, cheating on me or something?" I demanded, thinking back to that phone call he'd just had to sneak off to take yesterday. The fact that he'd gone out with True on Tuesday night without even telling me beforehand. Was I the biggest idiot on the planet? Veronica's words echoed in my head—don't be a doormat, keep him on a short leash. Apparently my leash wasn't short enough.

"Answer me, Orion. Because I am *not* going to ride around in a convertible at the homecoming game with some jerk who thinks he can play around behind my back. It's humiliating."

Orion's face went slack. "That's all you care about, isn't it? Homecoming."

"What?" I asked, feeling like the wind had been knocked out of me. Wasn't I supposed to be doing the accusing around here?

"I mean, do you care whether I'm cheating on you because it would mean there's something wrong between us, or do you only care because it would look bad to the world? To Veronica?" he demanded.

My face stung. Because he was right. I did care what Veronica and the rest of the world thought. I just never realized how bad it sounded until he spat it out at me like that.

"Don't—don't try to change the subject," I said.

Just then, Coach Morschauser blew his whistle long and loud. "Floros! Get your butt on the field!" he shouted.

"I gotta go," Orion said flatly. Then, without another word, he pulled his helmet on over his head and jogged away.

I blinked back tears as a cool autumn breeze blew my hair over my eyes. From my phone, Orion's handsome face smiled up at me.

Two minutes ago everything was fine. Everything was perfect. And now I felt hollow, and confused. What the heck had just happened?

"He's not cheating on you," Wallace said in that matter-of-fact tone of his.

"How would you know?" I asked, flicking my fingers under my eyes.

"I could tell by how shocked he was when you said it," Wallace told me. "Also, True would have said something to me."

"Are you sure?" I asked, sniffling.

"Yeah. I'm sure," Wallace said. "Sometimes guys check out other girls, even in front of their girlfriends. We can be hormonal that way. But they're not hooking up."

I followed him over to one of the benches near the end of the field. After fishing in his bag for a second, he came out with a package of tissues and handed me one.

"Allergy boy lives," I joked, giving my nose a quick blow.

He smiled. "Never leave home without them."

Out on the field, the guys lined up, and I saw Orion take the ball and slam into a couple of other guys. He was laid out on the ground for a second before someone helped him up.

"I feel like such an idiot," I said. "Did you hear him? He thinks the only thing I care about is homecoming."

I fiddled with the crumpled tissue between my palms. "What'm I going to do? If he breaks up with me, I'll die. I can't go to homecoming alone."

Wallace blew out a sigh. His feet bounced back and forth beneath the bench. "So . . . show him you care about more than homecoming."

I sniffled and touched the tissue to the tip of my nose. "How?"

"Well . . . for starters, do you even know what the wildcat is?"

An awful, prickly feeling tightened my throat as Coach Morschauser blew his whistle. "Like you do."

"Actually, I do." Wallace wore a familiar smug expression—the same one he used to wear on the rare occasions he beat me at MarioKart back in the day. "It's when a running back lines up in the quarterback position to take the snap. Then he either hands the ball off to another back, takes the ball downfield himself, or throws the ball to a receiver."

I blinked. Half the words he'd just used were gibberish to me. I tucked my hair behind my ear as a breeze scattered some fallen leaves across our feet. "Oookay. So?"

Wallace rolled his eyes. "So the fact that Coach Morschauser is trusting Orion to run it is a huge deal."

"Oh."

"Darla, do you know anything about football?" Wallace asked.

I slumped, the worn tissue an ugly ball in my palm. "Not really."

"So maybe you should learn. Maybe that'd be a good way to show him that homecoming isn't the only thing you care about. Show him you care about the stuff he likes. About, you know, him."

Right. Like I was going to take relationship advice from Wallace Bracken. He hadn't had a girlfriend since the fifth grade, when Christina Newan had gone on three group dates with him to the mall. I'd been there for every one of them, and they'd never even kissed.

Over on the field, they ran the same play again, and this time Orion busted through and raced to the end zone—at least I knew what an end zone was—thrusting his arms in the air.

"If you want, I'll teach you," Wallace offered, following my gaze. "It's not that complicated once you get the basics down."

"Why?" I asked. "Why would you do that for me?"

He grinned. "You know how I like a challenge."

The breeze blew his bangs back from his face and he shrugged, like all of this was so obvious. Suddenly I laughed. I couldn't help it. This whole situation made no sense. Wallace should have hated my guts, but he kept right on being nice to me.

"You really think you can teach me?" I asked.

"Did I not teach you algebra in fifth grade?" he replied.

"You did. Which I'm still grateful for, PS. AP calc is my favorite class."

"I know. I can tell. You get this look on your face when you're working a problem, like you're in a happy zone," he said. "It's pretty cool."

I blushed, but I wasn't sure why. Was he really watching me during calc class?

"So. Football tutoring?" he asked.

"Okay, fine," I said finally, wondering if I was completely out of my mind. "Just don't tell anyone."

He smiled. "Your secret's safe with me."

CHAPTER NINETEEN

True

"I'm telling you, it's a lost cause," Wallace said, talking to me through the speakers on my phone while I examined my look in front of my full-length mirror on Friday evening. I was wearing a blue, white, and silver football jersey over jeans. It had Orion's #22 stitched onto the front and his last name, FLOROS, across the shoulders. It was a new look for me—school-spirit chic—and I must say I was totally rocking it. "Darla's in love with Orion. She almost blew a gasket when she caught him checking you out yesterday."

I froze. "He did what?"

"He checked you out. Right in front of her."

I grinned at my reflection. Best. News. Ever.

"So what did you do?" I asked, reminding myself to focus. This was about Darla and Wallace, not me and Orion. But I still couldn't stop smiling.

"Oh, just offered to help her get back in with him by teaching her the intricacies of football. We're meeting up in five minutes so she can cram before the game." Wallace groaned. "What is wrong with me?"

"You volunteered to help her because you care about her," I told him, reaching for a shimmery lip gloss and swiping it across my lips.

"Correct me if I'm wrong, but helping the girl I like win back the guy she likes doesn't really advance my goals in any way," Wallace said.

I laughed. "It *seems* that way, but this is actually good. The more time you spend with her, the better. She'll get to see how selfless you can be and be reminded of how smart and funny you are. It's actually perfect."

"If you say so." Wallace did not sound convinced.

"True?" Hephaestus shouted up the stairs. "What're you doing up there? Plucking every last hair out of your body? Let's go!"

I rolled my eyes. "Wallace, I've gotta go. But I'll see you at the game."

"See ya."

Wallace clicked off. I gave my hair one last fluff, then turned and tromped down the stairs. Hephaestus smirked when he saw what I was wearing.

"Isn't that a tad desperate?" he asked.

"What? I'm his booster," I said, lifting my palms. "Now come on. I don't want to be late for the game. I need him to see me, front and center, cheering him on."

"You're the one who took an hour to line your eyes," Hephaestus replied under his breath. He tugged at the collar of the brand-new bright-blue LCHS sweatshirt I'd made him wear. "How're things coming with Wallace and Darla?"

"Fine. Great, even," I said as I reached for the door. "In fact, the two of them are getting together right now."

"It's impressive, I gotta say," Hephaestus told me. "How you just happened to find a match for the girl who's currently dating the guy you want."

"Isn't it, though?" I turned away from his knowing smirk. "Still nothing from Harmonia?"

"No. I'm starting to get concerned," he said, shoving his wheels hard to get over the doorstop. "Maybe we should try contacting her the way you did the first time. Or call on your father to see what's what."

Something moved in the corner of my eye, and I turned just in time to see Artemis step out of the shadows near the edge of the porch. Her straight white teeth were bared, her curls tumbling over the shoulders of a black leather jacket.

"Must be a cold day in the underworld if you're willing to go to Ares for help, Hephaestus," she said with a sneer.

I gripped the handle on Hephaestus's chair as Apollo moved in from the other side. His eyes were rimmed in red, his pale skin gone sallow over sunken cheeks. There was a feral look about him, as if he'd just crawled out of the desert after a week of tortured wandering.

"So. You've found us," I said, my confident voice betraying none of my terror.

Artemis's eyes narrowed like a cat's. "Deal with him," she said to her brother.

Apollo whipped a black hood out of his pocket and brought it down over Hephaestus's head so fast neither of us could stop it, yanking a cord to tighten it around his neck. Hephaestus reached back blindly, but Apollo shoved his chair off the one step to the path, and it tipped sideways, falling over with a clatter and throwing my friend on his side. Apollo jumped down next to him and kicked the chair away, leaving Hephaestus blind and struggling.

"True?" he called out.

"Hephaestus!" I took a step, but Artemis was on me. She

gripped my hair and held a blade against my throat. I felt a prick of pain just as the door opened behind us. Artemis whipped around, still clinging to me.

"Let her go," my mother spat through her teeth.

"Take one step closer and I will end her," Artemis said.

"I wouldn't do that," I said, barely able to speak, the blade was pressed so firmly against my windpipe.

"Oh really? Why not?" Artemis asked.

"Because if you kill me, you'll never see Orion again," I replied. "Not the Orion you loved."

"She speaks the truth, Artemis," my mother said, her slender fingers gripping the doorjamb on either side. She was clinging to her self-control by a slim thread. "Let her go and listen to her."

Apollo strolled back up onto the porch. I saw the look he gave Artemis. He didn't believe us and was silently telling her as much. But then, suddenly, the blade was released. Artemis shoved me toward my mother, who stopped me from hitting my knees. She cupped my face with her hands and I stared into her steady eyes for a moment, gleaning their strength before turning to face my enemies. Out on the sidewalk, a couple slowed, noticing Hephaestus, who was now sitting with his face covered, groping blindly for his chair.

"Talk," Artemis said, still holding the knife perilously close to my face.

"Help Hephaestus first," I said to Apollo.

He laughed.

"This is a busy street," I told him, nodding toward the small klatch of worried onlookers that was now gathering. "And you'll find that humans don't take kindly to people who abuse the physically challenged. You wouldn't want anyone calling the police."

Apollo glanced at the crowd. I could tell he didn't want to let me win or let the threat of human intervention cow him, but he wasn't stupid. He hopped down and untied the hood, yanking it off. Hephaestus sucked in a loud breath.

"Just a prank," he shouted gamely to our spectators, lifting a hand. "Nothing to see here."

Apollo righted Hephaestus's chair and returned to his sister's side, leaving Hephaestus to climb back in on his own. Hephaestus had a cut on his forehead, and when he touched his hand to it, his fingertips came back smeared with blood. I gritted my teeth.

"Now. Talk," Artemis said. "What do you mean, he's not the Orion I know?"

"When Zeus banished me here, it was with a specific goal and reward," I told her. "If I formed true love between three couples without my powers, I could have Orion back."

Her face colored at this. "He was never yours to begin with," she spat. "The moment you brought him down from the heavens you should have returned him to me."

As if he was a borrowed library book. As if his feelings meant nothing. I bit the inside of my cheek to keep from snapping her head off.

"Be that as it may, once you infiltrated the castle, Zeus had to send Orion here to protect our bargain, but he had to find a way to continue to keep us apart, even though we were so close together," I said.

Artemis and Apollo were blank-faced. Confused.

"The king erased his memory," Aphrodite supplied impatiently. "He doesn't remember who he is, let alone whom he has loved."

"If you kill me, Zeus has no reason to return Orion's memory to him," I said, eyeing Artemis's very impressive blade. "He won't know who you are. He won't know you were once his love. As far as he's concerned, he's a human guy with parents, a sister, and a varsity jacket. Not to mention a steady girlfriend," I added acerbically.

With a hefty groan of exertion, Hephaestus managed to climb back into his chair. He turned and popped the front of his wheels onto the shallow step, then shoved himself up to be nearer to us. The look he gave Apollo was a promise that he would one day return the favor. Apollo, wisely, looked away.

"So, what do you propose?" Artemis asked. "I simply let you get away with this betrayal? I just let you live after the pain and humiliation you've caused me?"

"No. I propose a bargain," I replied, holding her gaze. "You stop stalking me and let me form true love between one more couple. Once I do, Orion will awake from his stupor, and we'll ask him which one of us he truly loves."

"And when he chooses me? Then I get to kill you?" Artemis demanded, an amused smile on her lips.

"No. If he chooses you, I will wish you all the joy in the universe and get back to my job," I said as confidently as possible. "Because unlike Hera, you and I both know that if I am dead, then true love suffers. And if true love suffers, so will the women of this world. You do still care about your charges, don't you, Goddess Protector of Women?"

Artemis lowered her knife and took a step back. "You knew the queen gave me her blessing to kill you?"

Now it was my turn to smirk. "I do still have my friends on Mount Olympus."

"We believe that the queen wouldn't mind seeing either of you dead," Aphrodite told her.

"You're wrong," Artemis said. "The queen is on my side."

"Think about it, Artemis. She knows of your growing powers," Hephaestus said. "Of Eros's abilities. The two of you are a threat to her throne. But she knows she can't smite you herself without inciting Zeus's wrath, so she sent you here to deal with Eros, hoping one or the both of you would die and take care of the problem for her."

Artemis took this in. I could see her mind working, not wanting to believe the truth. Finally she looked to her brother. His thin-lipped expression said it all. He didn't want to trust us, but he knew the queen well.

"Forget about the queen and her plans." I closed the space between myself and Artemis, no longer feeling threatened. "Search your heart, Artemis. What is it that really matters to you? If it's winning Orion back, this is the only way. If it's exacting revenge on me, don't you think that you running off with the man I love will be horrible enough for me to witness? Isn't that the best revenge you could imagine?"

My throat constricted. Because there was the possibility, the tiniest possibility, that Orion would choose Artemis. And the worst of it was that his choosing her would be my fault. It was I who had matched them in the first place. I had manufactured their love with my arrows on a lark. That was what would hurt more than anything. If only I had known then that I would one day love him myself.

But I couldn't think about that now. Artemis had to be convinced.

"I don't like it," Apollo said through his teeth.

"Of course you don't. It means you get no blood spatter out of it," Hephaestus shot back.

"I don't like it because what if he doesn't pick you, sister?" Apollo said.

Artemis's jaw dropped indignantly, and I almost laughed until Aphrodite's steadying hands came down on my shoulders.

"How dare you?" Artemis blurted. "Of course he'll choose me. We were lovers for years. He's known Eros for mere months." She sheathed her knife in a hip holster and gazed coolly at me. "Our love was true. It was pure. I'm certain he'll pick me."

"Let us shake on it, then." I thrust my hand at her. Her grip was as strong as ever.

"We have a deal."

I was just letting out a sigh of relief when she withdrew her fingers and glanced at the silver watch clamped to her wrist. "It's half past seven now. I'll give you eight days. That's about as long as I can last on this rock. After eight days, the deal is off."

"You can't be serious, sister," Apollo countered. "Please tell me you're not relegating me to this hell for that long."

Artemis ignored him, her dark eyes glowering at me.

"Next Saturday, Eros. If you can't manage your job by then, your blood is mine."

CHAPTER TWENTY

Darla

"Okay, so there are four downs, which means the offense has four chances to get ten yards."

I took a sip of hot chocolate as I looked over the tiny diagram of a football field on Wallace's iPad, letting one of the mini marshmallows melt on my tongue. I hardly ever ate anything sweet, and this stuff was like heaven in a Styrofoam mug. We were sitting at the picnic tables near Havemill High School's refreshment stand, which was, like, half the size of Lake Carmody's. It was manned by a bunch of face-painted freshmen, who were doing some kind of choreographed dance behind the counter and shrieking with laughter every ten seconds while I tried to concentrate.

Somewhere inside the school, getting his football gear on, was Orion. I hadn't spoken to him since our tiff earlier, but I was going to corner him after the game and apologize. And before then, I was going to cheer my heart out for him to show him how much I cared.

Which I did. And I also knew I couldn't win homecoming without him. Not that I'd be mentioning that part.

"But on the fourth down, they usually kick it away." I put my cup down and rubbed my hands together between my legs to chase off the chill. "Why? Why not use all the downs you've got?"

"It really depends where you are on the field and how many yards you'd need to get for a first down. If you're way back here, of course you're going to punt it," Wallace said, pointing at the 20 on the image, "because if you try for the first down and don't get it, then your opponent has awesome field position."

"Why?" I asked.

Wallace closed in on the twenty yard line by swiping his fingers across the screen. "Because if you don't get the first down, the other team automatically gets the ball, and look how close they'd be to a touchdown."

"Oh! Okay." I took another sip of hot chocolate. "So if you punt it all the way down here, they have to go across the whole field to get a touchdown," I said, stabbing at the far end zone.

Wallace's face lit up, and for a second he looked exactly as he had back in fifth grade when he was cute and hyper, constantly spouting facts because he was just so excited that he had learned them.

"Exactly!" he said. "Now, what are your other options on fourth down?" he asked, leaning his chest into the edge of the table.

"You can either go for the first down, which I guess you'd only do if you had less than a yard or were really close to a touchdown or there was hardly any time left."

"Good. Or?" Wallace prompted me.

"Or you can . . ." The word was on the tip of my tongue. I looked out across the field, where both our team and the opposing team were running onto the field for warm-up. The yellow goalposts rose up against the darkening sky. "You can kick a field goal!"

"Yes! You've got it!" Wallace lifted a hand and I high-fived him, even though I knew that was totally dorky. It seemed appropriate, considering we were talking sports. I pushed myself up and did a hip-waggling dance, enjoying my moment. Orion was going to be so psyched that I could actually have a conversation about this.

"How many points for a field goal?" Wallace quizzed me, watching my moves with a smirk.

"*Trois!*" I said, holding up three fingers.

"And for a touchdown?"

"*Sept!* No! That was a trick question!" I said, pointing at him. "You get six, but then one if you kick the extra point and two if you go for the two-point thingie."

Wallace laughed. "That thingie would be called a conversion."

"And you *also* get two points for a safety!" I announced, then stopped dancing. "Which I still don't understand."

"But you're getting there." Wallace folded his iPad into its cover and stood up as a long whistle sounded down on the field. "Before you know it, you'll be a football savant."

"Booyah," I said, and reached out my fist. Wallace looked surprised. This was our move. Something we used to do whenever we made a breakthrough studying.

"Come on! Don't leave me hanging!" I said.

He tilted his head and touched his fist to mine, then we both exploded them, bringing them back over our shoulders. I giggled and held his gaze for a long moment, feeling nostalgic. I wondered what life would have been like if Veronica had never taken an interest in me. If I'd stayed Darbot the Geek for the last four years. Would I even be at a football game right now? Would Wallace and I have been friends nonstop since middle school?

"Thanks, Wallace," I said, reaching for my flimsy mug. "It was really nice of you to meet me here so early and do this."

Wallace smiled. It was a nice smile. I kind of liked the way his one front tooth sort of overlapped the other just a touch. "Anytime. Seriously."

On impulse I reached in for a hug. Wallace hugged me back with one arm, and I felt a tiny flutter of something. It was like muscle memory. My body remembered this, what it was like to be close to him.

Then someone nearby cleared her throat in a very familiar and kind of aggressive way. I turned around, sloshing chocolate over the rim of the cup. Sure enough, Veronica was standing three feet behind me. She looked down at the chocolate puddle between us like it was acid.

"Hey, V!" I trilled, feeling as if I'd just stepped on a land mine. One false move and I was vapor.

"D." Her voice was low, serious, sarcastic. Yeah. She could do that with one letter.

"I'm gonna head over and meet up with the rest of the boosters." Wallace gathered his stuff, his head suddenly bowed so low you'd think the queen had just shown up and he was nothing but a lowly serf.

Which, let's face it, was basically the deal.

"Um, okay. See you over there."

As soon as he was gone, Veronica stepped over the chocolate splatter and faced me, toe-to-toe. "What. Was that?"

"Nothing," I said, putting my hot chocolate down and reaching for my Tory Burch bag. I felt a pang realizing I'd have to abandon the rest of my drink if I didn't want to sit through Veronica's endless comments on sugar and calories. "Wallace was just trying to explain football to me so I can understand what Orion's talking about after the game."

Veronica's eyebrows rose. "Really? Because from where I was standing, it looked more like flirting than explaining."

"What?" My face burned like I'd had a bad reaction to a chemical peel. "No. He wasn't flirting."

Veronica rolled her eyes and walked past me. She was wearing four-inch platforms and towered over me in my kitten heels.

"Please. Wall-E was flirting with you, and you were totally flirting back. I know a good flirt when I see one."

She paused and turned to face me, her eyes flicking over my outfit. "And what are you wearing? I thought we made a plan."

My heart fluttered nervously. We *had* made a plan, but this time, I was the one who'd decided to go "caz," as she would say.

"It's a football game," I said, crossing my arms over my cable-knit sweater, which I'd paired with skinny jeans. Veronica had worn the silk knickers, white tank, and faux-fur crop vest we'd agreed on, and she looked . . . cold. "I figured it was better to be comfortable."

"If that's the kind of look your new boy toy likes," she said, wrinkling her nose.

"V. We were *not* flirting. I swear."

"Please. You go ahead and hang out with the riffraff if you want," she said, wiggling her fingers in the general direction of the bleachers. "Then you'll have *no* shot at queen."

She turned around again, her blond hair flying, and strode across the asphalt toward the visiting bleachers. I was so stunned, it took me a second to move. Had Veronica just said what I thought she'd said? I mean, not in so many words, but it was implied . . .

Holy crap. Veronica Vine *was* threatened by me!

Gripping my bag to my side, I jogged to catch up. The Havemill band chose that moment to march around the corner toward the field, and we had to stop to let them go by in all their tasseled and big-hatted glory.

I hid a smile behind my hand, trying as hard as I could to flatten it out, to turn my lips down. I bit my tongue, I pinched my side, I brought my heel down on my own toes, but nothing worked. I couldn't stop myself from grinning.

"What's wrong with you?" Veronica asked as the last bass drum marched on by. "Your face is all weird."

"Is it?" I asked, trying not to laugh.

Veronica Vine was threatened by me. The formerly dorky Darbot the Geek. Veronica Vine thought I could beat her.

"Never mind." Veronica rolled her eyes again and checked her phone. "Come on. Mariah and Kenna are saving us seats with the seniors."

"But I'm supposed to sit with the boosters," I said, matching her steps.

"Whatever. It's your social suicide."

Then she strode off ahead of me, her chin held high, as if I wasn't even there. Which, for that one moment, was fine by me. Because it meant I could smile as much as I wanted.

If Veronica thought I had a shot at queen, then it had to be true. She'd never felt threatened by anyone in her life. But I couldn't sit back and rest on my laurels, whatever that expression meant. Now was the time to get really serious about campaigning. I had to figure out a way to step up my game, and I knew exactly who to go to if I wanted to brainstorm ideas.

Orion and his teammates stood in a huddle at the sidelines, his last name FLOROS in big blue letters on the back of his jersey. I strode down the track toward the team, then passed them right by and jogged up the steps to the bleachers.

"Wallace," I said, dropping down on the bench next to him. "It's time to kick this thing up a notch."

CHAPTER TWENTY-ONE

Orion

We were down by six with one minute left in the game, lined up on Havemill's thirty-two yard line. Coach hadn't used the wildcat yet tonight, and if there was ever a time to do it, it was now. He called a time-out, and the whistle blew. We walked over to the sidelines, pads squeaking, breath panting. My chest pads had shifted somewhere in the last few plays, and something was sticking into my ribs. I yanked on the pads as I glanced up at the stands.

Darla was there. Right smack in the middle of the boosters. Even after that stupid fight we'd had yesterday. The fight I had totally turned around on her because she'd completely caught me checking out True.

I was such an asshole. And there she was, cheering for me. And guess who was nowhere to be found? True Olympia. Hadn't been there all game. I mean, WTF? She was supposed to be my booster.

"Bring it in, guys. Bring it in," Coach said as we gathered around him near the bench. He looked right at me, and my heart basically stopped. This was it. I knew it. "Floros, it's all you," he said. "We're gonna snap it to you and you're gonna take it upfield. Marrott, you line up in the wide receiver slot."

"Got it, Coach," Peter said.

"Granger, you'd best block number fifty-five like Floros here is carrying your mama across the line, you got me?"

"Yes, sir," Donnie Granger said, giving me a confident nod.

"All right, then. Let's win this thing," Coach said. "Hands in."

We piled our hands in the middle of the circle. My heart was pounding, like, a mile a second. The whole game rested on my shoulders. It was on me.

"Win on three. Ready?" Coach said. "One, two, three!"

"Win!" the team shouted.

The stands went crazy. Almost everyone was on their feet. As I turned toward the field again, I saw Darla, jumping up and down between Claudia and Wallace. My jaw clenched. I was about to be the hero of this game. And True wasn't going to be here to see it.

"Sonofabitch," I said through my teeth.

Why couldn't I get that girl out of my head? The hottest chick in the junior class was right there in the stands, practically dancing with nerves for me, and I was thinking about a random person who couldn't even be bothered to show up.

"You all right, dude?" Peter asked me.

"M'fine," I grumbled. "Let's do this."

Peter and Donnie exchanged a look but didn't say anything to me as we lined up in the wildcat. The defense noticed my position and started to shout to one another in confusion, which was kind of the point. Donnie, who was the center, counted off and snapped the ball and just like that, it was in my hands. I gritted my teeth, put my shoulders down, and ran straight ahead. There was nothing but bodies ahead of me. I was about to crash into another wall, like I hadn't had enough of that feeling lately. But at the last second, Donnie shoved his man aside and I saw a hole. It was a small opening, but I turned sideways and slid through, jumping over someone's ankle and dodging an outstretched arm. Suddenly I was in the clear. Seeing nothing but the goal line ahead of me, I turned on the speed. Dirt flew up behind my cleats. My ragged breathing filled my helmet.

"Go!" the crowd screamed as one. "Go! Go! Go!"

On the scoreboard, the seconds ticked down. Forty-five, forty-four, forty-three. I crossed the goal line with exactly forty-one seconds left in the game and threw my hands in the air. The fans went nuts. My teammates swarmed me.

I looked over at the crowd while my friends slapped my shoulders and rubbed my helmet and shouted my name. Darla blew me a kiss, and I lifted the ball in the air for her.

That was it. I decided right then and there. I was done playing. I was done flirting. I wasn't going to be that guy. Everything in my life was golden until I let True Olympia infiltrate my thoughts, but that was over. I had an amazing girlfriend. A girlfriend who was here for me. From here on out, I was only about her.

CHAPTER TWENTY-TWO

True

Inside his private bathroom, I touched a swab drenched with alcohol to Hephaestus's cut. He winced and so did I.

"Sorry," I said.

"It's okay."

"No, I mean I'm sorry. About all of this." I turned around to lean back against the ceramic sink, tossing the swab into the garbage can. "You shouldn't be getting caught in the middle of my squabbles with Artemis. You probably had a perfectly peaceful life before I got myself banished here."

Hephaestus eyed me. "Actually, it was kind of nice. Living on the beach, hanging out with the ladies . . . no listening to your constant whining about Orion . . ."

I shoved his arm and he made a fist, about to fake-hit me back, but suddenly his hands dropped. He cocked his head toward his room.

"What?" I asked. "What is it?"

"It's Harmonia." He spun his chair around. "She's calling."

My heart skipped excitedly as we rushed through the door and past his bed, the ancient floors creaking and groaning beneath us. The intricately decorated metal mirror above his desk glowed.

Hephaestus pushed himself out of his chair and touched the frame. Before his butt even hit the seat again, Harmonia had appeared. The sight of her beautiful face brought both a burst of joy and a slice of pain that was almost more than I could bear. Harmonia had been my best friend and confidante throughout my existence. Being banished to Earth without her was its own special form of torture, as was seeing her now but not being able to touch her.

"Eros, Hephaestus, it's good to see you." Her auburn hair hung in loose waves over her shoulders, with daisies woven throughout its strands. "I come with a message from the queen."

Hephaestus and I exchanged an alarmed look.

"So she knows you're in communication with us?" Hephaestus asked. "That we've been speaking behind her back?"

Harmonia's face was still. Too still. "She knows."

"Has she threatened you, sister?" I asked, leaning in toward the mirror. "If anything were to happen to you because you helped me—"

"No. In fact, the queen claims she is happy to have a go-between now," Harmonia replied. "Which is why I am here."

"Did she summon you?" I asked. "Did you actually see her?"

Harmonia nodded slightly, and something in her eyes shifted. She was scared and trying to hide it. I could feel it in my bones. I knew her better than anyone, and I knew it to be true.

"Yes. She allowed me into her chambers briefly today." Harmonia licked her pink lips. "She's sending me to Earth to speak with you on her behalf. To speak with all of you, Artemis and Apollo included."

I gripped the handle on the back of Hephaestus's chair. "Harmonia, what is it?" I asked. "What's wrong?"

"Nothing, my sister," she said, tucking her chin and looking me in the eye. "Everything will be explained when I get there."

"And when will that be?" I asked.

"Tomorrow night. You, Hephaestus, Artemis, and Apollo are to meet me at the town square at midnight. Will you come?"

"Of course we will," I said.

"I'm to see you?" Hephaestus asked, breathless. I could practically feel his nerves jumping like trampoline artists. "In the flesh?"

For the first time, Harmonia smiled. "Yes, my love. The wait is finally over."

A choking sound escaped Hephaestus's lips and he convulsed, tears streaming down his face. He stopped himself quickly, bringing the side of his clenched hand to his lips and gamely holding his emotions inside, but I knew it was a battle for him. He had awaited this day for generations. He was about to be reunited with his love.

I was so happy for the two of them, my heart was fit to burst, but there was still that question pinching the back of my mind. Why was Harmonia frightened?

"Harmonia, I—"

She looked behind her suddenly, her hair whipping. "I have to go," she told us. "But I will see you both tomorrow. I promise, one way or another, I will answer your questions then."

The mirror fogged over, then cleared, and I was staring at my own reflection. Hephaestus covered his face with both hands and cried. The sight of him, this masculine man curled up in his chair like a weeping child, was more than I could take. I knew he would get ahold of himself well before this meeting with Harmonia, but for now I felt that the only thing to do was to leave him to it. I backed slowly, quietly, out of the room and closed the door.

Alone in the hallway, I blew out a breath. Whatever was bothering Harmonia, she would find a way to tell me when I saw her.

CHAPTER TWENTY-THREE
Darla

Pizza City was jammed after the game, but I didn't mind. It meant Orion and I had to squeeze together on one side of what was technically a table made for two, while Veronica and Josh squeezed in on the other. We'd been there for fifteen minutes, and Orion had his arm around me the entire time. Plus, he kept playing with my hair and touching my leg under the table. I wasn't sure if it was me or the win or what, but whatever had put him in this lovey-dovey mood, I was cool with it.

"I still can't believe you won," Veronica said, reaching for her water. "That was an amazing play, Orion."

"Agreed," Josh said. "I thought you were gonna bite it and then you just vaulted over that guy's leg." He shook his head, impressed. "Total top-ten material."

"Thanks. But we'd still be playing if Ross hadn't made that kick. And if it wasn't for Donnie, I'd still be pulling my face mask out of the dirt."

Josh and I laughed. Veronica made a disgusted face.

"Honestly, I was a little worried when you started the second half way down at your own one yard line. I still don't know how

Peter managed to scramble away from that defensive end. I swear I thought they were gonna get a safety."

I reached for my pizza, trying not to preen. I couldn't believe I had just gotten through that entire speech without messing up once. Wallace would have been so proud.

"Wow. Have you been watching ESPN or something?" Orion asked.

I took a bite off the tip of my slice, enjoying his shock, and lifted my shoulders. "Maybe."

My phone beeped, and I glanced at the text. It was from Wallace. Veronica lifted up in her seat to try to see, so I turned the screen away from her.

SENT OUR IDEA TO UR MOM'S ASSISTANT. SHE SAID THEY'LL BE DELIVERED IN AM.

"Who's that?" Orion asked, munching on some pepperoni he'd stolen off my plate.

"Oh, nobody," I said, shoving the phone away. Wallace and I had spent half the game going over the schedule for the pancake breakfast tomorrow and brainstorming campaign ideas. I loved the one we'd landed on, but I wanted to wait to share it with Orion. This whole night was about showing him that homecoming wasn't the only thing on my mind.

Veronica smirked. "Just her own personal ESPN."

"Huh?" Orion asked.

I blanched. Yes, Orion knew that Wallace had been helping me out with the homecoming numbers, but I didn't want him to think what Veronica thought—that we'd been flirting. And knowing Veronica, she'd find a way to make it sound even worse than that.

"Darla's vast football knowledge didn't come from ESPN," Veronica said, sitting up straight. "She's just been spending every free minute with—"

"Orion! Oh my God! Great game!"

Saved by the cheerleading squad. I shot Veronica a wide-eyed glance as Josie Morrissey and some of her sophomore friends gathered at the end of our table.

"Thanks, ladies," Orion said, squeezing my shoulder. I smiled and took a sip of diet soda, draining the last dregs. Orion instantly signaled the waitress. "More Diet Coke, please?"

"Thanks, baby!" I cooed.

"Anytime, sweetness," he replied, giving me a quick kiss.

"Aw! You guys are so adorable. We're totally voting for you two for king and queen," Josie said, gesturing around at her friends.

Veronica's jaw dropped. Josh shifted uncomfortably and jammed half a slice into his mouth. Then Josie seemed to realize who we were with.

"Oh, no offense," she said to Veronica. "But you can only vote for one guy and one girl!"

Giggling, she and her posse went up to the counter to order their food. Orion gave an amused snort and I hid my smile behind a napkin, wiping at my lips for so long it was definitely suspicious.

"Don't get excited," Veronica said. "It's only, like, five votes."

I put the napkin down. "I know. Please. If anyone's gonna win who's not a senior, it's gonna be you."

Orion gave me a weird look. What? It had just come out of me. Like a reflex. It didn't matter that I knew otherwise. If there was ever a moment to appease Veronica, it was now. Two minutes ago she'd been on the verge of skewering me. Besides, he knew I was never going to tell her about Wallace's numbers. The girl would've chomped off my head with her Invisaligned teeth.

Veronica lifted a shoulder, but I could tell she was pleased. "We'll see."

Then Orion got a text. He checked his phone, and I saw True's name before he shoved it back in his pocket.

"Who was that?" I asked, holding my breath.

"Just True, texting about the place mats. We're picking them up first thing in the morning." He kissed my temple. "I think you're gonna love them."

God, I couldn't wait until football season was over. Then those two would have no reason to communicate with each other.

"Well. I guess it's on, homecoming court style," Josh said.

"It so is," Orion replied.

They bumped fists, then went right back to eating. The waitress delivered my fresh soda and I lifted it toward Veronica, trying to shove True out of my mind. At least she wasn't nominated for homecoming queen. Then I might have had to kill her.

"May the best couple win?" I said.

"Sure," Veronica replied, clinking her water glass with mine. Her eyes slid over me and Orion, as if she was maybe seeing us for the first time. "May the best couple win."

CHAPTER TWENTY-FOUR

Orion

I got out of my car outside the Graphic Shop on Saturday morning, asking myself for the ten millionth time what I was doing there. True texts and I jump? What was that about?

But then I remembered, for the ten millionth time, she couldn't pick up three heavy boxes of place mats by herself, and we were supposed to be doing this together. I was here because I was fulfilling an obligation to the team. I was not here for True. I was *not* here for True.

"Orion! Hey! You made it!"

And there was True. She came striding up the tree-lined street with her hair streaming behind her, looking totally beautiful in jeans and a flowing white top. Would it be so bad if I just took her up in my arms and kissed her? Just one little kiss?

My fingers and teeth clenched. There was something seriously wrong with me. Why couldn't I get my head on straight? Darla and I had a good thing going. She'd been watching ESPN for me, for God's sake. Until last night I didn't think she even knew what ESPN was. I just had to focus. Get the place mats into my car and get out.

True's face fell as I walked right past her and yanked open the door of the shop.

"Is something wrong?" she asked.

"Nope. All good."

The air inside the small, bright store was freezing, and the whole place smelled like dry paper and tangy ink. A copy machine whirred against the back wall, spitting out red flyers. There was no one behind the counter.

True walked up behind me and touched my arm. "What's wrong?"

A sizzle of attraction sliced through me, and I flinched away. "Don't do that!"

She looked as if I'd just punched her. For a second she shrank back, but then she shoved her hands under her arms and held on to herself. "Do what?"

"Touch me," I said. "Don't touch me. Just don't."

"Orion, did I do something wrong?" she asked. "I'm only trying to—"

"Where were you last night?" I asked, then immediately wanted to take it back.

True blinked, her beautiful brow creasing over those stunning blue eyes. "Last night?"

"Never mind. Forget it." I noticed a silver bell on the desk and brought my hand down on it. Hard. The ring reverberated throughout the shop.

"Be right out!" someone shouted.

"No. There's no forget it," True said. "If you're going to yell at me, at least tell me what it's about."

"The game," I reminded her. "We had a huge game, and you weren't there."

"That's what you're upset about?" she blurted. "Are you kidding me?"

Okay, so she was right. It sounded beyond stupid when I said it out loud. But there was no taking it back now, so I just barreled ahead like a whiny child.

"Yes!" I said. "That's what I'm upset about. I had an awesome game and you weren't there. I even scored the winning touchdown."

The look True gave me made me think of the way a kindergarten teacher might look at a five-year-old who's just finger-painted her favorite skirt—condescending, amused, and annoyed at the same time. Yep. I was definitely acting like a whiny child.

"If you knew what was really going on here, you'd—"

"I'd what?" I asked. "Why don't you tell me?"

"No! You know what?" True spat, throwing her hands up. "So I missed one game! Big deal! Get over it! I'm not your girlfriend, remember?"

My cheeks stung as if she'd just slapped me as hard as she could on both sides at the same frickin' time. Because she was right, of course. I was treating her the way a disappointed boyfriend might treat her. Someone who had a reasonable expectation to be her number one priority.

"Maybe not," I said, struggling for something to say to save face. "But you're supposed to be my booster."

"Um . . . hi?" A tall, broad guy with a red beard and curly red hair walked tentatively to the counter. "Can I help you?"

"We're from the LCH Boosters," True said. "You have some place mats for us?"

"Yeah! Yes. Right here." He gestured to a pile of three large white boxes. "They're all paid for already, so I'll help you out to your car."

"Thanks," I muttered, grabbing the box on the top.

True took the second and the big guy grabbed the third, holding the door open for us with his foot. We loaded everything into the small trunk of my car—it just fit—and I slammed the back.

"Thank you!" True shouted to the guy as he went back inside.

He gave us a wave, and then we were alone. I couldn't even look True in the eye. My face felt hot, and the back of my neck was sticky. I yanked open the door and got in behind the wheel, ready to bail. But before I could even start the engine, True was climbing in on the passenger side.

"What're you doing?" I demanded.

"Going to school for the pancake breakfast. Or were you planning to make me walk?"

She clicked her seat belt and stared straight out through the windshield. So much for staying away from her.

CHAPTER TWENTY-FIVE

True

We were silent for the entire seven-and-a-half-minute drive to the school. I had to force myself to breathe. Force myself to focus. His anger didn't matter. He was not the Orion I knew. He was not the Orion I wanted. If I could just get Darla and Wallace to fall in love, he'd return to me. We'd be together. Everything would be as it should.

He pulled the car around the side of the school into a small lot near the cafeteria and killed the engine. I waited for him to look at me. To apologize. To say something to break the awkward silence. But instead he opened the door and started to get out.

"So that's it? You're just going to go?" I demanded.

"What do you want from me?" he shot back, so quickly it was as if the words had been on the tip of his tongue the whole ride long.

Gods, he was handsome. Even more so when he was angry. His cheeks seemed more chiseled when he jutted out his chin, and his eyes smoldered.

"Don't you dare try to tell me that your little tirade back there was about the fact that your booster ditched you for one game," I said, and he slammed the car door again, cocooning us inside. "Let's talk about what's really going on here."

He lifted his head as if he had no clue what I was on about. "Okay. What do you think is really going on?"

"You!" I said, shoving his shoulder. "You and me! There's clearly something between us, and don't tell me you haven't felt it, because I know that you have."

He shook his head, looking through the windshield. Down in the main parking lot, more cars were beginning to arrive. The boosters were convening to set up before the guests and fans got there.

"You're crazy," Orion said.

"No, Orion, I'm not," I replied, softening my voice slightly. "You have feelings for me. Why don't you just admit it?"

At that moment we both heard a laugh, and suddenly Wallace and Darla walked out the side door of the cafeteria.

"Duck!"

Orion grabbed me and shoved me down, my head in his lap, then folded himself over my back.

"She knows your car!" I hissed.

"But she doesn't have to know we're in it!" he hissed back.

I rolled my eyes, but once the initial panic was over, I started to feel. Feel the weight of his body pressing against mine. The warmth of him so close. I breathed in the scent of denim and leather and held it inside my lungs until I went light-headed. After a few seconds, Orion hazarded a glance up and out.

"They're gone."

He sat up, then slumped down in his seat as far as he could get. I lifted my head and glanced down at the parking lot. Wallace and Darla were chatting with a man outside a white florist van. They laughed. She shoved him. He blushed and shoved her back. They were *so* flirting, and it was so cute. My pulse began to race for real. This was happening. It was really happening.

Then they started to turn. I dove down again, my cheek against Orion's thigh, my face turned toward the steering wheel. My fingertips automatically gripped the fabric of his jeans. I hadn't been this close to him in heaven knew how long, and I relished every moment, every sensation, every touch.

"True." He said my name like a question, like a plea, like a demand.

I turned over so that my feet were on the ground, but my back was across the console. My hair trailed down between his legs. It wasn't comfortable, but now I was looking at him. Looking at Orion. My Orion.

He lifted his right arm, the leather sleeve of his jacket squeaking, and gently touched my face. My heart pounded.

"True," he said again, and this time his voice was full of emotion. Full of love. He lifted me toward him, and my breath caught. "I can't."

And then he kissed me.

Tears sprang to my eyes. Tears of relief, of joy, of sheer ecstasy. I clung to him and kissed him back with everything I had. I'd waited for this moment for what felt like an eternity. Ever since I'd been torn away from him back at the palace, and even more since the day he'd been sent to Earth and hadn't known me. Orion's tongue parted my lips and I moaned. I clutched him to me, wanting to feel every inch of him.

"True," he whispered, tilting his head as he pulled me to him once more.

"Orion," I replied, barely able to speak. "My Orion."

My body burned for him as I found his lips again. I held on to him so tightly I thought my fingers might break. He was mine again. He was mine. And I would never let him go.

Then his phone chimed.

Orion instantly pulled back. Our lips parted so quickly they made a sucking noise. He fumbled for his phone, shaking.

"It's from Darla," he said, his voice throaty.

I looked through the window again. Darla, Wallace, and the florist were walking toward the front of the school, toting small vases bright with blue-and-white flowers. They hadn't yet noticed Orion's car.

"'Where are you guys?'" Orion read. "'We need help with setup.'"

I slumped down and covered my mouth with my hand. I hadn't a clue what to say. What to do. My brain felt as if it was floating on a sea of murky water.

"What the hell'm I doing?" he said under his breath, pocketing his phone. He moved to open the door, and I grabbed for his hand.

"Orion, no. Please. We have to—"

"I can't, True," he said, looking down at me, his expression pained. "I don't want to cheat on her. I don't want to be that guy. This was a mistake. I'm sorry. Wait a minute or two, then come in. I'll come back for the boxes later."

If only I'd had my powers, I could have stopped him—locked him inside with me until he admitted his love for me. But I couldn't do that, and Orion opened the door and was gone. Five seconds. In five seconds we'd gone from kissing like our lives depended on it, to him being gone. The world around me seemed empty, like I was trapped in some sort of sun-dappled abyss.

Slowly I opened the car door.

With a deep breath, I stepped out onto the parking lot's asphalt surface, my legs shaky beneath me. My lips still tingled from the kiss, and I reached up to touch them gingerly. It had really happened. It hadn't been a dream.

But now that I'd felt his kiss again, now that I'd tasted him and touched him and breathed him in, I needed him even more. I had to finish this, and I had to do it soon. Because if I couldn't be with Orion, I was going to go mad. Plain and simple. Then it wouldn't matter what Artemis did or didn't do to me. Without Orion, all was lost.

CHAPTER TWENTY-SIX

Orion

"Oh my gosh! Did you see that? What a catch!"

Darla grabbed my arm and shook it. We were hanging by the stoves in the kitchen at the back of the cafeteria, waiting for the school chef—who was an entirely silent old guy with an earring and a skinny black mustache named Geraldo—to load up two more trays of pancakes. The players, cheerleaders, fans, and parents were pretty much on their third helpings by now, but still hankering for more. The tiny TV mounted to the wall was playing college football highlights on ESPN. I had sort-of-kind-of seen the catch, but sort-of-kind-of not. Because my mind kept replaying that kiss with True over and over again, making me feel either nauseous or heart-poundingly turned on with no warning.

"That game was crazy," Darla said, leaning against the wall. "Did you see it?"

She grabbed a piece of bacon out of one of the trays and crunched into it, then picked up another and handed it to me. I thanked her and ate it like the good boyfriend I was pretending to be. On the other side of the propped-open door into the cafeteria, dozens of kids from school sat around eating and laughing and gossiping, but of course the only person I saw was True. She was mopping up a puddle of maple syrup, her long hair pulled back in a bun.

"Orion?"

"Sorry," I said, blinking. I somehow felt like I'd just woken up. "What?"

"I said, did you see the Michigan game on Thursday?" She gestured at the TV. Geraldo flipped a pancake onto a stack of about ten and transferred the whole thing into a wide silver tray.

Last weekend if you'd told me that Darla would have seen a football game I hadn't seen and that she'd be psyched to talk to me about it, I would have laughed so hard I would have ruptured something.

But here she was, looking at me all bright-eyed and eager. She was spending her Saturday morning at a Boosters pancake breakfast instead of sleeping in or working at the boutique she loved, and she was vibing on ESPN. It was obvious to the world that she was trying. Which meant it was well past time for me to stop thinking about True. The kiss was a mistake. It was a blip. Darla was my girlfriend. My homecoming date. I should start treating her like she was.

I reached for her hand. She looked at me, startled, and popped the last bit of bacon into her mouth.

"Hey, listen. Do you want to do some campaigning tomorrow?" I suggested. "It's supposed to be nice out, so everyone will probably be hanging out in town. Maybe we could walk around and, like, press the flesh or whatever."

Darla couldn't have looked more stunned if I'd dropped down on my knee and popped the question.

"Really? I'd love to!" she said. "I can't believe it!"

Geraldo added more pancakes to the tray, then pushed it in our direction. Which I took as my cue to go. I lifted one tray and Darla took the other.

"You don't have to sound so shocked," I said with a laugh as we walked through to the cafeteria. The line for more pancakes was already a mile long. We brought them to the serving table, where Claudia, Peter, Wallace, and some other people were holding down the fort.

Darla wiped her hands on her white apron and turned to me. Underneath that apron she was wearing gray leggings and an over-size LCHS sweatshirt, her hair pulled to the right in a side ponytail. I noticed for the first time that she was also almost makeup free—nothing but some shimmer stuff on her lips. She looked pretty this way. Younger. Like she wasn't trying so hard.

"Sorry. I just figured if someone was going to bring up home-coming today, it would be me," she said with a wry laugh. We walked back to the kitchen for the smaller trays of bacon. "But guess what? Wallace came up with this great idea."

From the big front pocket on her sweatshirt, she pulled out a folded piece of paper and held it out to me. Printed on it were two sides of what looked like business cards. The first side was a pretty black-and-white picture of Darla. The image below it showed the second side, which read *Darla Shayne for Homecoming Queen. All friend requests accepted!* Underneath was her Facebook URL.

"I don't get it," I said.

"We're not supposed to give out gifts or anything, right?" Darla said, biting her lip. "So we were trying to figure out what we could do virtually, and everyone wants more friends on Facebook, so we're going to have these business cards printed and hand them out. Actually, my mom's assistant is rush printing them and bring-ing them over tonight."

I laughed and shook my head. "It's brilliant. You can give them something without actually giving them something."

"Exactly!" Darla said with a grin. "I'm glad you like it, because we had some made up for you, too."

She pulled out another page, this one showing my card. On it was the picture she'd taken at practice the other day, right before we'd bitten each other's heads off. I actually felt touched, even though I didn't care about winning homecoming king. She totally didn't have to do this, especially considering everything I'd said to her that day.

"Darla, this is really cool," I said, looking her in the eye. "Thank you."

I leaned in and touched my lips to hers. My whole face felt tight as I remembered vividly the last place my lips had been, and I pulled back quickly, but Darla didn't seem to notice.

"No kissing in my kitchen," Geraldo said tonelessly, speaking for the first time in the last hour.

"Sorry," I said, turning beet red.

Darla laughed.

I bet 90 percent of the guys at my school would have killed to be in this situation—kissing two hot girls in one day—but I wanted to crawl under a rock and wait until they both graduated just so that I wouldn't have to deal anymore.

"So why don't we hit Goddess tomorrow and hand some out?" Darla suggested, folding the pages back into her pocket.

I tasted bile in the back of my throat. "Goddess?"

As if on cue, True's laugh sounded through the cafeteria and bounced around inside my chest like it was trying to find a cozy spot to rest.

"Yeah." She shrugged and grabbed a tray of bacon, balancing it between her hip and arm. "That's where pretty much everyone will be, right? We can go there and then hit Moe's and Pizza City."

"Makes sense," I said, reaching for a second tray filled with sausages.

"Maybe I'll ask Wallace to come too," she said. "He could do some polling and see how we're doing."

"Sounds like a plan."

I reached for her free hand and squeezed. Maybe this was like a test from the universe. Or my penance or whatever. Go to the place True worked and be the perfect boyfriend to Darla. If that was what I had to do to prove myself, then I'd do it. I didn't want to feel guilty anymore. I wanted everything to go back to the way it was a couple of weeks ago, when my world was golden, uncomplicated, carefree.

"Thanks, Orion," Darla said, leaning in to kiss my cheek. "This is gonna be so much fun."

"Yeah," I said, trying to ignore the way the pancakes I'd devoured earlier were sitting like a rock-solid lump in my stomach. "So much fun."

Darla and I spent the whole day together, doing homework at her house, going for a walk, watching TV. Basically me being the best boyfriend I could possibly be. When I left Darla's around ten o'clock, I was exhausted, even though we hadn't really done much. Apparently juggling feelings for two girls took a lot out of a guy. My car was parked on the street in front of her house, and when I came around the tall bushes at the edge of her yard, there was a girl standing next to it. She looked up when she heard me coming, and I realized it wasn't just any girl. It was the girl from True's gang, wearing a leather jacket with shiny gray sleeves and the tightest pants I'd ever seen.

"Hello, Orion," she said calmly. "I knew I would find you if I followed Eros. I hope you don't mind me waiting until dark to approach you."

"Who the hell is Eros?" I took a step back. "How do you know my name?"

Her brow creased. "They told me you wouldn't remember me, but I had to see it for myself."

"Remember you?" I asked, glancing around. Had she brought anyone else with her, or was she alone?

"It doesn't matter now," she said. "The queen will fix everything."

Suddenly she lunged at me and grabbed my wrist. "I have him!" she shouted at the sky. "Bring us home!"

I ripped my arm out of her grasp and backed away. "You're crazy."

The girl looked down at her palm. It shook like my thighs after a squat workout. "No," she said through her teeth. "No! No! No!"

Slowly she clenched her fingers into fists at her sides. I backed up even farther. Girl looked like she was about to blow.

"You gave me your word!" she screamed at the top of her lungs. Not at me, but at the world. At least, that was what it seemed like. She turned in a circle, bent at the waist, just raging.

"Orion?" The front door of Darla's house swung open. She stood on the step, framed by the light. "Is everything okay?"

"Go inside," I said, jogging toward her as I ripped out my phone. Whatever was going on with this girl, I didn't want Darla to get caught up in it. "Go inside and we'll call the police."

But by the time I got to the door and looked back, the girl was already gone.

CHAPTER TWENTY-SEVEN

True

I stood shivering next to the war monument at the center of Lake Carmody, unsure as to whether my shakes were due to fear, excitement, or the serious temperature drop. Next to me, Hephaestus was subdued and serious, his eyes trained on some crack in the brick walkway as he breathed in and out at a steady rhythm. For the last ten minutes I dared not speak and risk breaking him out of whatever trance he'd put himself into in order to survive these last moments before Harmonia would appear, but I couldn't contain myself any longer.

"What do you think she's going to say?" I blurted.

"I don't know," Hephaestus replied, his voice thin.

I paced back and forth in front of him, my boots crunching over fallen leaves. "Do you think Zeus is going to let us come home?"

"I don't know," he repeated.

"Well, do you think Hera's annoyed with us for making a deal with Artemis?" I asked.

"I don't know!"

Hephaestus's shout echoed throughout the deserted park. He pressed his lips together and glared up at me. "I'm sorry, True. I'm barely holding it together here. What time is it?"

"It's eleven fifty-nine," I told him after a glance at the clock tower above the post office across the street.

At that moment, Artemis and Apollo crested the stairs leading up to the park, their steps timed in perfect unison. Each wore a formfitting black leather jacket and tight black pants with black flat boots. For the first time I wondered where on Earth they were getting their clothing. I hoped they hadn't beaten some poor hipsters to death to get it.

"We're here," Artemis said with a scowl. "Where's your sister?"

"I have a bad feeling about this," Apollo said, his head pivoting from side to side as if he were no more than a mechanized puppet. A boil of a pimple had erupted on his chin, and his left eye kept twitching. Life on Earth was not agreeing with him. "What if they intend to ambush us?"

"Harmonia, part of an ambush?" Hephaestus said with a snort. "You've forgotten who you're dealing with."

Suddenly a stiff wind kicked up, sending the leaves at our feet into a fantastic, swirling vortex. I lifted my hands to shield my face from the whipping debris but was still nicked below the ear by a particularly sharp stem. Then, just as suddenly as it began, the wind stopped, and Harmonia stood before us. She wore a white dress with cinched waist and capped sleeves, her hair pulled back from her face on the sides. The sight of her left me speechless, but it didn't stop me from flinging myself into her arms.

"Eros," she said quietly, burying her face in my hair as she clung to me, her cool fingertips pressing into my back. "It's so good to see you."

I pulled away and we held on to each other's elbows. Her skin felt as silky and smooth as ever, the blush on her cheeks high and bright. She smiled at me—a reassuring, patient, loving smile—then turned and knelt before Hephaestus. There was so much love in her eyes as she gazed up at him, I couldn't believe I'd never seen it before. He reached down and cupped her face with both hands, his fingers trembling.

"My love," Harmonia breathed.

"I can't believe it," he said, smiling through tears. "I can't believe you're really here."

She stood up, slid onto his lap, and kissed him. My heart swelled and I pressed my palms against my chest, one on top of the other. Thousands of years of longing went into that kiss. Anyone could have felt it. I was hardly able to contain my own tears.

"Can we get on with this?" Apollo groused.

Harmonia pulled back, still gazing admiringly at Hephaestus, but he shot a scathing look at Apollo that made him pause.

"What?" Apollo said. "We're here for a reason, are we not? What news does Hera send? Is she restoring my powers so I can smite Eros?"

He rubbed his hands together in anticipation, shifting his weight from foot to foot as his mouth and eye twitched. He looked like some sort of evil imp, his pupils dilated, his movements jerky. The old, scheming Apollo was threatening enough, but this new Apollo—the one who seemed to be holding on by a thread—was a whole new kind of terrifying. He seemed as if he could snap at any moment.

"No." Harmonia stood, smoothing the front of her dress. Hephaestus reached over and took her hand, clearly unable to let her go, now that he had her near him again. Harmonia looked me in the eye. "But she knows of this pact you two have made, and she's not happy."

"Oh, really?" Artemis blurted, speaking up for the first time. "You're here to tell us *we've* angered the *queen*?"

"Yes. You and Apollo pushed her and pushed her about Orion for a fortnight, and then, when she finally heard you, she took your side." Harmonia gently tugged her hand away from Hephaestus and approached the twins. "She gave you what you wanted—a chance to spill Eros's blood and win back Orion—and instead you make a pact for peace."

Harmonia looked over her shoulder at me, calming me with her eyes. She was the queen's mouthpiece right now. Hera was listening to every word. I knew Harmonia didn't agree with anything she was being forced to say.

"Is that what she told you? That she gave me what I wanted?" Artemis spat. "What I wanted was Orion, and she gave me her word that as soon as I had him in my clutches, she would bring us back to Mount Olympus, but she lied."

"What?" Apollo snapped.

"I had Orion in hand tonight," Artemis told us, her nostrils flaring. "I called to Hera to bring us home."

"You did *what*?" I demanded. "We made a pact!"

"I had to see him for myself. Witness this memory loss you spoke of and make sure it was true," Artemis said, looking me up and down. "You would have done the same. Don't tell me you wouldn't."

I clenched my teeth, seething, but unable to deny her words.

"But when I saw him, I realized I couldn't just let him go, so I tried to take him home, but Hera forsook me."

"Is he all right?" I demanded. "Did you hurt him?"

Artemis turned on me, her eyes on fire. "I would never hurt Orion. How dare you ask such a thing?"

"Was it not you who pierced his skull with an arrow?" I shot back.

I knew it was a low blow even as the words spilled from my mouth, but I was too angry, too upset, to stop myself.

"Because *he* tricked me!" Artemis cried, pointing at Apollo. "You know what that did to me! You know how I suffered!"

"Enough!" Apollo roared. "I will not hear this!" He lunged for me, the thirst for vengeance dripping from his tongue, but Harmonia lifted a hand, sending a lightning bolt zipping across the park, where it exploded at his feet. Artemis screamed. Somewhere nearby a car's brakes squealed. In the commotion, Harmonia grabbed me and whispered in my ear.

"The queen doesn't care which one of you dies, but she doesn't intend to bring the other home," she said furtively. "She's forsaken you both, Eros, but one of you will die, and one will be banished. Please make sure it is you who lives. Please."

"But she can't do that," I breathed. "Zeus will bring me home. Me and Orion."

"Not if she has her way. And she is determined to have her way. Please don't chance it, Eros. As much as it pains me to say it, you must kill Artemis. You must prepare yourself."

As she released me, the thundering explosion caused by her outburst died off, but the frantic pounding of my heart had only just begun. It was either die or be banished forever. If I lived, I would never see my home again. Never match couples from my earthen window. Never get my powers back.

I staggered backward to the edge of the monument and sat on the cold, hard marble. Harmonia whipped around to face the twins.

"Come near my sister again in my presence and I will burn more than the toes of your shoes," she said imperiously, staring down her nose at Apollo. "This fight is to be between Eros and Artemis."

"I've never seen you resort to violence. Not once in our existence," Apollo said, as the last of the smoke danced its way toward the stars. "I rather like it on you, Harmonia."

Harmonia sniffed. "What say you, Artemis?"

"This is about Orion," Artemis replied, the color high on her cheeks. "It's about Orion's heart. Eros was right. We can't know whom he'll choose until she matches her couple and restores his memory. I will not fight her until that happens. Tell the queen I will not be a pawn in her little game."

"Artemis, sister, I beg of you," Apollo countered. "Hera has set her demands. Just end her and get it over with!"

"The queen was quite serious about this," Harmonia warned Artemis. "I would not test her."

"Oh, don't worry, Harmonia," Artemis said, moseying casually over to me with her hands clasped behind her back. "The queen will have her blood. But on *my* timeline. Eros will restore Orion's memory, she will watch him choose me, and then *he* will watch *her* die."

And with that, Artemis turned, took her brother's arm, and marched to the edge of the park. "Seven days, Eros! You have seven days."

Then they dipped down the hill and were gone. I bent forward, my head between my knees, and heaved in air. Harmonia's hands came down on my shoulders, and she crouched in front of me.

"Don't worry, Eros," she said. "Everything will be well. You have our father's blood in you."

I lifted my head to meet her eyes. She nodded ever so slightly, and my heart fluttered with hope. She was telling me to call on my father. To ask him to teach me how to fight.

"You are right, Harmonia," I said. "Perhaps all is not lost."

Together we rose to our feet, and Harmonia took Hephaestus's hand again. He brought it to his lips and kissed it. She smiled, but gently tugged her fingers away.

"There's something else you should know." Harmonia faced us as a doomed man might face his firing squad, chin lifted, but with fear in her eyes.

"Harmonia, what is it?" I asked.

"It's my fault," she said. "My fault that any of this happened. That our father found you and Orion in Maine, that he threatened Orion's life and you were forced to make the pact that got you banished here. It's all my fault, Eros, and I'm so sorry."

Harmonia bent her head forward and covered her face with her milky-white hands. Hephaestus and I exchanged an alarmed look. I hardly knew what to think.

"Your fault? How can that be?" Hephaestus asked finally.

"She's been spying on us," Harmonia said, her voice cracking. "The queen told me she's known for years that we've been communicating. She's listened in on every conversation we've had through our mirror since the turn of the century."

Hephaestus blanched. I could practically see his mind reeling, recalling what had been said, imagining the secrets and promises he and Harmonia had told and made. Private things. Personal things. The queen had heard every word.

"I kept your secret for months, Eros. I did," Harmonia told me, her eyes pleading. "But one night a few weeks ago I slipped and ended up telling Hephaestus where you and Orion were. The queen told the king, and he told Father. I'm so very sorry. If it weren't for me, you and Orion might be in Maine to this day, content in your love."

My palms were clammy as I stared at my sister. But even though she painted a pretty picture, I knew it wasn't true. I reached for her hand and squeezed.

"This is not your fault, Harmonia," I said. "You had no idea you were being watched. And if it wasn't for the mirror, we would have been found out some other way. Or Orion would have given in to the wanderlust he was starting to feel and struck out on his own."

"No. Never. Not without you," Harmonia told me.

I smiled. "Okay, maybe not without me. But I can't imagine we'd still be in our little paradise now. Or at least not for long. Things change. The world changes. We know that better than anyone."

"So you forgive me?" she asked.

"There's nothing to forgive."

Harmonia and I hugged for a long, long time. It was so good just to be near her again, I didn't want to let go. But eventually, Hephaestus cleared his throat. Harmonia laughed and took his hand.

"Look at the three of us, together again," she said. "Just like old times."

I smirked. "Yes, but I think it's time I leave you two alone."

"You needn't go, Eros," Harmonia said.

But I slipped away from her. As hard as it was to leave her, I knew that she and Hephaestus needed this.

"I'm sure you only have a short while to visit," I said. "What kind of love goddess would I be if I didn't leave you to it?"

Hephaestus shot me a grateful glance as I turned around and walked away. My knees shook beneath me and my heart felt about ready to give out, but I somehow kept moving. As soon as I was out of sight of my sister and her love, however, I lowered myself down on the nearest step.

Yes, it was a shock to know that Harmonia's loose lips had been instrumental in getting me banished, but what was done, was done. It was none of my concern. What mattered was that the queen wanted me dead. Me or Artemis. Apparently it didn't matter to her which. And when the queen wanted someone dead, she generally got her way.

CHAPTER TWENTY-EIGHT

True

I stood in the center of Goddess Cupcakes on Sunday afternoon, staring into space as I dumped ceramic plates into a plastic bin. Ever since last night's meeting with Harmonia, all I could think about was home, and what it meant to me. As I lay awake in the middle of the night, craving that feeling of security and comfort so acutely, I realized that my mind's eye was not filled with images of my chambers inside my mother's house, not of my earthen window. Not even Harmonia. When I thought of home, I saw only Orion. I saw our house in Maine, the small bedchamber, the rolling hills outside the windows. I saw him. His smile, his hands, his eyes, his hair. Home was Orion. Orion was home.

Yesterday's kiss had done nothing but solidify that fact for me. I didn't care whether I had to be mortal, whether I had to live out my days on this rock. As long as I was with Orion, everything would be okay.

"Tick-tock, Eros," Artemis whispered as I passed blindly by her table. "I don't know whether to root for you or against you."

"Then why don't you try shutting your mouth?" I suggested, dumping a coffee mug into the bin with a clatter.

My nemesis had been sitting at one of the corner tables since opening, sipping the same tea and tapping at her wrist every time our eyes met. Like she was doing right now as I turned my back on her.

I wondered what she'd do to me if she ever found out about Orion's and my lip-lock yesterday. Whatever it was, it wouldn't be pretty. And speaking of which, where was Orion? What was he thinking? Last night I'd been hoping against hope that he'd call, or better yet show up at my house and tell me he'd realized his mistake. That he wanted me. That he loved me. That he'd broken up with Darla—which would conveniently leave her free to be with Wallace. But thanks to Artemis and whatever bizarre scene had played out between the two of them, he'd probably spent the night in his bedroom, hiding under the covers.

My hand shook, and I dropped a plate back onto a table with a clatter. The two girls sitting there stared at me as if I'd offended them somehow. I took a deep breath. As long as I was stuck at work, there was nothing I could do to help Wallace and Darla along, and clearly I needed to distract myself from thinking about Orion. But how?

I picked up the plate and carefully placed it into my bin. It was a gorgeous, sunny fall day, and everyone in Lake Carmody had flooded downtown, hitting the shops and restaurants and parks hard and heavy. I had never seen Goddess Cupcakes so packed. Everywhere I looked, there were singletons just waiting to find a match. Slowly I smiled. Perhaps it was time to have a bit of fun.

Keegan Traylor had come in a few minutes earlier and now sat at the big window table with three of his friends. He was a jerk, but that didn't mean his friends didn't deserve to find love. I saw Josie Morrissey and two of her girlfriends about to snag the table nearest the bathroom and jumped into action.

"Oh, no, no, no. You girls don't want to sit here," I said, picking up Josie's plate and its contents—a PB&J cupcake—and balancing the bin against my hip.

"Why not?" Josie snapped.

Another special one. Maybe she and Keegan would hit it off. They both had hearts as black as tar.

"See that pipe right there?" I glanced at the ceiling. "Plumber says it could go at any time. He's coming to fix it tonight, but I wouldn't hedge my bets."

The three girls took a large step back. I pretended to ponder the crowded restaurant, like I didn't know exactly where to put them.

"Hey! What about that table?" I said, gesturing with the plate. "I'm sure those guys wouldn't mind sharing."

Josie's eyes lit up at the sight of the four St. Joe's varsity jackets. She applied some lip gloss, tossed her hair back, and led the charge. I bet my father would like her.

"Hey, guys." She leaned into the table, and every one of them checked out her tight shirt. "Have room for a few more?"

"Only if they all look like you," Keegan said, shoving a friend over.

Seriously, it was like shooting oversexed fish in a barrel. I placed Josie's plate on the table and left them to it. Maybe Josie's sweet-looking blond friend and the cute buzz-cut kid in the corner would hit it off.

"Excuse me? Are there any tables free?"

One of the English teachers from school stood nearby with a cup of coffee and a salted caramel cupcake, a novel tucked under her arm. She was pretty—about forty—with jet-black hair, an artistic sense of style, and no wedding band.

Artemis tapped her wrist. I heaved an impatient sigh and tried to ignore my timekeeper. Mr. Carlson, the school librarian, was sitting at a table near the wall with his daughter, Zadie, both of them engrossed in their own reading.

Mr. Carlson was not sporting a wedding ring either.

"We're pretty jammed today, but it looks like there's an empty seat at Mr. Carlson's table," I said, lifting my chin.

The woman hesitated. "I couldn't interrupt him and his daughter."

"They don't exactly look like they're in the midst of a tense discussion." I laughed lightly. Or at least I tried to. With Artemis's eyes on me, everything seemed to be coming out strained. "Follow me."

I moved sideways through the tight space between occupied chairs and stepped over someone's tuba case on my way to the Carlsons' table. The teacher took the longer route, sticking to the outskirts of the café and watching me with a sort of nervous anticipation.

"Hi, Mr. Carlson?" I said.

He looked up from his book and smiled. Man had an awesome smile. His dozens of long black braids fell free over his shoulders, unlike at school, when he wore them back in a ponytail, and he was wearing a polo shirt and jeans, rather than his usual button-down and tie. The shirt totally showed off his arms, and I saw the edge of a dark tattoo peeking out from under one sleeve.

"True," he said pleasantly. "How are you today?"

"I'm fine, thanks. Listen . . . the place is pretty busy, and I noticed you have an extra chair at your table. Would you mind if . . ."

I looked over at the teacher, who had just arrived at my side, clutching her book tightly to her side.

"It's Ms. Day. Amelia," she said, tilting her head apologetically.

"Hello, Maurice," she said to Mr. Carlson. "I don't want to interrupt. . . ."

"Oh, hi, Amelia." Mr. Carlson sat up straight. "You need a seat? Of course! Please, join us!"

"Thanks." Amelia's smile practically glowed. "That's very kind of you."

"Hi, Ms. Day!" Zadie said enthusiastically. She was wearing a white dress with short sleeves that made her look younger than her fourteen years, and her many Hello Kitty bracelets slid down her arm as she reached for her iced tea.

Amelia shot me a grateful look as she placed her cup and plate on the table. "Thank you, True."

"Anytime," I said as they settled in, looking like the perfect erudite family. "You guys let me know if you need anything."

I glanced around, making sure not to look directly at Artemis so I could maintain this cautiously optimistic feeling brewing inside me. Maybe being permanently banished to Earth wouldn't be so awful. Not if I could help people find happiness.

Then the door to the shop opened, and in stepped Orion. The sight of him after our encounter yesterday took my breath away. He was wearing a dark-blue sweater with a thick white stripe across the chest, and his glossy hair was freshly washed and brushed back from his strong cheekbones. As he walked toward me, Artemis's body went rigid, her eyes wide, like a dog who'd just spotted a bone. I gave her a warning look, and she didn't move. Luckily, Orion didn't notice her.

When Orion's eyes met mine, I saw the pain and hesitation there. He spotted Darla's friends—Veronica and the two other girls they were always with—sitting at the center of the room. Time seemed to stop as he stood there, considering. Then, finally, as if he couldn't fight it, he approached. I reached up to touch my hair self-consciously. What was he was going to say? That he was in love with Darla? That he was in love with me? I wondered, I wondered, I wondered. And then, he was there.

"Hey," he said.

"Hey," I replied.

"Listen, about yesterday . . ."

My heart filled my throat. "Yeah?"

Orion glanced behind him at Veronica and her cohorts. They blatantly stared him down. I could hardly breathe, and he was stalling. Artemis was still as stone. The silver arrow around my neck burned a hole in my skin.

"You were right," Orion said, lowering his voice. His gaze darted to my chest, to the spot where the arrow was tucked beneath my sweater. "I do have feelings for you."

My heart caught. This was it! He loved me! He was going to break up with Darla so we could be together.

"But I don't know where they came from," he continued under his breath. "I've been having all these . . . I don't even know what they are. Daydreams? Flashbacks?" He laughed sarcastically. "No. They can't be flashbacks. I didn't know you until a couple weeks ago."

I could hardly breathe. Was he actually remembering things from before? Remembering us? I grabbed his wrist. "Orion, what do you—"

"What the hell is this?"

The whole café fell silent. Apollo stood near the door, which was still swinging shut, his feet in a fighter's stance, his fists clenched at his sides. The black button-down he wore was open too deep at the neck, exposing the hair on his chest and his defined muscles. His acne had gotten worse, traveling down the bridge of his nose and across one cheek, and his lips twitched as he glanced at his sister, who, for the first time in her vain existence, looked like she wanted to disappear.

"You're allowing this to happen?" he demanded of her.

"What do you want me to do? He has no clue who I am."

"You again?" Orion stepped in front of me as if to protect me, which melted my heart like a glob of ice cream on a hot stove. "True, that girl is crazy. You should get out of here."

I glanced around the crowded shop. Mr. Carlson stood up from his table, sensing something was about to happen. A couple of Orion's teammates sat on high alert, a close eye on Apollo. All these people. If Apollo snapped, they could be hurt. But what was I supposed to do?

Apollo approached us, shoving aside chairs that were occupied by customers and knocking one man over in the process. Someone squealed. Apollo looked at me over Orion's squared shoulders.

"My sister may have struck a deal with you, but don't think that doesn't mean I won't end you right here. Harmonia's not around to save you anymore."

Orion lifted his chin. "Dude, back off or I'll call the cops."

"Son? I'd do as he says," Mr. Carlson said, stepping up behind Apollo.

Apollo ignored him. He looked Orion in the eye and snorted, stepping so close to him Orion had to tilt his head back to keep from kissing Apollo on the lips. "So pathetic you are. I'll never understand what they see in you."

"I said back off," Orion said firmly, shoving Apollo back with two hands. Apollo slammed Mr. Carlson in the shoulder, and he reeled back.

"Daddy!" Zadie shouted.

Apollo pulled his arm back for a punch and Veronica screamed, but Artemis was on him like a pouncing jaguar, grabbing his wrist with both hands before he could strike.

"Brother, let's go."

He whipped his arm out of her grasp but let it fall. Then he leaned past Orion, bringing his mouth ever so close to my ear. The tendons in his neck were taut, and I could feel tiny pulses of tension vibrating off him. One wrong move and he was going to snap. His breath smelled like rotten fruit.

"You may not care for your own safety, but I know you care for his," he whispered. "I've ended him before. Anger me, and I'll do it again."

"Apollo!" Artemis snapped.

He stood up straight, smiled wickedly at me, and walked backward toward the door, deftly stepping over backpacks and chair legs as he went. His eyes never left mine, and it wasn't until the door closed behind them that I finally breathed again.

"Are you kids okay?" Mr. Carlson asked.

"We're fine. Thanks, Mr. C." Orion turned to me, his face lined with concern. "True? What did he say to you?"

My whole body shook. I couldn't look Orion in the eye. Apollo, as ever, knew how to strike where it hurt. He'd threatened Orion's life. Even though his sister loved him, he'd threatened him. And I knew he would make good on that threat. He'd caused Orion's death once before when she loved him. There was nothing to stop him from doing it again.

I was putting him in danger right now, simply by continuing in his presence.

"I have to go," I said, taking a step back.

"Wait. True—"

"I'm sorry," I told him, meeting his gaze just long enough to feel my heart break. "I have to go."

It wasn't until I had locked myself into the tiny employee bathroom that I finally allowed myself to cry.

CHAPTER TWENTY-NINE
Darla

Wallace reached for the door of Goddess Cupcakes on Sunday afternoon, and it opened right into his hand.

"Son of a!" He pulled his arm into his chest, almost dropping his iPad as he bounced around in pain.

"Wallace! Are you okay?" I blurted, reaching for him. His knuckles were bright red. "We might need to get you some ice."

"No. It's fine." He shook his fingers out. "I'm good."

Orion stepped out onto the sidewalk, distracted. He looked like he'd just thrown up—totally pale and tense. Which was a shame because otherwise, nice outfit.

"Sorry, man. You okay?" he asked.

"Yeah. Fine." Wallace winced as he flexed and curled his fingers. "May never play the piano again, but it's not like I wanted to anyway."

"Where're you going?" I asked Orion, glancing inside the cupcake shop, which was, as predicted, slam-packed. "We just got here."

"I'm sorry. I'm really not feeling well," Orion told me, glancing over his shoulder. "I think you're gonna have to do this one without me."

"Oh no! Really?" I asked. "But look! Everyone from school is here."

I had so been looking forward to this—working the crowded hangouts as a couple, holding hands and chatting people up. Nobody ever campaigned outside of school, so when Orion had suggested it, I was sure it was really going to bump up our numbers. And now this.

"Well, if you're sick . . . ," Wallace said in a leading way, looking at me pointedly.

And suddenly I felt like an ass. Three days ago Orion had accused me of having a one-track mind for homecoming, and now here I was, proving him right.

"God, sorry. Of course. If you're not feeling well, of course you should go home. I'll call you after."

"Okay." Orion nodded, his eyes off somewhere down the street. "I'll talk to you later."

He gave me a quick, dry kiss on the cheek and speed-walked toward his car, which was parked at the curb, its cherry-red paint job gleaming in the autumn sun.

"Guess it's just you and me then," I said to Wallace.

He lifted his eyebrows in surprise. "You sure? You still want to do this?"

"Why not?" I asked. "Homecoming's in six days. It's now or never."

I yanked open the door and held it for Wallace. There was a distinct buzz in the air inside the shop. It was noisier than usual, and everyone seemed to be gossiping. But then again, that wasn't so odd. Almost every person in the room was a teenager. Gossiping was our national pastime. I pulled out a fistful of my cards and was about to start working the room, when I saw Veronica at a center table with Kenna and Mariah. She spotted me at the exact same moment.

"Hey, D. I didn't know you were gonna be here," she said.

Mariah and Kenna looked away. That was when I got that icky feeling in my stomach. Clearly they'd made a plan to meet up here today, and the plan hadn't involved me.

"Me neither," I said, walking slowly to their table. "I mean, I didn't know you were going to be here either."

Her eyes flicked past me and took on that glint that I knew so well. The one that meant she was about to eviscerate someone. I almost sidestepped in front of Wallace, as if I could possibly stop a word-bullet in midair.

"And with Wallace Bracken. Wow. You two sure have been spending a lot of time together," she said loudly.

A couple of guys from the soccer team snickered. My face flushed.

"We came to campaign, actually," I told her. Wallace stared down at his iPad with his jaw clenched, but I could tell he wasn't really looking at it.

"Oh really? Shouldn't you be doing that with your boyfriend?" Veronica said pointedly.

She glanced around at some of the kids from our school to make sure they were paying attention. Why was she doing this to me? But then, of course, I knew. Veronica saw me as a real threat in the homecoming race. She'd as much as said so before the game on Friday, and Josie had pretty much sealed it when she'd said she was going to vote for me. It looked like Veronica had finally decided to declare war.

And I was officially terrified. Yes, I had fantasized about winning. Yes, I had imagined what it would feel like to be declared more popular, prettier, better than Veronica Vine. But my best friend was not about to go down without a fight. And if there was one place no one wanted to be, it was in Veronica Vine's way.

"He said he wasn't feeling well," I told her quietly.

Mariah perked up. "Yeah, well, you should have seen what just—"

Veronica brought her hand down on Mariah's arm, and Mariah's mouth snapped shot.

"Maybe it was the sight of you slumming it with the dork of the century that made him nauseous," Veronica said, earning a few laughs. "But then again, I guess it's okay, since he was in here two minutes ago having a very intense conversation with that True freak. Maybe the four of you can set up a date for a loser foursome."

"Burn!" the guys from the soccer team shouted, slapping hands.

My stomach flopped over and wheezed as Veronica took a casual sip of her coffee. *Say you're just kidding,* I willed her silently. *Take it back.*

Part of me knew I should walk away. That I shouldn't stand here and let her humiliate me like this. But it was a teeny-tiny part. The rest of me knew I needed her. I needed her to laugh it off and invite me to join them. I didn't want her to leave me out in the cold. I loathed myself for it, but I couldn't stop feeling that way.

"Oh, look," Veronica said with a smirk. "I made him flee."

I turned around just in time to see Wallace shove open the door to the shop and walk out. Not that I could blame him. He was probably having traumatic flashbacks to Veronica's seventh-grade torture.

Veronica looked up at me and smiled. But it wasn't a wicked smile or a victorious smile. It was a nice smile. A welcoming smile.

Instantly my insides began to relax. How did she do that? How did she switch gears so quickly?

"Want to sit? I'll split my red velvet with you," she said.

The defiant part of me still screamed to turn my back on her and bail, but it was far, far too weak. When I sank into the chair, it was with total and utter relief. Everything was forgotten. Orion, Wallace, homecoming, the two pounds of business cards in my bag. Everything.

I hadn't lost Veronica. I hadn't lost my place. At that moment, that was the only thing that mattered.

CHAPTER THIRTY

True

I shoved open the gate at the side of our house on Sunday afternoon after my shift, sick to death of crying, sick to death of living in fear of Artemis and Apollo and their whims. Apollo couldn't just walk into Goddess and threaten Orion's life. This game was officially on.

Looking up at the clear blue sky, I stepped to the center of the small, square yard.

"Ares, mighty God of War, I beseech thee, come to me in my time of need."

A fierce wind whipped through the trees, sending orange and brown leaves swirling toward the sky, and Father appeared before me. He wore a brown sleeveless shirt, black pants, and black boots and was covered with smears of blood and inky tar. Sand clung to every bit of exposed skin and had settled into the folds of his clothes.

"That was fast," I said. "Where were you?"

"The desert. Always the desert these days." He dusted his arms off and sucked in a breath, his nostrils wide. "What am I doing here?"

"Harmonia told me that Hera has no intention of allowing me or Artemis to return to Mount Olympus," I said, stepping closer to him.

"It's true. She fears you, Eros. I told you this. She fears your growing powers. Yours and those of Artemis," he said succinctly. "She thinks the fact that you regained your powers even while banished to Earth might mean that you're on your way to becoming an upper goddess."

I lost my breath, nearly doubling over at the waist. "What? Is that even possible?"

My father turned up his meaty palms. "All things are possible. You know that. The queen does not take kindly to pretenders to her throne. She might be able to keep you in check while you're banished to Earth, but back on Mount Olympus, you'll be at full strength."

My mind reeled. An upper goddess? I had never dreamed . . . Well, okay, I had dreamed, but that was all, because as far as I knew, no one had ever ascended from one caste to the next. To be an upper goddess . . . that was a lot of power. Did I even want that much power?

No. There was no lust for more authority or clout within me. My job, my calling, was to create and nurture love.

"I have no desire to take the queen's throne," I told my father. "I only wish to return to my rightful place among the gods. I am no threat to her."

"Of course you're not," my father replied. "You have a pure soul. You'd never rise up against the upper gods, because you do not crave power. You crave love. Artemis, on the other hand . . ."

"So why not blame *her*? Why not simply smite *her*?" I asked, pacing angrily, moodily, toward the almost bare magnolia tree. "What do I have to do with anything?"

"I know your true soul, my daughter, but Hera does not," my father said, wiping his palms quickly against his backside. "Hera believes, and has always believed, that everyone is out to get her.

The very idea that two lesser goddesses might one day wield enough power to overtake her position as queen . . . she can't abide that."

I plucked a curled red leaf from a tiny, shivering branch and held its stem between my thumb and forefinger. It looked like a small, withered heart.

"Will Zeus still return Orion's memory if I succeed in my original mission?" I asked.

"I believe he will," my father said. "He doesn't like Hera's posturing, but he seems willing to let her have her way with you and Artemis. Happy wife, happy life, you know. Also, he doesn't relish your growing power any more than she does."

I shook my head. Power. It was always about power with these upper gods.

"Should you succeed, however, I'm sure he'll return your mortal to you," he continued. "If only to save face."

My jaw clenched in determination. "Then I must win."

My father's eyes widened. "Are you telling me you're ready to do battle?"

"Apollo has threatened Orion's life," I told him.

Ares laughed. "Of course. When it's your existence on the line, you don't care, but as soon as that mortal is threatened—"

"I love him!" I shouted, throwing the leaf to the wind.

"It's rather shortsighted to be more worried about him than yourself," my father spat. "He'll be dead in a mere seventy years now that you've rescued him from the stars. You have an eternal purpose to fulfill."

He wasn't wrong. But whenever I pictured Orion's face, my purpose didn't matter.

"I *will* kill Artemis if it is the only way for me and Orion to be together," I told my father. "He is the only thing that truly matters to me. Even if I must be made mortal and banished to Earth to have him."

My father shook his head, rolling his eyes at what he perceived to be my weakness. I squared my shoulders and stood before him, straightening myself to my full height.

"Father . . . even if you don't agree with my motives . . . I want you to teach me to fight."

His eyebrows darted up, and a spark of intrigue lit his eyes. Instantly his entire posture relaxed, and he did something I'd only rarely seen him do. He smiled.

"Finally."

An hour later, my muscles were shaking, I had a cut above my lip that refused to stop bleeding, and I couldn't feel my toes. That had to be a bad sign. I bent over the bench in the rear corner of our yard, clinging to my ribs, trying to keep them inside my body, as I was sure they were cracked and about to poke their way through my skin.

"Mercy!" I shouted, holding up a hand as my father advanced. I turned around and sat.

"Do you know who'll show no mercy?" my father said. "Artemis. She'll gut you where you sit."

"I just need a five-minute break," I told him, my hair dripping salty liquid onto my sneakers.

"No. You need to concentrate, Eros," my father said, backing up with his feet switching front to back, front to back, like a true boxer. "You're not blocking."

I shoved myself up. "You're punching too fast."

His fists dropped. "Do you have any idea how much I'm holding back?" He squatted in front of me, hardly winded. "Listen to me.

Artemis is not as experienced a fighter as I am. You need to watch her eyes. If you see where she's looking, you can anticipate her next move. Now try."

I took a deep breath, which hurt like hell, and stood up with raised fists. A drip of blood tickled my top lip, and I licked it away. I stared into my father's eyes. They darted to the left side of my face. I reached up and blocked his punch.

"There! You see?"

I smiled slightly. "Okay. Try it again."

He blinked and went for my gut. I jumped back, then lunged forward and threw an uppercut. My father leaned away from it, but I still caught the very tip of his chin. I heard the satisfying clack as his bottom teeth met his uppers.

"Very good!" he cried with a grin.

Then he threw a right hook. I blocked it. He tried a body blow and I blocked most of that, too, though he caught my ribs again. I reeled away, coughing, which only made the pain worse. My father stood up straight and dropped his arms.

"Perhaps we should stop. I don't want you to be injured if Artemis happens to change your timeline on a whim. You need to be in top form."

"You want to stop now? Just when I'm getting it? Besides, you can simply heal me when we're done here."

He tilted his head. "Excellent point."

Ignoring the pain as best I could, I darted forward, throwing an elbow at his face, which he easily deflected. He pushed me off him and hit me with a three-punch combination, but caught only the sides of my forearms. I reached back and threw the quickest, hardest punch I had within me, right at his face. It hit home, and his chin darted skyward. He staggered back. I brought my hands to my mouth and held my breath.

"Father? I'm sorry! I didn't think that would work!"

He caught himself before going down and shook his head as if to clear his vision. When his eyes met mine again, I saw the dazed pride behind them, and my heart swelled ten sizes, healing my bruised ribs.

"My daughter," he said, rubbing his cheekbone. "I think you're ready."

CHAPTER THIRTY-ONE

Orion

I waited for True by her locker Monday morning. A huge black-and-white picture of me and Darla stared me down from a home-coming poster across the hall. I'd talked to Darla quickly last night, claiming I still felt sick. Which was not a total lie. There was clearly something wrong with me. Saturday night I'd promised myself to commit to Darla, but as soon as I'd laid eyes on True on Sunday, I couldn't stop myself from talking to her. Telling her I had feelings for her. It was like I couldn't control myself.

There was no more denying it. I sucked.

But even though I knew that, I couldn't stop thinking about True, especially after the way that asshole had confronted her at Goddess yesterday. What the hell did he mean when he said he didn't understand what they saw in me? Why did him and that girl act like they knew me? And what the hell had he said to True to make her run from me like that?

Darla's sparkling eyes bored a hole through my chest. I turned away from the poster as True came around the corner.

She was wearing jeans and a plain black T-shirt with a wide neck, her hair pulled back from her face, which was pale and dry-looking. The second she saw me, she froze, and when I approached, she started looking around for an escape route.

"Hey," I said. "You're okay."

She cleared her throat. "Yeah. Yes, I'm fine. You?"

"I'm fine."

"Good."

She stepped around me to get to her locker and turned the knob with trembling fingers. I saw a couple of sophomore girls watching us and trying to pretend like they weren't.

"True, what the hell is going on?" I said under my breath, leaning into the locker next to hers. "What did that guy say to you yesterday? Did he threaten you?"

She let out this sound through her nose that was half snort, half laugh. "No. He didn't do that."

There was a loud slam down the hall, and she flinched. She was acting scared, and she looked . . . haunted. My heart began to pound.

"Did he hurt you?" I hissed. "True. You have to call the police."

"The police can't do anything, Orion." She took out a couple of books and held them against her chest.

"Why not? They helped you once before, right? Maybe they can do it again."

I reached for her wrist, but True angled away from me. "Don't touch me!" she said through her teeth.

I was going to explode from frustration. "Just tell me what's going on."

True took a deep breath and blew it out. "Just leave me alone, Orion. Please."

"What?" I felt as if I'd woken up in some alternate reality. Two days ago she'd been begging me to admit my feelings for her and

I'd been telling *her* not to touch *me*. "True, this is insane. I thought that you—"

"No," she said firmly, setting her chin. "Whatever you thought, it's over. You were right. You have a girlfriend, and she doesn't deserve this." Her chin quivered, but this time, she held my gaze. I felt the sting of her words and tried not to look away. "So please, from now on, just stay away from me."

She slammed her locker so hard I felt the reverberations inside my chest. I reached for her arm again as she strode by me, but she hugged it against her. And that was it. No further explanation. No discussion. She was just fine leaving it at that. Leaving me totally and mind-bendingly confused.

What the hell had happened in two days to make her do a complete one-eighty?

"True, wait," I said loudly.

"Leave me alone!" she shouted back.

Then she ducked into the science wing and was gone.

CHAPTER THIRTY-TWO

True

As I came around the corner, Orion still calling my name, my eyes blurred so badly I couldn't see straight. Suddenly Hephaestus appeared in front of me.

"What's wrong?" he asked.

"I have to hide."

A door behind him opened and a rotund janitor stepped out, moseying off toward the back of the school. Hephaestus caught the door before it could close.

"In here," he hissed.

We both ducked inside.

"Thank you," I whispered, as the door closed. "I couldn't let Orion catch up to me."

Hephaestus nodded his understanding. Artemis and Apollo were banned from the school, of course, but I couldn't take the chance that Apollo would somehow find out Orion and I were still talking. I pressed myself back against a shelf full of industrial cleaner and held my breath. After a few minutes had passed, my body relaxed. The coast seemed to be clear.

"Are you okay?" Hephaestus asked.

"No!" I blurted. I had thought I could control my feelings, but apparently not. "No, I am not all right. Everything is against me. Every*one*! Zeus claims that he wants me to succeed but sends Orion here to distract me. Apollo would take any excuse to kill Orion. Artemis wants me dead. Hera wants me dead and sends my own sister to tell me. Just about the only person willing to help at this point is my father! How have I come to this?"

"I'm still here," Hephaestus told me patiently.

I took a deep breath and shot him a sorrowful look. Out of steam, I sank to the floor, bringing my knees up under my chin. "Of course. You are still here. I'm sorry."

He lifted his shoulders. "It's all right. If you've gotta have a breakdown, have a breakdown. As long as you pull yourself back up again."

"He was just coming around," I muttered, staring at the brown, mucky water in the yellow mop bucket next to me. "He was going to tell me he wanted to be with me yesterday. I'm sure of it."

"You're missing the bigger picture here," Hephaestus said, folding his hands in his lap. "This Orion is not your Orion, remember? You want your Orion back. And the only way to get him is to match your last couple."

"Is it so wrong to want this Orion to love me in the meantime?" I asked, my voice a pathetic whimper. "I just want him back, Hephaestus. I just want him back."

"No. It's not wrong," Hephaestus said. "But from an outsider's perspective . . . it kind of seems like a waste of time."

I stared at the wheels on Hephaestus's chair, the chrome gleaming even in the relative darkness.

"You're right," I said with a sigh, pressing my chin into my kneecap. "Are you always right?"

He pretended to ponder this. "Mostly."

I laughed, and he reached out a hand to help me to my feet. I shoved my sweaty palms down my thighs and grabbed my bag, which had ended up in the corner with a stack of paper towel rolls.

"Focus on Wallace and Darla," Hephaestus instructed. "On forming the true love you were sent here to inspire. You'll feel better if you're being productive."

"Thanks, Hephaestus," I said, squeezing his hand as the first bell rang. "I don't know what I'd do without you."

CHAPTER THIRTY-THREE

Darla

Standing on Wallace's doorstep was just weird. I hadn't been there in forever, and nothing had changed. They still had the elaborate welcome mat with the cursive *B* at its center. There were still two planters next to the door with no plants in them—just dirt—like always. When I rang the doorbell and it sang that familiar classical song, it took me right back to those summers in grade school when we used to go swimming in his pool with his babysitter and get locked out and have to run around to the front of the house, shivering in our wet bathing suits, to ring the doorbell.

But it was also weird because I wasn't entirely sure what I was doing there. Did I really care about Wallace Bracken enough to come check on him? Did I really give a crap if he hated me?

I saw him peek out the side window, and my heart caught. Okay. Maybe I did. He opened the door.

"Hey," he said plainly.

"Hey."

I could see the grand piano on the other side of the foyer and smell something amazing baking in the kitchen at the back of the house. I waited, but Wallace didn't invite me in.

"So, I've never seen anyone bolt out of their classes as fast as you did today," I began.

He nodded, one hand in the pocket of his plaid hipster pants. "Yep. I kind of didn't want to talk to you."

That was the thing about Wallace. He didn't sugarcoat things.

"If this is about yesterday, I'm sorry about what Veronica said," I began, fiddling with the rings on my right hand. "She can be such a bitch."

It felt brave to say that out loud, even though she wasn't there.

"True. But she was also right," Wallace said, putting his hand on the door handle. "You really shouldn't be seen with me."

My brow knit. "What?"

"I took a poll today, and while most of the unpopular kids would still vote for you if they saw you hanging out with me, a majority of the popular kids—and the kids who really want to be popular—said they'd be less likely to vote for you."

I felt like my heart was being squeezed like an orange. He'd asked people this? He'd actually gone around school and made people tell him whether he was ruining my chances at homecoming queen and they'd said yes? To his face? What was wrong with people?

Somewhere deep inside the kitchen there was a crash. We both flinched. "I'm okay!" his mother yelled. "I'm fine!"

"Wallace, that's insane," I said finally, because I didn't know what else to say.

He shrugged, averting his eyes. "Maybe, but from the beginning this has been about getting you elected, and if you want to get elected, you should stay away from me. Go be with your boyfriend. You know that's what you need to do if you want to be queen."

He made me sound so callous. Like homecoming queen was

the only thing I cared about. Which, okay, it was something I cared about in a huge way, but right at that moment, standing there with him, it seemed so dumb. Why did he have to have his feelings hurt just so that I could get a plastic crown?

"Wallace, come on," I said. "I wouldn't even be in this thing if it weren't for you."

He chuckled. "You are so wrong. You were always in this thing. And Orion is a much bigger asset to you than I am." His eyes flicked past me toward my house. "And there he is now."

I glanced over my shoulder and sure enough, Orion's car was pulling into my driveway. We hadn't seen each other much today. I'd heard about the intense conversation he and True had that morning in the hall—the second in two days—and I didn't know how to bring it up with him and not end up in a fight. So I'd spent most of the lunch period avoiding the table by walking around, handing out my Facebook cards. Then, when the bell finally rang, he'd bolted. It was like we'd made a mutual avoidance pact. But now, there he was, rising out of his car like some supermodel, slipping his sunglasses from his eyes as he squinted over at us.

"Go talk to him," Wallace advised me. "Get this thing back on track."

I gave Orion a quick wave, telling him to stay there and wait for me. "Wallace, I'm—"

But I didn't get a chance to finish my apology. The door had already closed in my face.

CHAPTER THIRTY-FOUR

Orion

I held my breath as Darla cut across the lawn next door to hers—the lawn that apparently belonged to that Wallace kid—her arms crossed over her chest. She was so beautiful. Beautiful, smart, energetic, creative, funny. True was right. She didn't deserve to be treated the way I was treating her. Something that was going to end right now. I had picked Darla. Of all the girls at Lake Carmody High, I'd asked her out. I'd asked her to homecoming. I wasn't going to screw this up by letting True become a distraction.

Which I couldn't do anyway, considering she wanted nothing to do with me.

I smiled when she got to the driveway, ready to be the perfect boyfriend again.

"Are you finally going to tell me what's going on with you and True Olympia?" Darla demanded. Her brown eyes flashed as she lifted her pretty chin. No one could do righteous indignation like Darla Shayne.

"I'm sorry . . . what?" I asked.

"It's a small school, Orion. People talk. They text. They tweet. I know you went to visit her at work yesterday before I got there, and I know you had some kind of fight with her this morning. You're making me look like a total idiot." She paused, and something shifted in her expression. "No, you know what? I don't care about that. You're making me *feel* like a total idiot. And I don't like feeling that way."

Okay. This was not good. I wasn't sure what I was expecting when I came over here, but it wasn't this.

"I'm sorry," I said earnestly. "There is *nothing* going on with me and True. I promise. She doesn't even want to be friends with me anymore, and she's right. We have nothing in common."

Darla sniffed and flipped her hair off her shoulder, staring off across the driveway. Her body language was arctic.

"What do you want me to say?" I asked. "I like you, Darla. A lot. I really do. You know that, right?"

"Do I?" She looked me up and down, shifting her weight from one high-heeled shoe to the other. "So prove it. Actions speak louder than words."

Prove it? How? I felt like I was being quizzed on some awful TV show, and my life depended on whatever answer I would give. Prove it. Okay. I leaned in to kiss her. She leaned back. Honestly, she looked disgusted.

"That is *not* what I meant!"

I let out a groan of frustration. This was nuts. Maybe I should just give up on girls. Clearly, I didn't understand them. Clearly, I had no clue what any of them wanted. One minute True was all over me, the next she was shoving me away and running. Meanwhile, Darla had been basically pawing me ever since I met her, lately even telling me what she wanted and where to be and when, and now she was keeping me at arm's length and expecting me to figure it out myself.

Desperately I looked around, as if the sky would somehow offer up an answer, and then I saw the pom-pom hanging from my rear-view mirror. Something True had tied to my first spirit basket.

"I've got it!" I announced.

I whipped out my phone and hit the speed-dial button for Peter Marrott. He picked up right away.

"Hey, man," he said. "What's up?"

"Hey, Peter," I replied while Darla eyed me like I was cracked in the head. "Are you with Claudia right now?"

"Yep."

"Can I talk to her?" I asked.

There were some muffled noises, and then I heard a huff of air. "Orion?" Claudia said. "What's going on?"

"Nothing. I just want Darla Shayne to be my booster from now on."

Darla stopped breathing. I saw the light return to her eyes. A little bit, at least.

"Ooookay. So you want me to, what? Fire True?" Claudia asked.

"If you don't mind," I said. "If not, I can tell her. It's not a problem."

Which was a lie, of course. Telling True I was replacing her with Darla would mean getting her to talk to me, which didn't seem like much of a possibility anymore. But I'd find a way if I had to.

"No, it's fine. I'll take care of it. Anything else?"

"No, that's it. Thanks, Claudia."

I hung up the phone and looked Darla in the eye. "So?"

A smile finally broke across her face. She flung her arms around me and buried her nose in my shoulder. "Thank you," she said. "That was perfect. You are perfect."

I tried to shrug, which didn't really happen what with her clinging to me. "I have my moments."

Then I leaned in to kiss her, and it was a perfect kiss. We were a perfect couple. And from now on, I was going to concentrate on that. True was not a part of my past, she was not a part of my present, and she would never be a part of my future.

CHAPTER THIRTY-FIVE

True

My eyes were sore as I stared out the front window of Goddess Cupcakes on Monday evening. As hard as I tried to take Hephaestus's advice and put Orion out of my mind, I'd kept randomly leaking sorrowful tears all day long. To make matters worse, Wallace had spent the entire lunch period polling with his iPad, and when I'd tried to ask him how things were going with Darla, he'd scurried off with his head down, muttering something about crunching numbers. I'd made no progress with my couple, and I couldn't seem to pull myself up from this pit of despair into which I'd sunk. As I watched families trot by toting pizza boxes, groups of friends texting and laughing, and couples strolling without a care in the world, I couldn't help thinking of something Orion—*my* Orion—had once said to me.

"I'd rather spend whatever short time I have here with you than hang among the stars, watching life go on without me. Watching you go on without me."

At the time, we'd laughed over the extreme melodrama of his words, but now I felt them to my core. The only thing I wanted was to be with him. And now I was watching the world go by without him by my side.

I was just about to drown my sorrows in a black coffee when Wallace walked in. Deep within my chest I felt the slightest sparkle of hope. News. At least I was about to get news.

"I'm done," Wallace announced. "Stick a fork in me."

My heart sank. "What do you mean, you're done?"

Wallace plucked the napkin dispenser off the counter in front of me and fiddled with it, pushing the napkins all the way in until they bounced back out again.

"Darla and me? We're never gonna be together," he said. "I thought we were from different social worlds? Turns out most people think we're from two different species. It's not gonna happen. I already told her I thought she was better off with Orion."

No. No, no, no. He couldn't give up now. He and Darla were meant for each other. It was written across their faces whenever they were together. I could feel their connection in my bones. How could they just ignore it? Because other people didn't approve?

"But Wallace, you can't let others dictate your life . . . your happiness," I said desperately. "Please don't do this. Don't give up. You have to—"

"I don't want to talk about it, True," he said, replacing the napkins with a clatter. "I just came to tell you it's over. And to order a triple chocolate to go."

He hazarded a smile. I felt like I was going to throw up. What was I going to do? How was I going to fix this? Gods, if only I had my arrows. Then this would be a done deal, and I'd know I'd done the right thing by matching them. But that was not an option. I needed a new plan. I needed to regroup. I needed to stop hyperventilating.

"True?" Wallace eyed me with concern. "Are you okay?"

"Yeah. Yes. I'm fine." I took a deep breath. "One triple chocolate, coming up."

I served Wallace his cupcake, and he headed out just as Tasha came in, tugging off her jacket. Perfect. My replacement. I needed to get out of this place, stat. I needed some air, some time to think. I pulled my phone from my pocket and texted Hephaestus. Tasha was here to relieve me, so it was time to go home. Goddess was in walking distance to the house, but he and my mother had insisted that I shouldn't walk around town on my own anymore, not after Apollo's threat. Hephaestus had essentially volunteered to become my driver and bodyguard.

DONE FOR THE NIGHT. CAN YOU COME?

He texted back almost instantly.

FIFTEEN MINS.

I trudged into the back room, where Dominic sat at his desk, crunching numbers with a calculator and pencil. Over in the kitchen I could hear a couple of the bakers laughing and banging around, cleaning up after today's work and prepping for tomorrow's. I clocked out on the computer, then headed to the break room to exchange my apron for my jacket and my duffel bag. The bow and arrows clattered around inside it as the door closed behind me.

"Headed out?" Dominic asked, swiveling around in his chair.

"Yep. See you on Thursday."

Dominic's eyes narrowed at my bag. "You keep bringing that to work. What's in there, anyway?"

"Just some workout gear," I told him, patting the side of the black canvas bag self-consciously. "Headed to the gym."

His eyes traveled suspiciously away from the bag and up to meet mine. I held my breath. He would be well within his rights to look inside the bag. This was his business. I was his employee. He held my gaze for a long ten seconds, and I knew he didn't believe me. Then, finally, he returned his attention to his ledger.

"Have a good night!" he said, lifting a dismissive hand.

I breathed out. "You too!"

The back door had just slammed behind me when I saw something move out of the corner of my vision, and then I was on the ground. Pain crackled down my right cheek as it collided with the hard asphalt, and I skidded sideways, slamming the top of my head into a solid metal drainpipe. When I looked up, I saw flashing stars and behind them, the hovering figure of my good friend Apollo.

"This ends now," he growled.

He dragged me to my feet and pulled back a hand, but as he shifted his weight forward, I ducked and spun, getting behind him. I lifted a foot, let out a guttural cry, and kicked him as hard as I could in the small of his back, sending him sprawling face-first on the ground. I turned and lunged for my bag to get my bow, but Apollo grabbed my hair at the top of my head and yanked me backward.

"What are you doing?" I demanded.

He flung me away and I faced him, my fingers itching for my bow and arrows, but Apollo stood between me and my bag now. I had no chance of getting to them unless I incapacitated him first.

"I can't take this place anymore," he spat, "and as far as I can tell, if you die, I get to go home. So now you're going to die."

He attempted a roundhouse kick to my head, but I ducked and swept his standing leg out from under him. His head hit the ground with a crack and he stared at the sky, breathless. Finally he coughed.

"You can't kill me," I hissed. "Hera wants me to fight Artemis, not you."

He laughed through his heaving rasps and brought his hands to his chest. "As if I care what the queen wants."

He stood up slowly, and I took a few paces back, glancing left and right. My instincts told me to flee, but he would only chase me down, and by then we might be out on the street, sparring in public. I couldn't have that. I couldn't put people in danger.

"You've been practicing," Apollo said.

"There you go again," I said. "Stating the obvious."

With a sudden growl, Apollo threw himself at me. I tried to duck out of the way, but his shoulder collided with my jaw and he drove me backward into the brick wall, knocking the air out of me. Then, for good measure, he drove his fist into my gut, right in the center of my rib cage. The pain as I tried to suck in air was beyond all comprehension.

"Turnabout's fair play," he said in my ear.

I heaved in one breath, finally, and he hit me with a cross punch so hard I heard my cheekbone crack. When I fell sideways, I took the garbage can with me. At that moment, the back door flew open and Dominic stepped out.

"What the hell is—" His eyes widened when he saw me there, lying on my side on the ground with Apollo hovering above me. "What are you doing?" he shouted at Apollo. "Get out of here or I'll call the police."

Apollo rose to his full height, which was a good foot taller than Dominic, and sneered. "You dare command me, mortal?"

"Don't!" I said through my teeth.

"Get the hell out of here!" Dominic shouted again, pulling his phone out and starting to dial.

Apollo looked down at me with an evil smile on. "I suppose we can finish this another time. Looks like it's going to be even easier than I thought."

Then he ran off, jumping over the upended garbage can and disappearing around the corner of the building.

"True?" Dominic asked, crouching in front of me. "True? Are you all right? Can you sit up?"

I nodded and, ever so carefully, pushed myself up so that I was leaning back against the wall. I breathed in, but the air got caught inside my tight chest and I coughed, holding on to my ribs as my cheek radiated pain through my skull.

"I'll get you some ice. And water." Dominic hopped to his feet, surprisingly spry for a mortal of his age. "Who was that guy?"

A million possible answers flitted through my mind. Old friend. Old enemy. But I wasn't sure I could explain any of it to his satisfaction, so I simply lifted my shoulders, which hurt like hell.

"No idea," I lied.

He didn't believe it. He'd heard what Apollo had said to me. But he let it go. As soon as he was inside, I heard the singular rumble of Hephaestus's van and allowed myself to go limp. The cavalry was on its way.

CHAPTER THIRTY-SIX

True

I felt the pain in my face before I was even fully awake. Trying to avoid it, I rolled onto my opposite side, and one of my ribs exploded. At least, that was what it felt like. I opened my eyes and winced. In my debilitated state the night before, I'd forgotten to close the curtains on my east-facing window, and the sunlight was blinding. I raised one hand against it and winced. There wasn't one part of my body that didn't ache.

Letting out a groan, I rolled onto my back and tried to sit up. My ribs replied with another shock of pain. Everything hurt, but I was going to have to go about my day as if I was right as rain. I had to try to facilitate a reconciliation between Darla and Wallace. Those two were my only hope.

Finally, reluctantly, I opened my eyes and pushed myself up, doing it as quickly as possible, then eased myself back into my pillows. I didn't want to look at the sand timer, but I sadistically did it anyway. There was less than one quarter of the sand left in the top. I groaned again and looked away. That was when I saw something propped up against my desk chair, and my heart came to a screeching stop.

My quiver. My bow. My arrows. My magical weaponry. It was right there in front of me. This wasn't possible. It couldn't be.

I closed my eyes again, rubbed them, and blinked. Yep. Still there.

Ignoring the pain, I swung my legs out of bed and hobbled over to the chair. A note was attached to the strap by a black ribbon. It read simply:

All's fair in love and war. –A

Ares. Of course. He would never be able to bear it if his daughter lost in battle. Or, perhaps, he simply loved me and wanted me to live. Either way, I was grateful for the assistance.

I lifted my bow first, and the familiar, comforting heft of it sent a thrill of pleasure through my body. I clasped the leather handle in my fingers and laughed as they slid right into place, settling into the grooves they'd left after generation upon generation of use. Then I ran my fingers down the string and plucked it, watching it vibrate. I saw myself lounging at my earthen window, piercing the hearts of mortals from far above, inspiring endless love among the masses. My own heart swelled as I remembered what it felt like to be that free, that powerful, that in control.

I was Eros, creator of love on Earth. I was a goddess. For now, anyway.

"It's good to see you, old friend," I whispered.

Then I grabbed the quiver and knew something was wrong. It was too heavy. Far too heavy. So heavy it felt like my ribs were cracking again. I sat down on my bed and saw the cause. The quiver was filled with arrows—ten to be exact—but they were not my light-as-a-feather golden arrows, which were used for breeding love and making matches. They were my leaden arrows, the ones I used far less often and certainly never at a clip of ten at a time. These arrows bred hatred.

I took a deep breath and sighed. Of course my father would leave my hatred arrows. This way I could win by death, rather than by forging love.

But it did make sense. It would have been too easy if my golden arrows had suddenly appeared. I could have walked out of this room and made the mailman fall in love with a bus driver and my work here would be done—a slight against our bargain that Zeus would surely notice. Besides, I realized as I ran my fingers over the cold fletching on one of the arrows, these could be helpful too. With these arrows I could end Artemis and Apollo with a mere snap of the string. They were one of the few weapons ever forged that could stop a god's or goddess's heart with one strike.

I lay back on my bed again, drawing my bow with me, holding it against my sore chest and ribs. It felt good in my hands. It felt like home. Just clinging to it gave me a surge of white-hot hope.

I could do this. I could survive this. I would prevail.

I heard my mother's hair dryer roar to life in the bathroom. It was time to get up and move gingerly through my day. I pushed myself out of bed and went to the closet, placing my beloved bow and its evil arrows inside, where they could easily be reached.

Even with my many aches and pains and the memories of my ignominious fight with Apollo last night, I felt better now. Confident. Just knowing my bow was with me was a tremendous boost. Holding it had made me feel myself again. And when I was Eros, Goddess of Love, nothing could stop me.

CHAPTER THIRTY-SEVEN

Orion

Mr. Crouch, the photography teacher, had breath that smelled like pea soup. I wasn't sure I'd ever had pea soup before, but that was the image that came disgustingly to mind every time he leaned in close to me and Darla on Tuesday afternoon. Green, mealy goo. It was too bad they couldn't have had Greg take these shots, but he was already booked. Right now he was up on the field, getting ready to take the official team pics for football and Boosters.

"Put your arm around her from behind," Crouch told me, and I watched his stubble-covered Adam's apple bob over the top of the too-tight collar of his plaid shirt. "Act like you like her."

Darla and I laughed nervously. He really couldn't have said anything worse, considering how tense we'd been around each other today. Even after telling Claudia I wanted Darla as my booster, I felt like everything I said or did could be the wrong thing. I'd never had a fight with a girlfriend before, and I didn't know how to deal, so I'd spent most of the day keeping my mouth shut and smiling, just hoping that before long everything would go back to the way it had been. Easy. Uncomplicated. Fun.

Now I put my arm around Darla and held her close against my

chest, her hair tangling on the thick weave of my sweater. It was so awkward, standing here with everyone else, posing. I wondered how the kids who weren't couples were handling being paired up and asked to grope each other for the camera. Mr. Crouch moved on to Josh and Veronica, who stood behind us in line at the center of the gym.

"See? These two know what they're doing. Perfectly in sync."

I felt Darla clench. "You okay?" I whispered.

"Fine." She turned to smile at me, lost her balance, and brought the very sharp tip of her very high heel down on top of my foot. It hurt. A lot. I broke from the line, hopping like an idiot and cursing under my breath.

"Mr. Floros?" Principal Peterson hovered near the door to the locker room, looking bored. "Are we going to have to be here all day?"

"No. No, sir. I'm fine." I touched my foot gingerly to the ground and snatched it back up again, then hobbled back over to Darla. One hand covered her mouth.

"I'm so sorry!" she hissed. "Are you okay?"

"M'fine," I mumbled, forcing a smile as I slid in behind her again. Veronica smirked. Sometimes I really wondered what Josh saw in that girl. Actually, I wondered that every single day.

"As long as you can run this weekend," Josh joked as the photographer dealt with the seniors.

I clenched my teeth. "Shouldn't be a problem."

"Okay, on the count of three, everyone smile their best home-coming smile!" Mr. Crouch backed up with his camera until he was far enough to get the wide shot. He'd clicked off a few when the bell rang. In ten minutes we were going to be late for football practice, which would not make Coach Morschauser happy. To him, homecoming was about the game, not the dance. At this point I kind of wished that were true.

At least we'd gotten out of ninth period for the photo shoot. Art class would've been a nightmare. True probably hated me more than ever after being fired as my booster, and I didn't even want to deal with my arrow painting and what it might mean.

"That's it! We've got it!" Crouch raised his camera in triumph. "Great shot, people. You're free to go."

The line of candidates broke up, and the gym filled with conversation and laughter. Darla and I went to the bleachers to pick up our bags.

"So I wanted to ask you . . . what do you want in your spirit basket?" she asked, taking out her phone to make notes.

"Oh, you know what I like," I said, recalling, much to my guilt, the day True had told me what she was going to put in my basket and somehow guessed every one of my favorite things.

Darla's brow knit. "Brownies? Cookies? Candy bars?"

"Sure. That sounds fine," I said, trying to be diplomatic or whatever as I lifted my football gear onto my shoulder. No rocking the boat for me. "Whatever you think."

"But I want to get it right for you," Darla said, following me across the gym like a reporter on a hot story. "It's my first spirit basket."

"Darla, honestly. Just get whatever," I told her. "It's really not that big of a deal."

Darla stopped in her tracks. She, Veronica, and Josh stared at me as if I'd just insulted each of their mothers. Obviously, I'd done something wrong. But what? I didn't want her to stress over something as silly as a spirit basket. What was the problem with that?

"What?" I said, lifting my shoulders. "It's supposed to be fun. You don't have to take everything so seriously."

"I didn't realize I was such a downer," Darla said, shoving her phone into her bag. "I thought I was just trying to be a good girlfriend. Or do you still want True to be your booster?"

Right. Okay. Clearly, keeping my mouth shut and smiling had been the right policy.

"Darla. You know I don't want that."

I reached for her hand, but she turned away from me and grabbed Veronica. "Come on, V. We're going to the mall."

"Don't you have Boosters?" I asked.

"Yeah, well, suddenly I don't feel like going."

Veronica seemed impressed. She shot me a withering glance over her shoulder as the two of them walked away.

"I'm sure I'll love whatever you make for me!" I shouted after Darla. "Honestly!"

But they didn't stop. I heard the creak of the gym lobby door followed by its loud, very final slam. Josh gave me this look like, *Dude*.

"What? What did I do?" I demanded, my cluelessness making me sweat.

He shook his head and slapped me on the back, and we trudged together across the gym.

"We still going out to get our tuxes tonight?" Josh asked me.

I sighed, frustrated. "That's the plan."

"We'll stop by Darla's after so you can show her what you picked out," he said. "She'll love it so much she'll forgive you."

"Wow. That's not bad," I said. "What made you think of that?"

Josh smiled ruefully. "Date Veronica Vine long enough and you learn a few things about the female mind."

We both laughed, and I followed him into the locker room. I

just hoped that by the time I got to the field I was feeling more confident than I was right now. Just when I rededicated myself to Darla, everything I did was wrong.

A few days ago I had two amazing girls after me, and now they were both acting like they hated my guts. Where had it all gone wrong?

CHAPTER THIRTY-EIGHT

True

"Okay, everybody say 'cheese!'" Greg instructed.

I stood between Claudia and Wallace in a group of blue-clad boosters and smiled as best I could, considering Claudia had just told me that Orion had thrown me over in favor of Darla, and Wallace was acting like his dog had just died. I didn't care about Orion, I reminded myself. Or at least, I wasn't supposed to. Not this Orion. What I cared about was getting my Orion back. Which meant I had to corner Wallace and talk him into giving him and Darla a chance. The only thing that mattered was sparking true love between my third couple. And preparing myself for whatever might happen next.

But seriously, if Darla wanted to be Orion's booster so badly, then where was she? It didn't seem like she was very dedicated.

"Good job, everyone. Thanks!"

Greg gave us the thumbs-up and the rest of the boosters went over to the supply boxes to get out their paints, glitter, and glue for their über-important homecoming signs. I grabbed Wallace and pulled him around the far side of the snack bar, where we'd be out of sight of the rest of the club.

"Ow. Man, you have a strong grip." Wallace yanked his arm out of my grasp. "What's up?"

"We need to talk about Darla," I said, zipping my red hoodie up to my chin against the chill in the air.

Wallace looked at his feet. "I told you, I don't want to talk about that."

"Just tell me what you like about her," I said.

"Why?" He shrugged. "What's the point?"

"I'm just curious," I told him. "Talk. What's your favorite thing about her?"

"I don't know, she's very giving," he said, squirming. "She's always doing things for other people, and sometimes I think she doesn't even realize she's doing it. It's like it's in her DNA to care about other people."

"Okay. What else?"

"She's smart. Like, supersmart. She has the best math and science brain in the whole school." He paused. "Well, other than me."

"Of course," I said, surprised. I'd never imagined Darla as the brainy type. "Keep going."

Wallace raised his eyes to the heavens. He was losing patience with me, but I didn't care. Everything hinged on this. Everything.

"She's creative. She can make literally anything more beautiful. *She's* beautiful. And vulnerable. And totally unaware of how awesome she is." He pressed his hands over his face for a second, then dropped them.

"Why are you making me say all this?"

"Because I thought *you* should hear it," I said, gripping his shoulders and forcing him to look me in the eye. "I wanted you to hear how much she means to you. And don't you think *she* has a right to hear it too?"

Wallace stared at me for a long moment, considering. "What if she doesn't want to hear it?"

"What girl doesn't want to hear how awesome she is?" I asked with a laugh. "It's all anyone wants to hear, isn't it?"

Out on the track, the cheerleaders started to chant. "Get up and go! Get up and go! Get up and . . . GO!"

We locked eyes, then laughed. "See? Even the cheerleaders want you to tell her."

Wallace sighed. "I'll think about it."

"Good." That was all I could ask for. I knew Wallace well enough to know that he was a big thinker—a thorough thinker. And I knew he'd come to the right conclusion—that his love for her trumped everything else. It had to. Love was the only thing that mattered.

"Now let's go make some homecoming signs," I said, steering him around the corner. "Because you know those guys won't win this game unless we display the appropriate amount of glitter."

CHAPTER THIRTY-NINE

Darla

I stood in the middle of the square white dressing room after school on Tuesday in my underpants and strapless bra, staring at the three dresses Veronica and I had picked out. One was basic black with rhinestone straps that crossed in the back, one was red and slinky with a serious slit, and the last was a green strapless with an A-line tea-length skirt. It was the most flattering cut, but the color was semi-awful.

With a sigh, I checked the price tag. It was more expensive than the blue dress I had at home, the one I still loved even if it did make my hips look slightly large.

"Well? What do you think?" Veronica asked from the other side of the door.

"I'm not sure. Give me a minute."

"Try on the green one again," Veronica instructed.

I hung my head and covered my face with my hands. I knew I should go back out and keep searching, but I was sick of it. Sick of trying on dresses that didn't look exactly right. Sick of wondering which one might get me the most votes and win me homecoming queen. Sick of trying to predict which one Orion would like best.

Orion. Just thinking about him made me groan in frustration. One second he was acting like it was a huge, meaningful deal to ask me to be his booster, and the next it was like having me as his booster didn't even matter. Why did he have to be so hot and cold? So gray? So infuriatingly fickle and blasé about everything? If he were here right now, he probably wouldn't even have an opinion about the dresses. He'd probably tell me to "wear whatever."

I yanked the green dress down from the hanger and jammed my legs into it. The black crinoline itched at my skin as I zipped it up. When I looked at myself in the mirror, I heard a voice as clear as day in my mind, but it wasn't Orion's, it was Wallace's. And it said, "Wear the blue one. You love the blue one. The blue one makes you feel good. The blue one is you."

Weirdly, startlingly, in that moment, I wished Wallace was here to help me decide. I grabbed my phone and sent a quick text to his phone.

U AROUND 2NITE?

He texted right back. Boy always had his phone and his iPad nearby.

YEP. WHY?

Why? Why was a good question. I glanced around the tiny space, trying to think of a good excuse to see him when he'd basically told me that seeing him was a bad idea. Sticking out of my bag was the corner of the notebook where I'd been scratching out ideas for my homecoming speech tomorrow. My hands shook as I texted.

NEED 2 PRACTICE SPEECH. BE MY AUDIENCE? JUST US.

There was a long pause. He was ignoring me. He was going to say no. Tell me to ask Orion. I held my breath. Finally, an answer appeared.

SURE. WILL COME BY AROUND 8.

I exhaled, relieved.

"Let me see!" Veronica called out.

I shoved my phone deep into my bag and opened the door, ready to tell her I was done with this shopping sham, but her jaw dropped at the dress.

"See? That's the one. That highlights every one of your best features. Your tiny waist, your perfect calves, the green flecks in your eyes."

I turned toward the three-way mirror at the far end of the dressing room. It really was pretty. If it were only a little less . . .

Ugh. Forget it. No one was going to vote for the Wicked Witch of the West for homecoming queen.

"I don't know," I said, ducking back into my cubicle and closing the door again. As soon as the dress dropped to my feet, I felt lighter. "I think I'm just going to wear the one I have."

There was a long pause. Long enough for me to pull my jeans on and push one foot into its high-heeled boot. It was so long, my heart started to pound in anticipation.

"But it's the exact same color as mine," Veronica said eventually.

I rolled my eyes at her—something I'd only ever do when she couldn't see me—and pulled on my second boot.

"We can't stand up there right next to each other in the same color," Veronica continued. "Everyone knows we're best friends. We'll look like idiots. Like we didn't consult."

I pulled my T-shirt on and yanked open the door again. "So? We like our dresses," I said, my hair sticking to my face from the static. "Who cares what they think?"

"You didn't really just say that," Veronica replied, dropping her chin. "The only thing that matters is what they think. This is homecoming."

The frustration I'd been feeling all day burbled up inside my chest. But as Veronica stared me down, I realized it wasn't just frustration from today, it was frustration that had been building for a while. Veronica always got her way, no matter what. Why couldn't I have what I wanted, just this once? Why couldn't I be the one who got to choose? I wasn't Darbot the Geek anymore. I wasn't. I was Darla Shayne, and bitchy comments at Goddess the other day aside, I was supposed to be her best friend. Couldn't she give me this one little thing?

What would Veronica do? I thought, and almost laughed. Was I really going to use her own tactics on her?

I looked her in the eye and hoped she couldn't tell I was terrified. "Well, I got my dress first, so I think you should return yours."

Veronica let out a disbelieving snort. She readjusted the strap of her Louis Vuitton purse on her shoulder. "Wow. 'I had it first'? That's really your argument? What are we, five?"

"No. I just—"

"No, really, D. Very mature. I love that you're going to make me return my dress just because you've suddenly adopted the logic of a kindergartener," she ranted, walking past me. She paused near the door and looked back. "When did you get so selfish?"

"I'm not being selfish!" I countered, as the two girls in the dressing room next to mine started to giggle. "I just—"

"You just what? What, Darla?" Veronica asked, squaring off with me.

"Are you trying to sabotage me?" I asked.

The words came out like a squeak, but I couldn't believe they'd come out at all. I'd never accused Veronica of anything bad in my entire life. Never called her on how she'd treated Wallace. Never pointed out that she sometimes went back on plans that I'd thought were solid. Never scolded her for her comments on Mariah's weight or Kenna's frizzy hair. And clearly, Veronica had been aware of this too. For a long moment, we both just stood there, stunned.

"Are you kidding me?" Veronica snapped.

"I mean, you can't be serious about these dresses," I said, gesturing at the one on the floor. I was shaking, but I felt like I couldn't stop now. "And the pink one from the other day. And the way you treated me in front of everyone at Goddess. Not to mention the fact that you almost told Orion about me and Wallace hanging out."

"But you and Wallace *are* hanging out!" she countered. "And I sent you that dress because I know how much you like pink!"

I don't like pink. I only ever wear it because she once said it was my color.

"And as for Goddess, I was just doing you a favor. Showing you what your slumming behavior was going to get you. Did you not see how those people were laughing?"

"They weren't laughing until you started making awful jokes," I replied, though I was starting to lose my nerve.

"You know what, *D*? I was just trying to help you. Could you be any more ungrateful?" Veronica said, grabbing the two shopping bags she'd accrued from the floor, and a pair of jeans she'd decided to buy for herself. "I'll be up at the register. You have five minutes to find me there or you can call your precious Wall-E for a ride home."

"Veronica, wait," I said.

But she strode off, the security tag on the jeans smacking loudly against the wall as she took the corner too tightly. The two girls in the next dressing room held their breath for a moment, then cracked up laughing. I gazed at the pile of green silk and black tulle on the floor, feeling hot and completely confused.

Maybe she *was* just trying to help me. Maybe her help had just been a little off. Either way, I wouldn't even be here if it wasn't for her. I wouldn't be popular, I wouldn't have Orion, I wouldn't be nominated for homecoming queen. By making me her best friend back in middle school, she'd basically made *me*. I wasn't naive. I knew this. So maybe I was being ungrateful.

Would it really be that big of a deal to let her have the blue dress? Was it really going to matter? Maybe homecoming shouldn't be a war, with talk of battles and sabotage and beating the other person. Maybe it should just be fun.

I grabbed the dress off the floor and raced after her.

"Veronica, wait up!" I shouted.

But I didn't need to. She was still standing at the register, waiting for me. She smiled when she saw I was clutching the green dress.

"Good choice."

CHAPTER FORTY

Darla

"It really is a lovely cut, hon," my mother said, her semi-grainy image looking me up and down from my laptop screen as I stood in the middle of my room, wearing the green dress. "But I think something's wrong with my tint levels. Is that really the color?"

I groaned and trudged over to sit at the desk, head in my hand. "If you're seeing Emerald City, then yes, that's the real color."

"Well, it's a bit extreme, but if you like it—"

The doorbell rang, and I sat up straight. Was it already eight o'clock?

"Mom, I have to go," I said.

"Okay." She sighed and tilted her head, her brown wavy hair tumbling artfully over her shoulder. "I'm sorry I won't be there, sweetie. But I'll be home first thing on Sunday, and you can tell me everything."

"Sounds good." I was used to my mom not being there for things. It no longer broke my heart. This was our reality, and it had been for a really long time. I only felt the slightest twinge in the center of my chest when she apologized. "Safe flights!"

"Good night, hon."

We both leaned in toward the screen to air-kiss. Downstairs I heard Wallace's voice echoing in the entryway as Lisa let him in. I turned toward the mirror, fluffed my hair, curled my lip at the dress, then ran downstairs. My heart was pounding a little too quickly for a visit from Wallace, but I chose to ignore it.

"I don't know how long it's been since I've seen you," Lisa was saying to Wallace. "You've gotten so tall!"

"That's what happens," he said.

They both looked up when I was halfway down the staircase. Neither one of them smiled. Lisa had an apron on over her black pants and white shirt, which meant she was still cleaning up from dinner. I usually helped her—she'd wash and I'd dry—but tonight my mother's call had interrupted, and then I'd ended up putting on a fashion show for her.

"What're you wearing?" Wallace asked.

I knew it. Wallace hated the dress.

"I'll go get you guys a snack," Lisa said, disappearing quickly toward the back of the house before anyone could ask her opinion.

I took the last few steps slowly. "It's that bad?"

Wallace turned fully to face me, his hands in the pockets of his gray pin-striped pants, which were cuffed at the ankle. Only he could make those things work with a *Big Bang Theory* T-shirt and a pair of Chuck Ts.

"It's okay. I mean, it's fine. But I thought you liked the blue one."

"I did. I do." I turned and led him into the parlor, where I sat on the chintz love seat, the skirt pouffing out around me. "It's just, Veronica is going to be wearing that color, and she thinks . . . we both think . . . it would be a bad idea to stand up there looking like twins."

"Which is it?" Wallace asked, positioning himself in the center of the antique rug.

My brow knit. "What do you mean?"

"She thinks or you both think?" he said.

I bit my lip and looked away.

"I knew it!" Wallace announced, raising a finger as if he'd just discovered a new wrinkle in string theory.

"Knew what?"

"She bullied you, didn't she? She bullied you into picking out a dress you didn't like." His face turned pink and his nostrils flared. When he paced over to the fireplace, I half thought he was going to take down one of my mother's ceramic vases and throw it across the room. Instead he gripped the marble mantel like he needed it to stay afloat while the ship went down. "God, I hate that girl."

"Wallace, calm down," I said, rising from my seat. The back of the dress was so stiff it stayed bent out at an odd angle behind me. Embarrassed, I smoothed it—smacked it into submission, actually—but Wallace didn't notice. He was on a tear.

"No, you know what? It's not fair. Why are you even friends with her?" he demanded. "Please. Just tell me. I understand why you wanted to be back then, but now . . . It makes no sense to me."

"I know she said some things the other day that were not so nice—"

"Not so nice?" he blurted. "She suggested we take part in a loser foursome!"

My face burned at the memory, but I barreled on. "But she's not like that. Not all the time."

He brought his hands to his head, cupping the sides of his skull, which made his hair stand up on the top. "Yes! Yes she is! She totally has you brainwashed. It's because of her that we're not friends anymore. It's because of her that you have no clue how amazing you are. How amazing you've always, *always* been."

My breath caught. "I'm amazing?"

Wallace took two steps toward me, his eyes on mine. "Yes. You are. How could you not know that?"

I licked my lips, my mouth suddenly dry. "Wallace—"

"But I don't know, maybe it's not entirely her fault. Maybe it's just that no one's ever bothered to tell you. Because your dad bailed and your mom's never here and you have a boyfriend who, while well-meaning, is—let's face it—kind of a pretty-boy doof."

I was speechless. And when I realized my mouth was hanging open slightly, I snapped it closed.

"You, Darla Lea Shayne, are amazing," Wallace told me hotly. "You are smart. You're creative. You're stylish. You're giving. You're determined. You make everything beautiful. You don't have to be anyone's sidekick, because you kick ass on your own."

Wow. Was that really what he thought of me? I had never felt like I could kick ass on my own. I'd never even felt like I could stick up for myself, not really. Not without knowing Veronica would agree—that she'd have my back. But right then, right there, looking into Wallace's eyes, I did feel pretty strong. I felt indestructible, actually.

"Wallace," I said finally. "That was . . . thank you."

He took the teeny-tiniest step toward me, and my skin hummed. He was going to kiss me. Wallace Bracken was going to kiss me. But then something shifted in his expression, and the world seemed to pause until suddenly he backed away.

"I have to go," he said.

And he bolted for the door.

"What?" I breathed, needing a second to recover myself before I went after him. "Wallace, wait!"

We blew past Lisa, who was coming through the foyer with a

tray of chips, salsa, and bottled water. Wallace yanked open the door, and as his foot hit the threshold, I knew I couldn't let him go. I wasn't done with him yet.

"Wallace, stop!" I ordered.

I kick ass on my own. I kick ass on my own.

He looked back at me from the front step. I walked up to him, grabbed him by that stupid *Big Bang* shirt, and pulled him to me.

"If you won't do it, I will," I said.

And then I kissed him. I kissed Wallace Bracken, the guy my friends thought was a dork, the boy who Veronica had once teased to within an inch of his life, the kid who'd polled the school and found out he was a detriment to me.

I kissed him, and nothing had ever felt more right. Wallace took a second to respond, but when he did, his arms went around me and he held me close and the warmth of him, the sureness of him, made me feel safe and excited all at once. Wallace was my best friend. Why did I ever think he wasn't? He believed in me. He saw things in me I could hardly believe. I would have kissed him forever if I could have.

But then he pulled away.

"I really have to go," he said. "You—you have a boyfriend and I—I really have to go."

Orion. Crap. Homecoming. Crappity crap. My lips felt swollen as I watched Wallace cut across our lawn in the direction of his house.

"Wait! What about my speech?" I shouted after him. It was the reason he'd come over in the first place.

"I'm sure it's great!" he shouted, walking backward. "How could it not be? You wrote it!"

He disappeared into his house and slammed the door. Then I

went back inside to have the nervous breakdown I was clearly in need of having.

Tomorrow Orion and I would give our speeches, telling the student body why we should be king and queen. We would sit up onstage next to each other in the gym surrounded by posters of the two of us, hugging, smiling, kissing. We had conveyed the picture of the perfect couple to the world, and we had a really good chance of winning. This was my moment. The moment I'd been working toward for years.

And all I'd be thinking about while I was up there, all I'd be thinking about every second until then, was Wallace Bracken.

CHAPTER FORTY-ONE
Orion

Josh and I were completely silent as we watched Wallace Bracken break from a lip-lock with my girlfriend and take off for his house. The stereo inside my car blasted an annoyingly bass-heavy dance tune, and I reached up to click it off. The tux I'd rented for homecoming was hooked by its hanger from my headrest, hanging down behind my seat in its black plastic bag.

Wallace closed the door of his house. Eventually, after touching her lips with her fingertips and smiling, Darla went back inside too. She never saw us. My car was just behind the hedge down the hill from her house, so unless she'd turned to look right in our direction, she never would have.

"Dude," Josh said finally. "I'm sorry."

My hands gripped the steering wheel, wringing it like I should have been wringing Wallace's neck. You don't just kiss another guy's girl. You don't do that.

But then the white-hot flash of anger passed. My hands fell to my lap, and I realized . . . I felt nothing. Slightly betrayed, maybe, because I thought Darla really liked me, but I wasn't heartbroken. I didn't feel crushed.

"You all right?" Josh asked.

"Yeah," I said, rubbing my forehead.

"You gonna go talk to her?"

I glanced up at Darla's brick-faced house with its many windows and huge front porch, wishing I knew what she was thinking. It was just a kiss, and I knew as well as anyone how easily a kiss could happen without too much pre-thinking it, and it wasn't until afterward that you realized how much it could affect everyone around you. Maybe it was nothing. Maybe it had just happened. If that was the case, I could let it go. She'd already let me have one slipup—not that she knew that she had—but that meant I owed her one.

"Nah. Not tonight," I said.

Maybe she did like Wallace, or maybe she didn't. Who knew? But I didn't have to find out right this second. Tomorrow I'd ask her what was up. I'd find out what she wanted. Right now, I needed some time to think about what I was going to say.

I put the car in first, and quietly drove away.

CHAPTER FORTY-TWO

True

I was playing Bach's Prelude in C Major at the piano in Wallace's beautifully appointed foyer with its incredible acoustics, when he burst in through the front door. I had come over for dinner after he told me he was going to be meeting up with Darla, just to give him a last-minute pep talk.

"We kissed!" he shouted. His eyes were about to burst from his skull. "We actually kissed!"

Wow. It looked like my pep talk had worked. I got up from the piano bench as Wallace crossed toward me. He shoved his hair back, brought his fists to his mouth, turned in a circle. It was like he had no control of his body.

"Wallace, that's great!" I cheered, my heart as light as air. "Tell me everything."

"I told her," he said. "I told her how incredible I thought she was. And then I almost kissed her, but then I chickened out, and then *she* kissed *me*!"

Oh my Gods. Oh my *Gods!* Darla had kissed him. There simply couldn't have been a better outcome. Her feelings for him were confirmed. I felt like crowing my victory from the rooftops.

"I'm so happy for you, Wallace," I said.

And then, suddenly, his face fell. "Yeah, well. She still has a boy-friend."

"True." I nodded, a mischievous glint in my eyes. "But things change."

CHAPTER FORTY-THREE

Darla

My throat was so tight I could barely swallow. There were way too many people in the bleachers. I mean, really? That many people went to this school? And why did it seem like every one of the teachers who stood along the three non-bleacher walls of the gym was looking at me? Like maybe they couldn't believe I was really up there. I wiped my palms on my jeans as Josh sat down to rabid, psychotic applause from his teammates and the rest of the school. Veronica got up to make her speech, leaving a cloud of heavy perfume behind her.

"You okay?" Orion whispered to me.

The left side of my face suddenly felt a lot hotter than the right, as if his eyes were boring through my skin or something. Could he tell I'd kissed someone else? Did he know that was why I'd avoided him this morning? That I was planning on breaking up with him when this was done? I turned my iPad, where my speech was stored, over and over in my lap.

"Yeah. Fine."

"In conclusion, I believe I would make a fantastic homecoming queen and represent our school to the world," Veronica said.

What the hell did that even mean?

"When this is over, I think we should talk," Orion said.

Veronica's speech was over. Everyone was clapping. Which meant . . .

"Thank you, Miss Vine," Principal Peterson said. "And now, Darla Shayne."

"Yeah, okay," I told Orion.

I walked past Veronica, who was on her way back to her chair in her chic blue shirtdress and high-heeled boots. I was wearing my favorite jeans, flat riding boots, and a white V-neck sweater. My hair was up in a high ponytail and I wore stud earrings, but the diamond D still glittered around my neck. I felt comfortable. I felt like me. Which was what I was going to need if I was going to get through this.

My head swam as I stepped up to the microphone. The lights above the bleachers were trained right at my eyes. I opened my iPad and glanced at Wallace, who sat in the front row of the junior section. He was completely still, leaning forward over his knees with his hands laced together. There was something very confident about his posture, which I took as a good sign.

I cleared my throat and looked down at the words I'd typed up last night after Wallace had gone. I couldn't believe I was about to do this, but I'd made my decision. It was go time.

I kick ass on my own.

"Hi everyone, I'm Darla Shayne." My voice blasted back at me through the speakers, and I tried not to wince. "And I don't want to be elected homecoming queen."

There was a wave of uncomfortable laughter. Wallace sat up straight.

"I don't want to be elected homecoming queen because none of you really knows who I am, so your vote would be cast for someone who doesn't really exist," I continued, holding on to the sides of the podium to try to keep myself from shaking. "You probably think I'm the ditzy girl who dresses like her cooler best friend and landed the hot new guy, and maybe I sort of am that person, but that's not all I am."

I glanced over at Veronica and Orion. He looked stunned. She looked like she just swallowed her gum.

"I'm also a girl whose parents kind of suck, who spends half her time alone at her house watching Real Housewives and eating way too much ice cream."

That got a bigger laugh, which made me smile. I was doing this. I was really doing it. And it was working.

"I'm a girl who got a job at a boutique downtown because I love helping people find clothes that make them feel good, but also because I just wanted to get out of my big, empty, boring house."

I took a deep breath, knowing that for whatever reason, the next part was going to be hard to say, even though I knew how wrong it was that it was going to be hard to say. Because if you're a straight A student, why not tell the world? If you're going to graduate near the top of the class, why not own it? I took a breath.

"I'm smart," I said, and paused. "Even though I sometimes pretend I'm not. I'm great at math and science, and I especially love my calc class. I like to talk to people and I also really like to help people so, actually, if you ever need help in math or science, let me know."

More laughs. Wallace was grinning from ear to ear. Even True Olympia, who sat next to him, looked impressed.

"And, as it turns out, as of like a week ago, I'm also really into football."

The football team, clumped in the middle of the bleachers, went wild, along with the cheerleaders and the half of the school that cared about sports.

"The thing is, I'm still learning about myself," I continued. "So if I'm going to promise you anything, it's that whether or not I'm elected homecoming queen, I'm not going to pretend to be anything I'm not anymore. Thank you."

As I walked back to my seat, the volume of the applause nearly knocked me over. Even the teachers, who had mostly done nothing but give a respectful two-clap acknowledgment to the other speeches, were full-on applauding. I sat down in my chair between Orion and Veronica, smiling so wide my cheeks hurt.

"That was awesome," Orion said. "You totally nailed that. I'll be shocked if you don't win."

"Thanks," I said, feeling overwhelmed.

"Next up, we have Orion Floros."

Slowly Orion rose to his feet. He looked so broad and strong walking over to the podium, and it occurred to me that even though we'd been trying to act like we were in this together, I had no clue what he was going to say. I hadn't told him about my speech, and he hadn't told me about his.

Orion leaned toward the microphone, looked over at me, and smiled that killer smile that had floored me from day one.

"I think you guys should vote for Darla Shayne."

Then he sat down again, and the crowd went nuts. Stunned, I felt suddenly like I was choking on emotion. I couldn't believe he'd just done that for me. When just last night I'd been kissing another guy. How could I break up with him now?

My eyes searched the crowd and found Wallace again. He stared back at me, his expression unreadable. For some reason, that unreadable expression opened me up. It gave me the ability to breathe again.

I turned to look at Orion. "That was amazing," I said. "Thank you."

"Well, I know how much this thing means to you," he said.

I swallowed hard. There was that comment again. Like homecoming was all that mattered to me. And maybe it had been, for a while. For forever. But it wasn't anymore. I was grateful to him for what he'd just done, but it didn't change anything. Not really.

"Orion, you were right, what you said before," I told him as Claudia took the microphone. "After this assembly, we really need to talk."

CHAPTER FORTY-FOUR

True

I was filling a to-go box with cupcakes for a middle-aged couple on Thursday night, when the door opened and Orion walked in. He was wearing a leather jacket over a white sweater, his hair freshly washed and still wet around the ears. I glanced past him at Artemis, who had taken up her vigil at the table near the window again. She followed his progress with suspicious eyes.

"Hey," Orion said as I handed the couple their cupcakes. "I need to talk to you."

"What is it?" I jammed the buttons on the register with a trembling finger.

"I'll wait," Orion said with a knowing, flirtatious smile.

I was fairly certain that Apollo hadn't told Artemis he'd threatened Orion's life. She would have killed him for it. But that didn't mean she wouldn't go back to wherever the two of them were holed up and tell him I was talking to Orion. And if she did, my love was as good as dead. I looked at my customers.

"That'll be ten fifty."

The man handed me twelve dollars. "Keep the change."

"Thank you!" I made change, dropped the extra in our tip jar, then slammed the drawer loudly and looked at Orion. I tried to keep my expression as cool as humanly possible.

"Darla and I broke up," he said. "After the assembly. I just . . . thought you should know."

Instantly Artemis was forgotten. The relief that filled me flooded out everything else. "Really?"

"Yes, really," he said with a laugh.

I knew this was a possibility, of course, but I could hardly believe it. It was over. The torture of seeing him with her every day was over. The wondering what they were doing when they were alone. The horrible turns of my imagination every time they drove off together or snuck into the back corner of the library together. But why was he telling me this? Did this mean he wanted to be with me? That my dream was finally, finally coming true?

Over Orion's shoulder, Artemis shifted to the edge of her bench. Her teeth were clenched, as if priming for a fight. I took a step back and hit the rear counter with my butt.

"Okay," I said.

"That's it? That's all you're going to say? Okay?" Orion asked.

"I'm very sorry it didn't work out with Darla, but I already told you . . . I've moved on." I raised my voice so Artemis could hear. "I told you it was over."

Orion's confidence sagged. "I know, but I figured—"

"Whatever you figured, you figured wrong," I snapped, hating every minute of this. The tears I held back were so hot I began to choke on them. "This is never going to happen, Orion. Get used to it."

I walked into the back room, leaving Orion stunned behind me. As soon as I got to the break room, I pressed my hands into the wall, letting the bumps in the bricks cut into my palms. I breathed in and out, in and out, telling myself it was okay. That everything was going to be fine.

Darla and Wallace had kissed. They were going to declare their love for each other soon. I was sure of it.

And once they did, Orion would be free to make his choice. He would be free to choose me.

CHAPTER FORTY-FIVE

Orion

Nothing felt real. I walked through my day on Friday like a zombie. Everyone else was hyped up for the pep rally ninth period, for the homecoming game that night, for the dance tomorrow, but the excitement couldn't touch me. It was like everything was happening around me and I was inside a bubble in the middle of it, just rolling along.

Darla had broken up with me, and True had completely ditched me. And to top it all off, last night I'd had the worst night's sleep imaginable. I kept falling into these horrifying, vivid dreams about wars and famines and genocides, as if I was actually there. Every time I woke up in a panicked sweat, I figured that had to be it—it had to be the last one—but then I'd fall back to sleep again and something even worse would play out inside my mind. The whole thing was so effed up that by four a.m. I'd decided I was done. I'd gone down to the kitchen and started chugging coffee so that I wouldn't pass out again.

Now that decision was coming back to haunt me. As I shuffled toward my car after school with happy, cheering, borderline-crazy kids streaming past me, I was crashing so hard I could barely see straight. I needed to get home and nap or there was no way I was going to be able to play tonight.

I clicked the button to unlock the doors and dropped the keys on my foot. They bounced off and landed two feet under the car.

"Crap."

I hit my knees and strained my shoulder to grab them. When I looked up again, a shadow had crossed over the sun. I froze when I saw who it was.

"Hello, Orion."

Her cool voice sent a chill right through me. It was that girl again—the one from True's old gang or whatever it was. She was looking at me like I was a steak and she was a starving tiger.

"Where the hell did you come from?" I asked, backing up a step. "Where's your sidekick?"

"He's not here," she said. "I came alone. I just couldn't stay away anymore."

"Why? What do you want with me?" I glanced past her toward the school, hoping one of the security guards would spot us. "If you think you can get through me to True, you can't. We're not even friends," I said bitterly.

"I don't care about her." She took a step closer to me.

"I care about you."

The tiny hairs on my arms stood on end. Suddenly I was wide-awake. Adrenaline, I guess. Girl was starting to freak me out again.

"Why? What the hell is going on?"

"I know you don't remember me, Orion, but you will. You and I . . . we were in love once."

I laughed harshly. "Now I know you're crazy. I don't even know your name."

She lowered her chin, giving me a patient sort of look. A cold breeze tugged her brown curls away from her face.

"I am Artemis," she said. "You do know me. You know things about me that would make a mortal girl blush."

I swallowed hard. What was I supposed to do here? How was I supposed to make her go away? Clearly she was unstable, so the best thing to do, probably, was get the hell out of there.

"I have to go," I said, yanking open the car door. "I have to get home."

She put her hand on my arm and held me. She was freakishly strong.

"Tomorrow night you will be asked to make a choice," she said, leaning in so close I could smell the lilac scent of her hair. "All I ask is that you remember what we had. That you think back to those days. It was a long time ago, but you were mine and I was yours and oh, how we loved."

"Okay, back off," I spat, swatting her arm away. I dropped into the driver's seat and slammed the door, relieved that she didn't put her hand between it and the car. I started the engine and rolled the window down. She hadn't moved an inch. "Next time I see you or your psychotic brother, I'm calling the police."

Artemis smirked and stood back while I revved the engine. "Until tomorrow, then."

I slammed the car into reverse and peeled out. My heart banged around inside my chest as I raced off, trying as hard as I could to focus on driving, even as I checked the rearview mirror over and over again.

This day could not have been any weirder, but at least I had one thing going for me. There was no way it could get worse.

CHAPTER FORTY-SIX

Darla

Take it all in, Darla, I said to myself as I stood next to the white, old-school Chevy convertible Orion and I were supposed to ride in during halftime. *This is it. This is your homecoming.*

I breathed in and out, kneading my hands in their elbow-length black gloves. The cars were parked along the visitor's side of the track, the elderly drivers standing in a klatch nearby, talking and occasionally laughing as one. Usually the stands emptied out at halftime, but the bleachers across the field were jammed with students and parents and teachers. We were waiting for the guys from the football team who were also on homecoming court to get cleaned up and come back out. Once they got here, we'd have the processional around the track, after which each of us would be presented with our prince and princess crowns—the ones we'd wear to the dance tomorrow night, hoping to have them replaced by the king or queen crown. My smile was so wide my lips hurt. I still couldn't believe I was here. It was actually happening. The whole scene was like something out of a movie, and I was one of the stars.

Yes, it would have been nice if I hadn't just broken up with the guy I was going to be riding the track with, but it had to be done.

My heart wasn't in it, and I was pretty sure his wasn't either. A few weeks ago all that mattered to me was having the hot guy at my side, showing that image of me to the world. But things had changed. I couldn't just be with a guy because he was going to look good in my homecoming pictures. I refused to be that shallow. It wasn't me. Not anymore.

"Hey there."

Wallace walked up behind me so silently, I didn't hear him until his finger came down on my bare shoulder. I whirled around, hand to heart. He was wearing a blue LCHS T-shirt with a black vest over it, along with a pair of rolled jeans and black lace-up shoes. His arms were held behind his back in a way that made it blatantly obvious he was hiding something back there. Knowing him, it was his iPad with some new poll numbers on it. There was fresh writing on his left arm, but I couldn't tell what it said.

"You scared the crap out of me!"

"I thought you were going to wear the blue dress," he said, looking me up and down in a neutral way. "Wasn't there a whole be-true-to-yourself theme to your speech?"

"Yes, but I realized that part of being true to myself was being a good friend." I smoothed the front of the green dress and smiled. "Let Veronica wear the blue and have her moment. I'm good."

Wallace smiled in a lopsided way. "You really are an original."

"Thanks," I said, grinning. "And don't you think the accessories sort of draw your eye away from the color?"

I raised one gloved arm, then the other, and touched the massive rhinestone-and-pearl necklace I'd borrowed from my mother's collection.

Wallace laughed. "Absolutely. So listen, there's a rumor going around that you broke up with Orion."

"I did," I said. "It just wasn't working anymore. Also, I kind of kissed this other guy."

"Did you?" Wallace played along. "Was he a cool guy?"

"Beyond cool," I said with a laugh.

"So . . . what would you say if this beyond-cool guy asked you to homecoming?" Wallace drew his arms out from behind his back and presented me with a gorgeous bouquet of white roses. My breath caught at the sight of them. His iPad was nowhere in sight.

"Wallace, I—"

"Her answer is no."

Veronica stood near the front grille of my homecoming car, wearing the red bombshell dress she had originally picked out. Her hair was slicked back from her face into a severe bun, and her lipstick matched the shade of her dress perfectly. No male in a fifty-mile radius was going to be capable of looking at anything other than her.

"I thought you were wearing the blue," I said.

Veronica sauntered around the car and came to stand next to me, swinging her little black bag on its rhinestone strap.

"Like I was going to take the chance we'd look like twins up there." Veronica sniffed. "You know me better than that."

Wallace and I exchanged a look. When it came to sabotage, the girl really was brilliant.

"As for your question, Wall-E," Veronica said, turning to him. "The answer is no. Darla will be going to homecoming with Orion. But kudos to you for shooting so high on the food chain."

"God, Veronica! Do you have to be so rude?" I blurted. It just came out of me, and I wasn't even scared. While she was momentarily stunned into silence, I smiled at Wallace. "I would love to go to homecoming with you."

"Have you completely lost your mind?" Veronica demanded. "You can't do that! Don't you get it? Whatever minuscule chance you had of winning this thing will be obliterated with him as your date."

"So? What do you care?" I said, arching one eyebrow. "You'll have a better chance of winning."

Veronica laughed a wry, nasty laugh. "Okay, fine. I didn't want to say this, but you leave me no choice."

At that moment, the homecoming princes from the football team crested the hill. They wore their uniforms but had taken out the padding, and none of them looked very happy. Orion was staring at the ground. He hadn't played that well in the first half. In fact, he'd lost yards four times and fumbled the ball away once. Josh saw us and whacked Orion with the back of his hand.

"I forgave your little breakdown at the mall the other day as some kind of PMS glitch, but this is not going to happen." She waggled her finger between me and Wallace. "You think you're so brilliant? Then do the math. If you go out with a dork, that makes *you* a dork."

My teeth clenched. "I think you need to check your work on that one, Veronica, because I've been hanging out with you for the last four years, but somehow, I haven't morphed into a total bitch."

Wallace laughed. Veronica's jaw dropped. Orion, who had just arrived with Josh, covered his mouth with his fist, but I saw the smile he was trying to hide.

"Veronica," Josh said, coming up behind her. "What the hell is going on?"

But Veronica was still focused on me. "How dare you—"

"You want to know how I dare?" I asked, my heart pounding like I was about to drive myself off a cliff. And maybe I was, but at the moment I didn't care. "I dare because I couldn't care less whether you want to be friends with me anymore. I've spent the last four years of my life doing everything you wanted, wearing what you told me to wear, liking what you liked, being where you wanted to be. And lately all you've done is treat me like crap. But you want to know who's never treated me like crap? Him!"

I pointed behind me at Wallace.

"So yes, I'm going to choose him over you," I told her, looking her up and down. I reached up under my mother's big necklace and yanked at the diamond D she'd given me last year. The thin chain broke easily, and I handed it back to her. The tiny diamonds sparkled under the field lights.

"What? What are you—" Veronica sputtered.

I pointed at the necklace in her palm with my gloved index finger. "It's a *D*," I said. "For dumped."

Wallace turned away, trying not to laugh in her face. Even after everything she'd done to him, and to me, and to half the student population, he managed to be discreet. Orion, however, didn't have such control. He was still chuckling when he came around the car to open the door for me.

"Your chariot, princess," he said.

"Thank you."

As Orion popped the door closed, I settled in atop the backseat like so many homecoming princesses had done before me, shaking with relief and glee and adrenaline. I only hoped that some of those princesses had felt as good as I felt right then. Wallace walked over and handed me my roses, which I cradled in the crook of my arm.

"Meet up at the Snack Shack for a milkshake later?" I asked.

Wallace pushed his hands into his pockets, and I could see what was written up his arm. *Darla Shayne* in big curly letters. He smiled when he saw I'd noticed.

"I am so there."

CHAPTER FORTY-SEVEN

Orion

Sitting in the back of that car, I did everything I was supposed to do. I waved at the crowd, I tried to look happy. But when the slow-moving vehicles passed under the blindingly lit scoreboard, I felt like total crap. We were losing 17–10, and it was partially my fault. No. Totally my fault. I had fumbled away the ball that the Orchard Hill High cornerback had picked up, which had eventually led to the touchdown that had put them ahead. I was a complete loser.

If only I had slept last night. If only I had been able to nap this afternoon. But like that was ever going to happen after that freak friend of True's had practically accosted me for the second time. To be honest, though, when I'd gone into my room and downed the blinds and lain on my bed, it wasn't her and her crazytown delusional comments that were playing in my mind. The only thing I could think about was True.

She liked me. I was sure of it. Forget everything she'd said in the last few days. When I thought about that kiss, I knew how she felt about me. The way she'd clung to me so tightly, the way her lips had searched mine, the way she'd said my name.

Orion. My Orion.

She liked me. Maybe even more than liked. So why did she keep pushing me away?

The caravan inched past the home stands. The crowd was going crazy for us, like we'd just come home from a war or something. The sustained cheering was honestly kind of hard to believe. Who the hell was I? I'd just moved here. I was losing the game for them. So why were they shouting my name? It made no sense. Maybe everything that I thought mattered was totally stupid. Maybe high school was totally stupid.

And then I saw her. I saw True. She was standing in the middle of the booster section on the bottom bleacher, and she wasn't cheering. She had her hands clasped under her chin, and she was watching me. Only me. When her eyes caught mine, she looked away for half a second, but then she looked back. We were moving by her, but I kept staring at her. I craned my neck so I could keep staring at her. And then, when it became impossible for me to twist any farther, I heard a voice in my mind. Not True's or Darla's or even my own. It was, weirdly, Artemis's.

You will be asked to make a choice, she said.

And just like that, I did. I flung my legs over the side of the car and jumped down. A few people gasped, but the driver kept on driving.

"Orion!" Darla shouted. "What're you doing?"

I jogged for the stands. My heart throbbed inside me, growing bigger with each beat. This was nuts. I knew it was. But it had to be done. It had to be. I would never stop thinking about her until I knew for sure.

Up the stairs I went, taking them two at a time. A few stunned people stood in my way and I turned sideways, sliding past them, taking a pom-pom to the face and almost tripping over someone's megaphone. As I got closer to True, she looked over her shoulder in a gesture I was starting to expect—True searching for a way out. But this time, I wasn't going to give her one.

I stepped right up to her, put one arm around her waist and the other hand around her neck, and kissed her.

"What the hell?" some guy said.

"Aw! That's so romantic!" a girl cooed.

For a second True went stiff, and I had this awful, sinking feeling that I was about to be kicked to the curb. But then, out of nowhere, she relaxed. She relaxed and her hands traveled up my sides and around my back. Thank God we'd taken our pads off to ride in the processional or she never would have been able to hold me as close as she did.

This was it. This was where I was supposed to be. As much fun as Darla and I had, I hated myself for wasting so much time with her. Time I could have spent here, with True, where I belonged.

Then, a voice called out over the loudspeaker.

"And now, your homecoming court will step up to receive their crowns!"

True pulled away from me. "You'd better go."

"I don't care," I said, breathless.

"No. You should go. Get your crown, Mr. Popular Homecoming Prince."

I laughed. "I'll go, but only if you say you'll go to the dance with me."

"Say yes!" Lauren Codry prompted from behind True. "Say yes!"

True glanced around uncertainly. Then her eyes trailed up to meet mine, and she smiled. "Oh, what the hell?"

Smiling from ear to ear, I kissed her one more time, then jogged across the field to the makeshift stage to receive my crown. On my way, I glanced one more time at the scoreboard, but now the numbers didn't bother me.

I had a feeling the second half was going to be a whole new ball game.

CHAPTER FORTY-EIGHT

True

It was past midnight when I snuck out the back door of the house with my bow and arrows, the night so eerily still I could have been at the bottom of the Aegean Sea. Ducking as best I could while loaded down with weaponry, I shoved through the back gate and raced toward the thickly wooded park at the far south end of town, keeping close to the hedges that lined the streets and crouching behind parked cars to avoid the few headlights that passed by. Once inside the tree line, I finally dared to look around. The jogging path was still, the park deserted. I was completely alone.

I walked until I found a clearing with a nice, fat oak tree near its perimeter. Then I took twenty paces back and loaded an arrow onto the bridge of my bow. A giddy bubble burbled up inside my throat as I pulled back and aimed. Holding my bow—the bow I'd wielded for countless millennia—I felt like a mother being reunited with a long-lost child. I couldn't have been more at peace, more content, more fulfilled. But then I remembered the reason I needed this weapon in the first place, and the giddiness died.

I let the arrow fly. It pierced the tree at the very center of its trunk. My aim was still true.

Taking a deep breath, I unsheathed another arrow. I had less than twenty-four hours until we reached Artemis's arbitrary deadline. Tonight Wallace had asked Darla to homecoming, and hopefully tomorrow, under the twinkling lights at the dance, they would seal their love. And the second Orion woke up from his Zeus-induced stupor and chose me, I was going to be ready.

Because there was no way I was going to let him go. That kiss tonight, the way he'd thrown himself out of that car for me, put his heart on the line in front of the entire school, it meant something to me. Wherever we were, whoever we were—whether goddess or human, mortal or immortal—we were meant to be together. Artemis could not win.

I lifted my bow, stared down the sight line, and imagined Artemis standing before me. I let fly. Another direct hit.

As I reached for the third arrow, someone very nearby clapped their hands. The noise was so loud in the thick of the night, it startled a few sleeping birds from their nest. I whirled around just as Artemis emerged from the trees. She wore skintight black pants and a black-and-gunmetal jacket, zipped to her chin, elongating her neck. Her brown hair was piled messily atop her head in a thick, haphazard bun.

"Well, well, well. You've still got it."

I flung my quiver to the center of my back and inched toward the tree, keeping my bow behind me.

"How did you find me?" I demanded, trying to keep her from getting a better look at the arrows still caught by the thick bark.

"You think Goddess is the only place for me to keep an eye on you?" Artemis tilted her head. "I've been watching your house. I saw you sneak out. The stalker lifestyle seems to suit me."

She advanced on me slowly, a challenge and a question in her eyes. I knew she was wondering why I hadn't drawn on her, and I tried to come up with some way, any way, to keep her from seeing the truth. If she knew I had these arrows, she'd know I'd gained an unfair advantage—that I could end her with one shot whether she were mortal or made Goddess again by Hera or anyone else. She'd know someone on the Mount was helping me. And worst of all, she'd know what to expect tomorrow night.

I forced myself to stop my backpedaling and took a wide-legged stance between her and my oak tree. "I thought I had another day. You should know that, considering what a diligent timekeeper you've become."

Artemis lifted her slim but strong shoulders. "Just figured I'd check up on you. See how your latest match is coming along. It must be going well if you feel able to take time out to come here for target practice."

"It's going very well," I replied. "By tomorrow night, Orion will be back to his old self and able to make his choice."

Of course, the current Orion had already made his. Remembering tonight's kiss again brought a blush to my cheeks. I hoped it was too dark for her to notice.

"And then we fight," Artemis said, the glee in her voice unmistakable.

Quick as lightning, she darted to my right—my weaker side. I reached out to stop her, but my ribs clenched in pain and I caught only the fabric on the elbow of her jacket. Artemis grabbed one of the arrows from the tree trunk and held it up, clutched in one black-gloved hand. Her face went gray as ash.

"This is a leaden arrow." Her eyes flicked to my face. "One of *your* leaden arrows."

I said nothing. My body quaked as I quickly considered my

options. Did I try to kill her now where she stood, or make a run for it? If I could only avoid her, only hold her off until Darla and Wallace sealed the deal, then there was still the possibility that Zeus would squire me and Orion home. That he would overrule Hera and save the day. There was still a flicker of hope.

Artemis raised her fist to my face, the ends of the arrow seeming to waver in the dim moonlight. "How did you get these?" she roared, her spittle dotting my cheeks. "How?"

Suddenly lights flicked across her face, and I heard a shout.

"Stop right there!"

A pair of flashlights bobbed toward us through the trees. I saw a flash of something, a gold badge, and heard the static of a radio.

"It's the police!" I hissed. "We have to run."

"I'm not afraid of them," she spat back.

"You should be. They've been looking for you two all week. If they lock you up, you're going to miss the fun tomorrow night."

Artemis gave me one last livid look before dropping the arrow and taking off into the trees. I ran in the opposite direction, hoping to confuse the police, knowing I could probably outrun them. At first I heard at least one of them crashing through the underbrush after me, but then he cursed under his breath and the light went dead. I could only imagine he'd fallen, but I refused to look back. I sprinted until I reached a sidewalk, then lifted my cotton hood over my head and turned my steps toward home.

It wasn't until I reached our front porch that I bothered to breathe. Artemis now knew that I had a weapon that could take her and her brother out, even if they somehow regained their powers before our fight. The element of surprise was gone. She was going to come to our battle prepared.

Suddenly the overhead light on the porch flicked on. The door opened, and there were my mother and Hephaestus.

"What is it?" my mother asked. "What's happened?"

I sighed and trudged past them into the house. "We're going to need a new plan."

CHAPTER FORTY-NINE

Darla

"You okay?" Wallace asked me.

I looked down at his hand, clasped around mine. He'd worn a dark-blue tie to match my blue dress, which was not only way prettier than the green, but far more comfortable. Especially with my one-inch black heels. When I stood up straight in them, Wallace and I saw exactly eye to eye.

"I'm good," I told him as Principal Peterson took the stage. My pulse raced convulsively, and there were parts of me sweating that really shouldn't have been sweating, but otherwise, I was fine. "Except this crown is really starting to itch my head."

I reached up and dug my fingertips into my scalp. Wallace smirked.

"Well, good thing you're about to get a new one, then," he said, knocking my shoulder with his.

"Ha-ha." I knocked him right back.

The voting had been closed about a half hour earlier, and a few sophomores had scurried out with the vote box, giggling the whole way. Wallace had been invited to help tally the votes again this year but had declined, so that he could stay by my side.

Thank God. Because if he hadn't, I definitely would have peed in my Spanx by now.

Suddenly the music died. Principal Peterson took the microphone off its stand and cleared his throat. Almost everyone turned to face the small stage, which was skirted by a dark-blue curtain. The blue, white, and silver balloon arch behind the principal had detached from the wall and was starting to peel forward slightly. A couple of the girls from the homecoming dance committee stood nearby, eyeing it warily.

"Can I have your attention, please?" the principal said, tugging at his too-tight collar. "This is the moment you've all been waiting for. The announcement of this year's Lake Carmody High School homecoming king and queen!"

Mariah and Kenna brushed by behind us, both of them casting beady glances at our held hands. Neither of them said a word to me, but Mariah gave me a little smile when Kenna's back was turned. I realized that I honestly had no idea who my friends were going to be on Monday morning, if I'd even have them, but right then I didn't care. Wallace was my best friend and now, sort of my boyfriend. Who needed anyone else?

"Hey, good luck."

I turned to find Charlie Cox, of all people, standing next to me with his arm around Katrina Ramos. She smiled shyly, looking ridiculously pretty in a dark-pink dress with a black lace overlay.

"I voted for you," she said.

My eyebrows shot up. "Really? Thanks. I love your dress."

"Yours, too," she replied. "It's the perfect color for the occasion."

Exactly.

Principal Peterson opened the silver envelope and withdrew a white card. My grip on Wallace's hand tightened.

"Your homecoming king and queen are . . ."

Darla Shayne. Say Darla Shayne, I begged silently.

"Peter Marrott and Claudia Catalfo!"

My chest deflated as the world erupted in applause. Just like that. All the work, all the hoping, all the drama—it came to nothing.

"Wow," Wallace said. "So much for my career in political polling." He turned to me and took my hand. "I'm so sorry that I got your hopes up."

"It's okay," I said, and meant it. I mean, it sucked, but I had a feeling it wouldn't suck for too long.

Wallace pulled me into a hug as blue, silver, and white balloons rained down from the ceiling. People whooped and cheered, kicking the balloons around as Peter and Claudia ascended the few steps to the stage.

"There's always next year," Wallace said in my ear.

And I laughed as two tiny tears squeezed out. "You know, I really don't think I want to go through this again."

Wallace pulled back. "Then we'll run someone else's campaign. Together. Because we really can't let Veronica Vine win."

I rolled my eyes. "Please. Can we talk about anything else?"

"How about how much I love you?"

My heart burst into a million tiny pieces and then zipped back together again, pounding one hard, strong beat, like nothing I'd ever felt before.

"You do?" I said.

"I always have," he told me matter-of-factly as a hundred people jostled around us to make room for the king and queen's first dance. "I think I probably always will."

I looked him in the eye, my hand flat on the lapel of his jacket. "Wallace, I—"

"You don't have to say anything," he said, tucking a lock of hair behind my ear. "I know it's probably a serious shock."

"No. I mean, it is, but . . . what's really shocking is . . . I love you, too."

And then, as the spotlight trailed Peter Marrott and Claudia Catalfo to the center of the dance floor, Wallace Bracken and I stood in the middle of the sea of nameless, faceless people and kissed for what felt like the very first time.

CHAPTER FIFTY

True

"This is it! This is it! They're going to kiss!"

I grabbed Hephaestus's shoulder, balling the black fabric of his suit jacket up in my hand. My bow and arrows were tucked safely into their case, which was hidden badly behind Hephaestus's butt. Luckily, my mother was chaperoning the dance—the better to keep an eye on me and do whatever her mortal self could do to protect me—and since we'd come in with her, none of the other chaperones had asked him what it was sticking out a foot from each side of his chair.

Slowly Darla leaned in to accept Wallace's kiss, the lights swirling around them, the dancers moving to block them from my view. Aphrodite watched from the far side of the room, her hands clutched in front of her. So far, Artemis and Apollo had yet to make themselves known, but they would undoubtedly be here, and I knew that they would come prepared.

"Where's Orion?" Hephaestus asked.

"I sent him to get us some snacks."

Orion smiled over at us from across the room, as if he knew we were talking about him. He looked unbelievably handsome in a dark gray suit, his brown hair freshly shorn.

Finally Wallace and Darla's lips touched, and then everything happened at once. Orion suddenly fainted, eliciting a scream from someone nearby, and the entire room went black.

"What the—" Hephaestus said.

A communal groan went up around the gym, and there were a few girls' squeals as well. I had taken one step in Orion's general direction when someone grabbed me from behind. I had barely a chance to gasp before I felt the ice-cold blade sinking into my side. Pain exploded into the depths of my stomach as I doubled over.

"This is almost too easy," Artemis growled in my ear.

I screeched and reached back to grab her behind her head. With everything I had in me, I flung her over my shoulder onto her back, then yanked the blade from my side, dropping it with a shaking hand to the floor. Blood soaked my fingers, but I was still breathing, still here.

"Hephaestus! My weapon!"

The lights came on. Hephaestus was slumped forward in his chair, out cold. Apollo hovered over him. Both he and Artemis, on the floor in front of me, wore breastplates made of steel forged in the deepest caves of Mount Etna—the only material on Earth or in the heavens that could stop my leaden arrows. It was their blue-black color that gave them away. Someone was helping the twins, just as my father had helped me. But no matter. I was prepared for this.

I yanked my case out in one swift motion and, before anyone could act, had the bow and arrow in my grasp. Apollo lunged for me, but instead of drawing on him, I raced across the room, where Orion was just pushing himself to his hands and knees. Girls scurried out of my way, boys grabbed their friends and darted into corners. Someone screamed as I loaded an arrow into the bridge and drew on Orion. He stood up and staggered back, his face white with shock.

"Eros?" he said.

Dear Gods, he knew me. My heart nearly exploded as I longed to throw myself into his arms. To kiss him with all the longing and despair and hope I'd felt for these last weeks of exile. But I couldn't do it. I had to stay strong. My fingers, slippery with blood, shook as I held the arrow fast between them.

"Eros! What are you doing?" Artemis cried, running up behind me.

"Everyone just calm down." The vice principal, Ms. Austin, walked over with her hands raised, wearing a brown dress that did nothing for her square frame. My mother was right behind her, her blue eyes sharp. "True, put down the weapon."

"I see you've protected yourself, Artemis," I said, blood gushing from my wound. "Unfortunately for you, I've come up with a new plan. Orion, I need you to look at Artemis."

"But—but you're hurt," he said, staring at the bloodstain that was rapidly growing across the front of my white dress.

"Just look at her!" I growled, even as my side convulsed with pain.

It took obvious effort for him to tear his eyes off me and look at her. She stood next to me, shaking from head to toe.

"If I prick Orion with this arrow while he gazes upon you, Artemis, he will be poisoned against you for all time."

"But you'll kill him!" she protested.

I shook my head. "All it takes to breed hatred is a flesh wound. I don't have to kill him to make him loathe you."

She took a step toward me and I inched the arrow toward his shoulder, gritting my teeth. "One false move and I'll do it. I swear."

Artemis froze.

"You need to choose, Orion," I said. "Do you love her, or do you love me?"

Apollo raced toward me with a growl of rage.

"Apollo, no!" My mother moved to intercept him, but he shoved her out of the way and into the wall of gaping students. Two guys grabbed her before she could hit the floor, and her face was red with anger.

"Stop where you are, Apollo!" I cried. "If I cut him with this, she will never get her answer."

"Like I care," Apollo replied.

He lunged for me, but Artemis turned around and kneed him in the groin so hard, he doubled over and fell at her feet. A few guys gasped, and some startled shouts echoed through the room.

"Choose, Orion," Artemis said. "It's time for you to choose."

My love drew himself up. His shoulders were thrown back, his chin raised in that haughty way I knew so well. He looked Artemis directly in the eye, and his expression softened. My heart skipped a beat and my fingers twitched. I'd lost him. I never would have thought it possible, but I'd lost him.

"I'm sorry, Artemis, but I love Eros," he said.

My heart overflowed and I took a step forward, but at that moment Artemis let out a battle cry like no other and launched herself off her feet. I turned to face her, hoping to get one arrow off and at least hit her in the leg, but I had let my guard down for that brief moment and I was too late. She tackled me to the ground, and my fingers slipped from the bow. My side tore in two as I watched the arrow arc feebly through the air, heading right for Orion's chest.

There were screeches, screams, gasps. People scattered. There was a clatter as something large fell to the gym floor.

And then the arrow stopped. It froze in midair. Artemis and I sat up together as the world went silent. I shoved myself to my feet. Every soul in the room except for me, Orion, Artemis, Apollo, and Aphrodite was as still as ice. I glanced at Hephaestus, who remained unconscious, and was gratified to see that he was breathing.

"What in the name of Zeus?" Orion stepped forward and touched the pad of one finger to the tip of the frozen arrow. Then he waved his hand in front of the vice principal's face, her mouth open in an arrested scream.

"What's happening?" Apollo groaned, pushing himself to his knees.

I glanced down at him. "I don't know."

It was then that Zeus, Hera, Ares, and Harmonia whirled into the gym, taking out half the balloon arrangements and sending glitter splattering against the frozen faces of a hundred unsuspecting mortals. Harmonia fell to her knees in front of Hephaestus while the three upper gods walked down the aisle I had created with my bow-wielding run.

Ares stepped up next to me and ran his hand over my wound, healing it and clearing the blood away. "Are you quite well, my daughter?"

"Quite," I replied, standing up straight.

The king and queen came to stand before the rest of us. Hera wore her black hair piled atop her head with a gold band crusted with diamonds running through it, her white gown pristine as ever. Zeus's blond beard was clipped short, his green eyes almost merry, as he paused before me in his classic Roman attire—laced sandals, leather breastplate and all.

My mother, father, Orion, and I bowed. Artemis and Apollo,

still on the floor, merely dipped their heads. Somewhere behind the king and queen, Hephaestus groaned.

"Well, Eros. You've made quite a mess of things, haven't you?" the king said.

"Have I? I think things were going well until a moment ago."

Artemis shoved herself off the ground and advanced on the queen. "You told me I could have him! You told me I would have my revenge!"

The queen raised a dismissive hand, passing it before Artemis's throat, and Artemis fell silent. Try as she might to shout, nothing emanated from her mouth. She clasped her hands over her neck and tried to choke out a sound, but it was fruitless.

"I tire of your incessant complaining," Hera said with a sniff.

"Well, I'll give you this," the king said, looking down his nose at me. "You've done as I asked. You've matched your three couples and proven yourself to be dedicated to your calling."

Hera glanced over her shoulder at Wallace and Darla. Their hands were clasped as they looked toward us, frozen in disbelief.

"An odd pairing, to be sure, but love is often . . . illogical," she said, glancing at her husband.

Zeus smirked, then gestured at Orion casually.

"Go ahead, Eros. You may now claim your prize."

I turned to Orion. A smile stretched across his handsome face. We stumbled into each other, our lips meeting messily, hungrily, ecstatically as my hands traveled his arms, his shoulders, his waist, his hair. He was back. My love had been returned to me. It had been so long since I'd touched him—the real him—I couldn't get enough.

Hephaestus was right all along. Those kisses with the other Orion had been amazing, but this . . . this was the real thing.

In the corner of my vision, Artemis fell to her knees, still clutching her throat as tears poured from her eyes.

"What about your deal with Artemis?" Apollo demanded, shoving himself unsteadily to his feet and advancing on the queen. "What happened to that?"

"The king and I discovered that our desires were in conflict," the queen said. "I wanted to do away with both of you," she said, casting a cool eye at me and Artemis. "But he claims that we gods and goddesses need a stronger presence, not a lesser one."

"My queen acted rashly," the king put in with a teasing smile. "Losing two young and dedicated goddesses would not only upset the balance of the universe, but it would weaken our power as a whole. Therefore, we've decided to let you both live."

I looked at my father. He barely contained an eye roll. Games. The king and queen loved to play games—with us, with each other, with the mortals of Earth. But at least this time, I had won. My hand was clutched inside Orion's and made me the victor.

"Where would the two lovebirds like to go?" Zeus asked me and Orion, plucking my leaden arrow from the air and twirling it in one hand. "Would you return to the Mount? Or to your love nest in Maine?"

I grasped Orion's hand even tighter, about to say yes. That cabin in Maine was where I'd been happier than anywhere else. But then I remembered how restless Orion had grown, being separated from human contact. My gaze traveled over the many familiar faces in the crowd—Peter and Claudia, Katrina and Charlie, and Wallace, Darla, Lauren, Mia, Josh, Gavin, even the awful Veronica. I'd begun to feel at home among these people. I enjoyed getting to know them and understand them. Did I really want to leave them now?

I looked into Orion's eyes, and he smiled. He knew exactly what I was thinking.

"What if we . . . wanted to stay here?" I asked. "For just a little while longer. I feel like I was just getting good at this."

"But what of the rest of the world?" Hera asked. "Lake Carmody, New Jersey, is not the only community deserving of your attentions."

"Of course not, my queen," I said. "But I do love this new depth of understanding that comes from really knowing the people I'm matching. What if I came home to Mount Olympus a few hours each day to breed love from my earthen window? Would that appease you?"

She tilted her head in acquiescence, her attitude toward me still cool.

"What say you, Orion? Do you like it here?" Zeus asked.

Orion's jaw dropped slightly, probably unable to believe the king had bothered asking what he wanted. Harmonia and Hephaestus approached our conference from behind the king and queen, holding hands.

"I'll happily go wherever Eros goes," Orion said, lifting my hand to kiss it. "As long as there is good hunting nearby."

Zeus stepped up to me and put out his hands, palm up. I released Orion and allowed the king to hold my hands in his.

"I'm proud of you, Eros. You showed true dedication, true understanding, and true heart in all this. You've set an example for everyone else on Mount Olympus to follow," he added, casting a wry glance at Apollo and Artemis. "But I need you to do me one favor."

"Anything, Your Highness," I said.

"Would you promise my wife that you won't use your growing

powers in an attempt to usurp her throne?" he said, turning sideways to see Hera. "She's become quite paranoid about you girls."

Hera sniffed and looked to the left, as if this line of conversation offended her. My gaze shifted past her, to where Hephaestus sat, kissing the back of Harmonia's hand, holding it like he would never let her go.

"Of course I will. On three conditions," I said.

Zeus raised his eyebrows, intrigued. "Let's not forget who you're talking to."

"I won't," I replied. "These are small requests."

He lifted his chin and drew back, crossing his arms over his chest. "Have at it, then."

"I want you to return Aphrodite to the Mount where she belongs," I said. "I want Artemis and Apollo to be banned from Orion's presence, and I want Hephaestus's powers to be returned and for him to be welcomed back home with open arms, so that he may be with my sister, Harmonia."

Zeus's eyes narrowed, and he nodded. "Done."

"What? Really?" Hephaestus raised his head, his whole face brightening with joy. Harmonia laughed, a musical, tinkling sound that lightened the entire room.

"I'd quit while you're ahead if I were you," my father said gruffly.

Hephaestus's mouth snapped shut, and he had the intelligence to look unnerved. I couldn't imagine how my new family was going to work with my mother's former husband now in love with her daughter, but they would figure it out somehow. Hopefully there would be no tossed lightning bolts or sojourns to Etna involved.

"Come now, my brethren. I tire of this place," Zeus said, crooking an arm. "Let us go home. Good luck to you, Eros."

He took Hera's hand and together, the king and queen whirled out along with Artemis and Apollo, who barely had time to screech his indignation before he was gone. My mother enveloped me in her perfumed arms, holding me tight to her chest.

"Thank you, Eros," she said, her eyes shining as she looked me over. "The king is right. You've done us proud."

"Thank you, Mother."

She reached up and tucked my hair behind my ear. "I'll see you soon?"

"Before you know it," I replied.

With a smile, she touched her lips to my forehead, then stepped back and whirled away, kicking up a tornado of glitter and streamers as she went. When the debris finally floated to the floor again, Hephaestus was wheeling toward me with Harmonia at his side.

"Nice work, True," he said with a mischievous glint in his eye. He extended one hand. "I'm going to miss being your sidekick."

I clasped his fingers with my own. "Well, you could always stay. . . ."

He let me go and reached for my sister's hand. "Not a chance."

We laughed, and then they both blew me a kiss and were gone. Orion drew me into his arms.

"So what now?" he asked.

Suddenly the music started up again, and the people around us flinched to life. My eyes widened, and I quickly kicked my bow beneath the long tablecloth on the snack table next to us. Ms. Austin looked around, baffled, as if she couldn't remember crossing the room, then shrugged and went back to her post by the door. Everyone else started to dance and eat and laugh and talk like nothing had happened. Clearly Zeus had altered their reality so that none of them recalled a thing.

"Okay, this is weird," Orion said, taking my hand.

"When the king says he's going to take care of something, he takes care of it," I said.

Orion laughed. "It is *so* good to see you."

"It is so good to be seen," I replied.

Then I reached back and unclasped his arrow from around my neck. He bowed his head slightly so I could reclasp it around his. He closed his eyes and sighed, savoring the feeling of the cool silver against his chest.

"I've missed this. I've missed us," he said, holding my hand. "It was like I knew there was a hole inside me, but I didn't know why, and now it's gone."

"You'll never have to miss me again, I promise."

I leaned in to kiss him, and the moment our lips met, a hand came down on his shoulder. I darted back, ever on the defensive, but it was just Peter, with Claudia at his heels, their new crowns glinting under the strobe lights. Charlie and Katrina stood beside them along with Wallace and Darla, who were flushed with the early stages of romantic bliss. All of them looked so beautiful and shimmering and happy, holding hands, arms around each other, smiling and beaming with love. And I'd done that. I'd helped them find each other.

"Are you two gonna stand there the whole night looking serious, or are you going to get out here and dance?" Charlie asked.

Orion laughed and lifted his shoulders at me. "I'm gonna say . . . dance?"

"We've never done that before," I remarked.

"Then let's go already," Darla said, rolling her eyes.

I held Orion's hand as we moved to the center of the floor. Orion held me against him as we began to dance.

"So, True Olympia," he said with a smirk. "You've completed your mission. How does it feel?"

"It feels good," I answered.

Orion twirled me around, and even though I was surrounded by happy couples, my eyes fell on plenty of forlorn faces, lonely hearts, souls just longing to be appreciated. I looked up at my love and smiled.

"But there's lots more work to be done."